WHO STOLE MY TWINS' IDENTITY?

Bill Duff

First Published 2009 by Appin Press, an imprint of
Countyvise Ltd.,
14 Appin Road, Birkenhead, Wirral CH41 9HH

British Library Cataloguing in Publication Data.
A catalogue record for this book is available from the
British Library.

ISBN 978 1 906205 34 8

BILL DUFF has recently retired from his role as a Fraud Specialist within the National Health Service and has used his knowledge to write novels with a fraud background. He lives in Liverpool and is married with two sons. His hobbies include walking which has taken him through many parts of Andalucia as well as being a member of Liverpool Brisk Walkers, which is reflected in his books.

Also by Bill Duff

Fraud Why Did They Do It?

ACKNOWLEDGEMENTS

The Institute of Counter Fraud Specialists (ICFS) and the Counter Fraud and Security Management Service (CFSMS) from both of which I was able to obtain research into fraud cases during my employment as a Fraud Specialist.

1

Wendy Carson was sitting in a high class New York restaurant with her American boyfriend, Frank Sinclair. They had just arrived the day before from London, where Wendy had left her job as a manager of a Nursing Agency in a London hospital having committed a massive fraud on the payroll system. She was also involved in identity fraud and was now enjoying the benefits of her criminal activities. She was quite pleased with the life that she would now be able to live. It was of no concern to Wendy that she had murdered a Polish immigrant to the United Kingdom who had failed to pay for her forged identity documents.

David Parish walked out of London Crown Court, where he had heard Judge William Lawson send Zoe Ferguson and Rik Jeffreys to prison for two years. They had also been ordered to repay a hundred thousand pounds within three months or face a further year in prison. The Judge had acknowledged the investigation undertaken by David in bringing these two fraudsters to Court. They had been part of a travel fraud conspiracy at Euston General Hospital and defrauded the Health Service of nearly three hundred thousand pounds. Their two fellow fraudsters were dead, one having been murdered in Spain and the second committed suicide on the evening before the trial should have taken place. David is a Fraud Consultant within both the Public and Private Sectors and investigates fraud within the Health Service, Local Authorities, Benefits Agencies and many Insurance Companies. His special knowledge and expertise in this field has led to him being called Mr Fraud by the Police and Senor Fraudo in his trips abroad, especially in Spain, where he has had a long relationship with Alisa Garcia, who is a Police Inspector in the Guardia Civil.

He made his way across London to the Euston General Hospital where he had arranged a meeting with the Director of Finance, Stuart Bradley, in order to update him on the result of the court case. On entering the Executive Offices, he spoke to Louise Elliot, who was the Personal Assistant to Stuart.

"Good afternoon Louise, how are you today?"
"I'm fine, thank you very much."
"Is Stuart in?"
"Yes, I'll let him know you're here."

Louise picked up the phone and dialled Stuart.
"Hello Louise."
"I've got David Parish here to see you. Shall I send him in?"
"Yes, will you bring in a couple of drinks?"
"Are you having tea?"
"Yes please Louise."
Louise turned to David.
"You can go through, would you like coffee?"
"Yes, thanks Louise."

David entered Stuart's office and shook hands.
"Well, what's happened to our friends Ferguson and Jeffreys?"
"They've been sent to prison for two years and have been told that they must repay a hundred thousand pounds within the next three months, or face another year in prison. When they were leaving the Court to be transferred to prison, Jeffreys yelled at Zoe Ferguson, telling her to give the money

back to avoid the extra year. It seems pretty clear that he hasn't got the money, which is what I expected. I don't know if she'll give the money back. Hopefully, when she sees what it's like in clink, she'll get hold of the money, which will, of course, eventually come back to the Hospital."

"The Judge obviously listened to what you had to say. It was your idea to increase their sentence if they didn't repay the money."

"That's right, but the Judge will say it was his idea. I asked our Barrister to approach the Judge a couple of weeks ago. He's obviously listened to the Barrister and thought it made a lot of sense."

"Have you got any more big investigations taking place?"

"I had a phone call from Michael Fox, the Director of Finance at Lancashire Health Trust and met with him to discuss a dentist. I'm working with Brian Lewis, a Fraud Specialist in Lancashire and we've got Finance Staff, Community Staff and the Dental Board helping us. We are looking at the dentist, who has claimed for providing treatment over the past five or six years. It transpires that there are many claims for deceased patients, fictitious patients, patients that are no longer registered with him and he's also claimed for work that he's never done. We thought he'd also fled to Spain, but we think he's just gone abroad on holiday and he should be back the day after tomorrow. I got my contacts in Spain to find him and they say he's booked at a hotel in Madrid with his family and they have already arranged the airport transfer in a couple of days."

"Is this contact your girlfriend in the Spanish Police?"

"No, it's actually Alisa's brother, Felipe, who's based in Murcia with La Policia but he has good contacts in Madrid. Alisa has got a twelve month secondment with the Spanish Police, looking at extradition issues between Spain and this country. She has a flat near Regents Park but most of the time she commutes from London and stays with me in Liverpool, although she is in London for the next few days."

"That's good and pretty convenient for you both. When I asked if you were busy, it's because something else has cropped up at this hospital. There's another big fraud that has been going on for a couple of years, at least."

"Go on, tell me more Stuart."

They were interrupted when Louise brought in the drinks.

Stuart looked at Louise but David could see from his face that he had a lot on his mind.

"Thanks Louise," he said before gathering some notes.

"There has been a fraud on the Nurse Bank payroll. As a result of the travel fraud that has just occurred, we had to admit that the systems we had in place for travel claims was poor and we were punished as a result. We spoke to our Internal Auditors and asked for a thorough audit on systems where a fraud was more likely to occur. They have been swarming all over us for the past few weeks but our own finance staff have also been looking at any unusual variations in the overall costs to the hospital compared to previous years. One area they looked at was the amount of money paid to Bank Nurses and noticed sizeable increases over the past two years. How up to date are you with the Bank Nurse procedures?"

"I know quite a bit about the Bank Nurses and have had to undertake a few investigations over the years, but fortunately, only for small amounts. The hospital's own employed nurses cover most shifts and they'll also work additional shifts in the form of overtime. If none of your own staff are available, then you go to the Nurse Bank. There are normally many names on the Nurse Bank, but they are often nurses who are not employed elsewhere, but to keep in touch and earn some extra money for working the odd shifts. The Bank also includes some staff from other hospitals, where no overtime is available and the staff who operate your Bank can often ring somebody up at the last minute, and get somebody to come in and cover a shift. It has always been an area where you may expect to find frauds on the timesheets that the nurses complete, but if the controls are tight, the chances of fraud lessen. I think you are going to tell me something bigger has happened."

"I'm afraid so. This is probably going to turn out as the biggest Health Service payroll scam. It only came to light yesterday, but it looks as though the manager of the Nurse Bank Agency is responsible for the fraud. We didn't know why the payroll expenditure had risen so high and when we started going through some of the names on the Bank listings, we couldn't link a few of them to the wards where they were supposed to have worked shifts. When we place nursing staff on the Bank Agency, we always do the appropriate checks on their status, qualifications and past employment history, just like we do for the staff who are fully employed by the hospital. We've found ten names relating to staff that've had no checks made. I got Mike Williams, our Director of Human Resources to check the names and they've got no records whatsoever. They've never appeared on the ward lists and have never worked on the wards. We haven't had time to check all the shifts, but it looks as though the wards never even required nursing staff on some of the dates that we've checked. All of these ten are down as working virtually full time during the past couple of years, but they don't exist. We've checked the total salaries paid to these ten fictitious people and it comes to nearly six hundred thousand pounds. They've been treated as Agency workers and there have been no deductions for tax and insurance."

"Who is the manager?"

"It was Wendy Carson, but she left last week."

"Did she know that checks were being made?"

"I don't know. We can do all the checks we need, either in Finance or Human Resources. She gave the required months notice, but had a few days holiday entitlement, which meant she finished at the end of last week. If she knew something was going on, would she have given the proper notice to leave? I doubt if she was aware that checks were being made, although she would have known that our Internal Auditors were working throughout the hospital and maybe she thought they might start checking on her department. I don't know her very well but we have met. My assistant, Simon Gardner, who you know from the travel fraud, does know her a little. Apparently, she has an American boyfriend and often visits him. He's often over here visiting her in this country. She does have a daughter, aged around twenty, from her previous marriage, but she's been divorced for years. I understand her mother is still alive and also lives fairly local."

"Do we know if she's still around or has she started a new job?"

"No, she didn't have a job to go to. She was going to visit her boyfriend in America and we think that she flew to the States yesterday. It was probably going to be a long visit and we think that she intends to stay in America."

"I need to know the full details of her bank account and the other ten, which were used to receive the salary payments over the past couple of years. I'll also need the full names, addresses and anything else you've got, before I contact the Banks and get them to freeze the accounts."

"Will they put stops on the bank accounts or will you need to get court orders first?"

"I am an accredited Fraud Investigator and have a Registered Licence and PIN. We are able to approach the Bank's Fraud Investigators, give the licence details, and they will then receive the cooperation of the Banks, who will place a temporary stop on the bank accounts. A stop may also be placed on any travellers' cheques that have been issued, leaving her with cash only."

"Simon Gardner has given me some details, which I think, has everything that you need."

Stuart then passed a folder containing the information to David who had a quick glance at the sheets of paper.

"This looks good enough to start. I'll contact Wendy Carson's Bank Investigator straight away. His name is Eric Page; he'll probably help with contacting the other Bank Investigators. There are only three Banks being used by Wendy and the other ten fictitious employees. I'll also need to speak to Peter Daley, who you know, helped with the travel fraud investigation. I was with him in the Crown Court this morning and told him that I'd probably see him again sometime, but we didn't think it would be this quick."

"That's okay. I'll arrange for you to have a meeting room in the Human Resources Department for as long as you want."

"Thanks Stuart, I'll go there now and make a few phone calls. I will stay at Alisa's flat for a few days while I'm working on this case."

2

David looked up the contact details for Eric Page and rang him on his mobile phone.

"Hello, Eric Page."

"Hello Eric, its David Parish."

"Mr Fraud, it's nice to hear from you. What can I do for you?"

"I've got a big payroll fraud concerning the Nurse Bank at Euston General Hospital. Initial indications suggest that we are talking about six hundred thousand pounds. We believe the person responsible was the person in charge of the Bank, but she's just left and we understand that she flew to the States yesterday. She arranged for ten names to be added to the payroll but they've never worked for the hospital. We don't know who operates these ten accounts but we've got ten different names, three are female and seven are male. I've got all the bank details, branches and the account numbers. The lady in charge was Wendy Carson and she banks with you. The other ten are only using three banks but different branches and one of the banks is yours. I would guess that she will allow these people to keep a proportion of the monthly salary, but she'll be given the rest on a regular basis. I would like you to put a stop on her account and see if there are any signs of the money. She may have other bank accounts and there's a chance she may have transferred money from her account with you."

"I'll need all the details quickly, can you email them to me?"

"Yes, I've got your email address. You'll have all the information in the next half an hour. Have you got my Fraud Investigators licence details?"

"Yes, it's all on file."

"Can I ask a favour?"

"Go on."

"Should I contact the other Bank's investigators or will it be easier for you?"

"No problem David. We're in close contact with all the other Bank's investigators. We'll start the ball rolling as soon as I've got your email. I'll get them to find out what they can about these account holders. From what you've said, apart from us, there's only two other banks involved, isn't there?"

"That's right. I'm in London today and will probably stay a few days at my girlfriend's flat. You can contact me on my mobile, you should have the number."

"Yes, I've got it on my computer. Are you on your own with this, or have you pulled somebody in to help you?"

"He doesn't know yet, but I'll be giving Peter Daley a ring as soon as I've sent you the email."

"Peter worked with you on that travel fraud, what's happened with that one?"

"They were in Crown Court this morning and they both got two years. If they don't pay a hundred thousand pounds back within three months, they'll get another year added on."

"Good one. I'll give you a ring as soon as I've got some information. It'll probably be within the next couple of hours."

"Thanks a lot Eric."

David then phoned Peter Daley on his direct line.

"Hello."

"Hi Peter, its David. You know that I said I'd be in touch if something cropped up."

"Yeah."

9

"I've just had a meeting with Stuart Bradley and updated him on Ferguson and Jeffreys. He then told me that another fraud has been discovered and this one is bigger than the last travel fraud. It involves the Nurse Bank payroll, false names have been added to the payroll and we're looking at a fraud of six hundred thousand pounds."

"When did they find that?"

"Yesterday, but he knew that I was coming to see him today, so he saved it for me. It looks like the fraud has been committed by the manager in charge of the Nurse Bank. She gave in her notice and left a couple of days ago. We understand she has a boyfriend in the States and flew there yesterday."

"I presume you are trying to freeze the bank accounts?"

"Yes, I've spoken to Eric Page. He's putting a stop on the accounts with his bank, which includes the manager of the Nurse Bank. He's also contacting the Investigators at the other banks and the stops should be going on the accounts at this moment. He'll find out anything he can do to help, and he should ring me back later today. I'm not sure how much I'll have to do, but will you be available if I need you?"

"No problem David. I'm not involved in anything that can't wait for a few days."

"We're going to have to work with the police on this case. You probably have a closer contact than me in London. Who's best to contact?"

"I'm quite friendly with Ross Edgar, an Inspector with the Metropolitan Police. Do you want me to speak to him now?"

"It'll do no harm. Once we've got all the information from Eric Page, we'll arrange a meeting."

"I'll give him a ring and let him know."

"Thanks Peter, I'll be in touch. Bye for now."

He then picked up his mobile and rang Alisa, who immediately recognised the number of the incoming phone call.

"Hola David. I didn't expect to hear from you until you returned home tonight."

"I'm not going home. I've got another fraud case in London and will be staying here for a few days. I'll be at your flat in a couple of hours if that's okay."

"Of course it's okay. I'm in work at the moment but I'll see you at the flat later. It might be after you've arrived, you've got the key haven't you?"

"Yes my love, I'll see you later."

"Bye Senor Fraudo."

David opened the file that Stuart Bradley had given him and undertook a thorough investigation. As always, the information provided by Simon Gardner from the Finance Department was of a high standard and gave David a full background of the frauds that had been undertaken. It was also evident that the Internal Auditors had been involved in the investigative work and were already insisting on some changes in the procedures that were the current practice in the hospital.

It was little more than an hour later when his mobile phone rang. He picked up the mobile and looked at the incoming number which he immediately recognised as that of Eric Page.

"Hi Eric, thanks for getting back to me so quickly."

"Oh, that's us Bank Investigators, we're so efficient."

"I know you Eric, and your colleagues. You'll be checking to see if you are in the clear, or if the hospital may have some comeback on you, in case you've made any type of cock up when you've opened the accounts."

"True, but it looks as though the Banks haven't done anything wrong at this stage, but we'll, no doubt, find out in due course."

"What have you found out so far?"

"We've frozen the accounts of Wendy Carson. She had five thousand, five hundred pounds in her current account and just over a hundred thousand in a deposit account. I have spoken to her branch and one of the staff remembered her coming into the branch a few days ago. She transferred eighty thousand pounds from her account to another account in her name at another bank. She also transferred twenty five thousand pounds to her daughter's account and another twenty five thousand pounds to her mother's account. Both of those have accounts with our bank."

"It sounds as though she thinks she'll be away for a while."

"Yep, but all the accounts have now been frozen. Her mother and daughter are not going to be too happy when they find out. The daughter hasn't got much money in her account apart from the twenty five thousand pounds but the grandmothers got about five thousand quid. The balance in the other account that Wendy Carson transferred eighty thousand pounds now stands at a hundred and fifty thousand pounds. That's been frozen as well. She's quite computer literate and has set up on line computer facilities with us and at the other bank. This means that she'll be able to transfer money between accounts and set up other bank details if she wants to. She might have already opened other bank accounts and set them up on the online banking system."

"Will you be able to find out if she adds any other accounts to the system?"

"Yes, we'll allow this to be completed and we'll know within a matter of minutes. She won't be able to transfer any money from her accounts and she won't be able to draw money from any cash machines. She has a credit card with this bank and that's also been blocked, and she has a credit card with her other bank but that's also been blocked. She also got five thousand dollars in traveller cheques which have also had a stop put on them. She also took a thousand dollars in cash, but there's nothing we can do about that."

"I've just been working out as you've been talking and you've managed to freeze about three hundred thousand pounds and put a stop on the travellers' cheques."

"That's right, but there's hardly any money in all the other accounts, that the monthly salary payments have been sent to by the hospital salary department. It looks as though the salary is credited and the moneys drawn out within a matter of days each month."

"I'm not surprised. She'll probably be taking a proportion of the monthly salary and let her fellow conspirators keep a share."

"I've asked all the other bank investigators to email me with details of the account holders including addresses, dates of birth, and any other background information. They'll also be talking to the staff in the branches to see if they can remember the account holders and obtain any descriptions and anything that can help us. I've also asked them all to copy you into the emails."

"Thanks a lot Eric. Peter Daley is contacting the Metropolitan Police and we'll have a meeting with them once I've got some more information from all the banks. We might require some help from the American Police in due course and it'll be easier if our police are involved. I do have some contacts in the States but my influence is not as strong as in Europe. When will Carson's mother and daughter find out that there accounts have been blocked?"

"We are going to write to them today. I presume that you will want to interview them as soon as possible?"

"Yes. If it's okay with you, I'll interview them with Peter. You can let them know in the letter that I'll be in touch within the next couple of days."

"That's fine, but I'll give them my contact number as well as yours in case they want to speak to somebody from the bank."

"That's okay. We will start the formal legal proceedings to have the money in the bank accounts returned to the Courts, who will then send it back to the hospital, but it'll take some time as you know."

"Once we've had the emails from the other banks, we'll speak again. They should let us have something by tomorrow. We'll probably need to meet at some time but there's no need at the moment."

"I'll speak to you tomorrow, hopefully. Thanks Eric."

"Cheers."

David gathered his paperwork and packed it into his bag together with his laptop. He then left the hospital and decided to walk to Alisa's flat near Regent's Park. The walk only took twenty minutes and as he passed Regent's Park Tube Station he saw Alisa who had just got off the Tube and was leaving the station. He quickly caught up with Alisa and as he approached he said.

"Good afternoon Miss Garcia. How are you?"

Alisa was initially startled but soon recognised the voice of David before turning around to give him a smile.

"I am very well Mr Parish," she replied before giving him a welcoming kiss.

They then walked the short distance to the flat, hand in hand.

Once they had entered the flat, took off their coats and put their baggage away, Alisa turned to David.

"Would you like to eat out tonight, I forgot to tell you that I've discovered a small family run Spanish Restaurant. It's only got ten tables and it's not far from Edgeware Road. I went there a couple of weeks ago with Sue from work and it's very nice?"

"I'd love to but will we get in at short notice?"

"It shouldn't be too busy tonight but I'll give them a ring."

Alisa picked up the phone and when it was answered, Alisa said.

"Do you have a table for two this evening at eight o'clock?"

When David heard Alisa say "Thank you, I'll see you later," he knew the table had been booked.

"That's booked and how is your new fraud case going?"

"It's a big fraud on a hospital payroll. We've managed to block a lot of bank accounts and we've frozen around three hundred thousand pounds, but that's only half of what's been taken. I should get much more information tomorrow and I'll decide what to do then."

"Do you know who has committed the fraud?"

"Yes, the main person is the manager who was in charge of the Nurse Bank. She left last week and we think she's gone to the United States."

"Is she married or got any family?"

"She's been divorced for years, but she's got a daughter who's about twenty and a mother. She's got an American boyfriend, which is why she's gone to the States."

"You should get some information from the daughter and mother."

"I know, I'll be seeing them in a couple of days."

David then laughed before speaking again.

"Who's in charge of this investigation Inspector Garcia, you or me?"

"You probably think you are, but she's gone to the States. If she'd gone to Spain, you'd be begging me for help by now."

Alisa grabbed hold of David and gave him a long kiss before he remarked.

"Should we go for a lie down in bed?"

"No, we'll never make it to the restaurant. I'm going for a shower."

"Should I join you?"

"Sit down David Parish and watch television until I've finished. You can wait till we get home after we've been to the restaurant."

"I won't forget."

"I'm sure you won't, Senor Fraudo but I should tell you that I've been to a self-defence class today."

"How did it go?"

"They asked me if I'd been to a self-defence class before and when I told them that I'd gone to classes in Spain for several years and had received many awards, they sat back and asked me all about it. They put me with the top group and I think I was probably one of the best in that group, but there were some different ideas although it was very similar to the training in Spain. I did say that I would only be here another couple of months at the most and if it was longer, they might have recommended a different class. He said they were short of some qualified trainers and did I want a job, but I declined. They were a nice group and I'll probably go again because I haven't been since I left Spain."

3

The following morning, David had only been in his room at Euston General Hospital for about twenty minutes when his mobile phone rang. He looked at the number of the incoming call but did not recognise the number.

"Hello, David Parish."

"Hello, my name's Pauline Carson. I've had a letter from my bank saying you've frozen my bank account. My Nan then rang me and she's had her account frozen as well. I've just spoken to a Mr Page and he said I should contact you. I know it's something to do with my Mum but I want to know what's going on. What's this all about?"

"I'm glad you've rang Miss Carson, I was going to ring you and your grandmother, Mrs Longridge, today to make appointments to speak to you. When would you like to meet?"

"I'd like to have a meeting today and I'll bring my Nan with me."

"How about two o'clock at Euston General Hospital. Do you know the hospital?"

"Yes, whereabouts?"

"The Human Resources Department. You will see the signs when you enter the hospital. If you go to reception and ask for David Parish, they will contact me. I will have a colleague with me. You are entitled to bring a legal representative if you wish, do you want one?"

"I haven't done anything wrong. I don't understand what this is all about."

"That's okay. I'll explain everything when we see you both at two o'clock."

"I'll see you then. Bye."

Peter Daley picked up his phone when it started ringing.

"Hello."

"Hello Peter, its David Parish."

"I've just had Wendy Carson's daughter on the phone. You don't know but Wendy transferred twenty five thousand pounds to both their accounts. She wants to know why her and her Grandmother's bank accounts have been frozen. She's coming in to see me with her Grandmother at two o'clock today. Can you get here in Human Resources at one o'clock and I'll go through what I've got by then?"

"Yes, I'll be there at one o'clock. Is it going to be a formal interview on tape?"

"No. I'll make it a fact finding interview. I did say she was allowed to bring a legal representative with her, but she just said she's done nothing wrong and wouldn't bother. She's just bringing her Nan. She didn't mention the twenty five thousand pounds, so it's possible she doesn't even know about it, but we'll find out later."

"I did speak to Ross Edgar and he said let him know when we need to meet and he'll do what he can. He's never met you and he knows about Mr Fraud, but he has met Alisa at a meeting about a month ago and knew of her connection to you. You can't go anywhere. I'll see you this afternoon David, bye for now."

During the morning David received copies of the emails that had been sent to Eric Page. He made a list of the ten names, addresses and dates of birth which were provided by the various banks. The Bank Investigators had also managed to obtain descriptions from branch staff concerning the ten account holders. He examined the list closely and noticed several duplications. The list contained two female names and ten male names, but the two female names were different but both had the same date of birth and the same address. The eight male names fell into a similar pattern, with different names, but there were clearly four sets of two, with each set having the same date of birth and the same address. The address listed for the female was also the same as one of the male names.

The descriptions were a bit vague in many cases but there seemed every possibility that the ten bank accounts were being operated by five people, each managing two accounts under different names but having the same address and date of birth. He looked at the date of birth of the female and quickly picked up his file on Wendy Carson. It came as no surprise that date of births were identical and there was every chance that Wendy Carson, herself, was operating two of the bank accounts. There were fairly similar descriptions, given by branch staff, but David had never seen Wendy Carson, so was unable to know if they were a match to Wendy.

He left the room were he was working and went to see Mike Williams, the Director of Human Resources. Mike was at his desk but the door to his office was open.

"Morning Mike, have you got a couple of minutes?"

"Of course, come in and have a seat."

"You know that I'm working on the payroll fraud?"

"Yes, Stuart Bradley did tell me and we had to provide you with an office to work in."

"I've got some descriptions of the people who have been operating the bank accounts. There is one female involved and it looks possible that she was operating two bank accounts. Both accounts have the same address and the same date of birth, but different names. Funny thing is that the date of birth is the same as Wendy Carson's. Did you know her?"

"Yes. What are the descriptions that you've got?"

"The age is right. They say about five foot eight inches, slim build, but she's strong and well toned, because she's heavily involved in Kung Fu or Jujitsu or that type of thing. She has long blonde wavy hair, plenty of make up, and always wore long dangling earrings."

"The description would probably fit plenty of people, but it does match Wendy. She was known to wear long dangling earrings and we would often joke with her about the earrings. It's probably Wendy. Can I help you with the others?"

David passed over his list and Mike glanced down at the information on the sheet.

"The address noted against the two female bank accounts is the same as that against one of the men. I know where that address is, it's close to where my brother lives. I might be wrong, but do you know Wendy has an American boyfriend?"

"Yes."

"I was going out for a drink with my brother and when we were going to the pub, we passed Wendy and her boyfriend. They were going into a house in that road and I mentioned to Wendy, a couple of days later, that I'd seen her. She said that's a house belonging to a friend of the boyfriend, and the boyfriend often stayed there when he was in England. I think the two men are from New York."

"That's interesting. Thanks for your help Mike."

"No problem."

David called at one of the shops in the hospital and picked up a sandwich and a drink for his lunch. He then returned to the room where he was working in Human Resources. Not long after finishing his lunch, Peter Daley came into the room.

"Hi David, here we go again."

"A few things have happened since I spoke to you on the phone Peter. You know the background and the fraud has been controlled by Wendy Carson, the Nurse Bank Manager. She's left and gone to see her boyfriend in the States, probably New

20

York. She added ten names to the payroll and paid them a monthly salary even though they didn't work at all. It looks as though each individual manages two bank accounts making five people involved in the fraud but I would guess that Wendy Carson is one of the five. We have got four addresses for the ten bank accounts and I was speaking to Mike Williams who reckons one of the addresses might belong to a friend of her boyfriend. This friend could be involved in the fraud and I think we'll need to have a chat with the police and get them to call on these four addresses. The quicker the better, I suppose, but we'll need the co-operation of Ross Edgar."

"He's okay, but he'll probably want to see us before they make any moves. Should I try and arrange a meeting after we've spoken to Carson's mother and daughter."

"That makes sense Peter, is it worth ringing him now, before the two ladies arrive?"

"Yes, I'll try and get hold of him now."

Peter picked up his mobile and dialled the phone number of Ross Edgar, who was quick to answer the phone.

"Hello, Ross Edgar."

"Hi Ross, its Peter Daley."

"Good afternoon Peter."

"I'm with David Parish now and it looks as though we have four addresses for the ten bank accounts, which have been used to operate the fraud. We're just about to have a fact finding interview with the mother and daughter of the lady that we believe has run the fraud. Is it possible to come and see you later, say four o'clock."

"Yes, that's okay. I presume that you will want us to make calls on those four addresses?"

"Yes, we haven't got any search warrants."

"We'll manage without. They may be false addresses."

"We know that, but bank statements have been sent to those addresses and we think the lady running the fraud may have been seen entering one of those addresses."

"Okay, I'll see you at four o'clock."

"Thanks Ross."

4

It was just before two o'clock when the receptionist from Human Resources knocked on the door and entered the room that David and Peter were working in.

"I have two ladies at reception waiting to see you, a Miss Carson and a Mrs Longridge. Shall I show them in?"

David replied.

"Yes please, thanks a lot."

The two ladies were shown into the room by the receptionist and David spoke to the ladies.

"My name is David Parish and this is my colleague Peter Daley. Please take a seat."

David looked at the younger lady.

"I presume you are Miss Carson and this is your grandmother Mrs Longridge?"

"Yes, that's right."

"The meeting today is what we call a fact finding meeting. I will explain what has happened and why your bank accounts have been frozen. I'm hoping that you will be able to help us but that is up to yourselves."

Pauline Carson suddenly interrupted.

"When I spoke to you this morning, all I knew was that I'd had a letter from my bank saying my account had been blocked. My Nan also phoned me and told me her account had been blocked as well. I phoned the man who sent the letters, Eric Page, and he told me you were completing an investigation and had the authority to request a hold put on our accounts. He told me to ring you which I did, but since then I went into the branch. I tried to draw some money out but I couldn't and when I spoke to the cashier, I found out that there is over twenty five thousand pounds in my account and it's the same with my Nan's account. I've got no idea where this money came from and neither has my Nan, but is that the reason why the accounts have been blocked?"

"The quick answer to your question is yes, but I need to explain in more detail. We are investigating a large fraud that has taken place at this hospital, and the person we want to question in connection with the fraud is your mother Wendy Carson."

"What do you mean, my Mum?"

Mary Longridge also raised her voice, shouting at David.

"My daughter's done nothing wrong. She's gone to America to stay with her boyfriend Frank."

"You have both had twenty five thousand pounds paid into your accounts. The money was transferred from the bank account of Wendy Carson."

Pauline looked shell shocked but managed to mumble.

"That can't be right."

"I'm sorry but it is true. It was transferred a few days ago and was credited to your accounts yesterday. We've also frozen your mother's accounts. Naturally, we want to contact your mother, but don't have any contact details and we do not know, at this stage, where she is staying in the United States. We are hoping that you may be able to give us this information and it's in her best interests that we contact her as soon as possible."

Mary then spoke in a calm voice.

"We haven't got any address or contact number, but Wendy should be in touch over the next couple of days and we'll speak to her and let you know what she has said. Are the police involved in this yet?"

"We have spoken to the Metropolitan Police and have a meeting later this afternoon. They will then issue an arrest warrant and will contact the police in the States. We understand that your daughter may be in New York and the Immigration Authorities will have an address where she is staying. I know that you might be able to contact Wendy, but the best thing for her to do is return to this country immediately. I think she'd be happier in this country rather than spending some time in an American prison or on the run from the American Police."

Pauline then spoke quietly.

"You've told us about the two lots of twenty five thousand pounds but what else has she done. There must be some mistake, my Mum was in a responsible position and was in charge of the Nurse bank. You said a large fraud but how large?"

"Have you noticed that your Mum has had a lot of money recently and been able to buy lots of things that may be expensive? Does she have lots of holidays?"

"I told you she's got a good job and she's well paid. I asked you how big is the fraud?"

"I'm sorry, but I can't give you any more information at this stage. Wendy has had her bank account frozen and won't be able to get any money out in the States."

"She took a lot of travellers' cheques."

"They're no good to her either. She'll find it pointless trying to cash them."

"Look. I can't give you any details on how to contact my mum. You must understand that, but I'll make contact and tell her that our accounts have been blocked and so have hers. I don't know what she's done but I'm going to tell her to come home."

"Will you give us the contact details; it'll make it easier for her in the long run?"

"You might be right but I'm not going to land her in trouble without speaking to her first. I've got your phone number."

Mary then spoke to David.

25

"Will you take back the twenty five thousand pounds from our accounts and let us have access because there is some of my own money in the account. I've got about five thousand pounds."

Pauline joined in the conversation.

"Yes, I've got a couple of hundred pounds and my salary is due in shortly."

"We can't release the stops on the accounts at this stage. We don't know if any other money has been given to you by Wendy in the past."

"Mum's never put any money in my account in the past. How long ago are you talking about?"

"I can't tell you that at this stage. Have you noticed if Wendy has transferred any money to you, Mrs Longridge?"

Pauline turned to her Nan.

"Has Mum put any money in your account besides the twenty five thousand?"

Mary refused to answer her granddaughter.

Pauline knew by her Nan's expression that the answer was probably yes, and started sobbing uncontrollably.

Peter passed Pauline a glass of water, which she sipped before getting control of her emotions.

"I'll speak to Mum, that's all I've got to say. Come on Nan, we'd better go. Will we hear from the Police?"

"I think there's every possibility," David said as he opened the door to let the two ladies out of the room.

Peter looked at David as he returned to the desk.

"Do you think they know?"

"My initial thoughts are that they didn't, but I think Grandma has had some money in the past. She mightn't have known it was the result of a fraud. They both know where Wendy is and they'll have contact details. Pauline will be speaking to Wendy within the next half an hour."

"They're about five or six hours behind us, so it'll be early morning in New York. Yeah, she'll be talking to her any time now."

"Let's go and see Ross Edgar. It's time to ask plenty of favours."

"Ross already knows what we're going to ask. He's probably even made enquiries with Immigration."

David and Peter caught the Tube and then made their way to the Police Station where Ross was based. They walked to the counter where a uniformed officer was looking at some paperwork.

Peter then spoke to the police officer.

"We have a meeting with Ross Edgar."

"And your names are?"

"Peter Daley and David Parish."

The officer picked up the phone and dialled the number for Ross.

"Hi Ross, I've got a Peter Daley and David Parish at the front office."

"Okay, I'll come down and collect them now."

"He's on his way down."

A couple of minutes later a plain clothes officer opened the door and said.

"Hello Peter, I presume this is the famous Mr Fraud? It's nice to meet you David."

They all shook hands and followed Ross upstairs to his office and sat around his desk when Ross spoke to David.

"Peter has given me some background information, but you'd better tell me again and give me an update on anything else that has cropped up since then. I know you've spoken to her daughter and mother."

"It's a payroll fraud which has cost the hospital around six hundred thousand pounds. The Nurse Bank Manager, Wendy

Carson, has operated the fraud and has added ten false names to the payroll. We reckon that she's got four people helping her and they've operated two bank accounts each. That's eight accounts and we think Wendy Carson has operated the other two accounts. I've got a list of the names and addresses used and I've also added Carson's home address which she shares with her daughter, Pauline. I've also added her mother Mary Longridge's address but the daughter and mother have not been used for the payroll fraud. Their bank accounts have been credited with twenty five thousand pounds each last week. It was transferred from the account of Wendy Carson."

David then passed the list, which also contained his and Peter's contact numbers, to Ross who quickly glanced down. He also passed files showing copies of the bank statements and details provided at the time the various bank accounts were opened.

"I see the addresses for the two female bank accounts are the same as one of the male addresses."

"Yes. We think the man at that address is a friend of Carson's boyfriend. Wendy and her boyfriend, Frank Sinclair, were seen walking along that road by a member of the hospital staff."

"I think that we'll go to these four addresses today but we'll leave the visits to her daughter and her mother until tomorrow. We'll see if we get anything from the others after our visits today. That's if they're in and haven't done a runner. I've got four uniformed lads who will go to two of the addresses and I'll cover the other two with three of my boys. I think I'll go to this address which is quoted four times, where one of your staff saw Carson and her boyfriend. We'll work with you David, and Peter, in this case and we'll let you know what's going on. I've got your mobile number and I'll give you a ring later. We'll all go on the visits now but it'll probably take a few hours. If we get hold of any of them, I think I'll bring them in and hold them overnight. We'll then interview them tomorrow and we might need you two around to sit in and make sure that we're fully updated on the fraud. I imagine that you'll be happy to disclose the bank statements and the other paperwork."

"That's no problem. Give me a ring tonight and I'll speak with Peter. We'll then arrange a time for tomorrow morning."

They all left the station together and as David and Peter made their way to the Tube station, they were quickly passed by four cars, two of which were the standard police vehicles containing the four uniformed policemen.

David and Peter made their way to different lines in the Tube Station in order to make their way home. As they parted David said to Peter.

"Hopefully, I'll give you a ring tonight once I've heard from Ross."

"Thanks David, I'll speak to you later."

Pauline Carson returned home and looked up the phone number she had to use to contact her mother, Wendy, in New York. She then dialled the number.

"Hello."

"Hello Mum, its Pauline."

"Oh Hi Pauline, everything okay?"

"No, not really Mum. I mean there's nothing wrong with me or Nan. There's been a problem with our bank accounts."

"What do you mean?"

"Both of our bank accounts have been frozen and we can't get any money out."

"Why not?"

"You transferred twenty five thousand pounds to our accounts didn't you?"

"Yes. It was a surprise and I did it because I wasn't sure when I'll be getting home. I thought it would be nice for you both to have some money."

"Where did you get the money from?"

"I had some savings and Frank gave me some money."

"You're not telling the truth Mum. We both had a letter from our bank telling us the accounts were frozen and I rang the bloke who sent the letter. He is a Fraud Investigator with the bank and he wouldn't tell me much apart from the fact the accounts were frozen. I was told to ring a David Parish who's a Fraud Consultant with the National Health Service and covers Euston General Hospital. I did ring him and he agreed to meet me and Nan at the hospital. When we got there, he was with another Fraud bloke from the Health Service and they told us why the bank accounts had been frozen. He didn't give us much detail but he said they were investigating a big fraud at the hospital and they were looking for you in connection with the fraud."

"Me? Why me?"

"I think you know why. They've also frozen your bank account and he said your travellers cheques weren't any good either."

"Oh no, what else has he done?"

"After our meeting, he was going to meet up with the police. They'd already spoken to them but they were going to contact the American Police. David Parish said you should return to this country as soon as possible as it would be better for you."

"Oh I'm sorry you and Mum have been involved. I was only trying to help you."

"Have you committed this fraud Mum?"

There was a silence and some sobbing at the end of the phone.

"Speak to me Mum. What have you done?"

"I'm sorry Pauline."

"What do you mean sorry?"

"I've been stupid. I did do something wrong at work. I found it easy and Frank helped me."

"So it's his fault. I could have guessed. Nan had about five thousand pounds in savings before you paid in the twenty five thousand and she can't touch that either. We've got no money."

"I'll sort something out. I've got another bank account with money in."

"They've probably frozen that as well."

"The hospital didn't know about that account."

"I bet the bank and the Fraud Investigators know about that account."

"They mightn't."

"Don't kid yourself. When are you coming home, you can't stay in New York, the American police will be arriving any time."

"I need to speak to Frank. Did the Fraud Investigator know where I'm staying?"

"I don't know. I didn't tell him and I didn't give him any phone number to contact you, but he didn't seem too worried. I was chatting to Nan and maybe Immigration will know or maybe the American Police already know Frank and where he lives."

"I'll give you a ring back later Pauline. I need to speak to Frank."

"Mum, come home."

"I'll speak to you later Pauline."

It was just before eight o'clock when David's mobile rang out.

"Hello, David Parish."

"Hi David, its Ross."

"Have you had any luck Ross?"

"I would say so. We called at all four addresses and eventually arrested four men. We had to call back a couple of times at one of the addresses before we managed to get hold of one of the blokes. We actually found some bank statements at all of the addresses and they are in different names to the people we've arrested. Three of them haven't said much, they just shrugged their shoulders, but we've got their correct identities and driving licences or passports. We haven't formally interviewed them yet, we'll do that tomorrow morning, but the bloke I arrested hasn't shut up. He was the friend of Wendy Carson's bloke, his name is Denis King and he's already told us that Carson was in charge, and he just operated the bank accounts and was given his cut of twenty five per cent of the salary. He then had a monthly meeting with Carson and gave her the seventy five per cent in cash. He wasn't under caution when he was telling us this but I'll bring up what he told us today, when we formally interview him tomorrow. I think he might have a lot to say and it'll be better if you joined me for this interview. Is that okay?"

"Yes, that's fine with me Ross."

"I'll also need Peter to be there and stand by to help the others if he's needed. Will you speak to him?"

"Sure, what time do you want us in tomorrow?"

"It'll be a late night tonight, how about half past ten?"

"That's okay. I'll let Peter know and we'll see you tomorrow morning. Thanks for your help Ross."

"No problem, it's all part of the job."

Alisa was sitting by David when he was talking on the phone and quipped.

"Have the Metropolitan Police been good for Senor Fraudo?"

"It looks as though they've had a good night. I've been asked to interview one of the blokes with Ross Edgar. They want Peter to stand by for the other interviews, so I'll give him a ring now. I think we'll have a nice bottle of Rioja afterwards."

"Is that all you want?"

"We'll see how we get on."

David then picked up his mobile and rang Peter Daley.

"Hello David."

"Hi Peter. They've picked up all four of the blokes and they're being kept in the cells overnight. One of them hasn't stopped blabbing and I'll be interviewing him with Ross tomorrow morning. Ross has asked that you help with one of the other interviews. He asked us to be there at half past ten tomorrow morning."

"That's no problem. Should I meet you there or should we have a pre-meeting?"

"It's probably worth having a quick chat beforehand. We'll have a coffee in the police canteen, how about ten o'clock?"

"I'll see you at the front office at ten o'clock."

"Cheers Peter, see you in the morning."

5

David had been out for an early morning walk before returning to Alisa's flat near Regents Park and as he entered the flat, Alisa was talking on the phone.

"He's just come in now. I'll put him on the phone."

"David, I was in a meeting today and met Darren O'Brien. He's a partner in the firm of solicitors, Howarth and Davies, and he worked with you on the travel fraud case at the hospital in London."

"Yes, I know Darren."

"He knew of our relationship and asked where you were. I told him you were in London and I gave him this number. He wanted to talk to you about something personal, but did not want to interrupt you at work."

Alisa handed David the telephone handset.

"Good evening Darren, what can I do for you?"

"Hi David, this is a family matter and we would like to pick your brain."

"You can try."

"I don't know if you've heard of Sally O'Brien?"

David thought for a few seconds.

"Do you mean Sally O'Brien, the news reporter on television?"

"Yes, well Sally is my sister."

"I didn't know that, you have someone famous in the family."

"I thought you knew everything."

"I must've failed on that one. She's quite high profile for one of the children's charities isn't she?"

"Yes she is. It's along story David and I'd like to arrange a meeting with you and Sally, but the brief background is as follows. Sally had a relationship about twenty years ago with a bloke, Ron Thomas, who we thought was a bit of a bad one. Anyhow, Sally ended up having twin boys, but one day they'd been out and he was driving the car. He was driving quite fast and Sally told him to slow down, but it was too late. He crashed the car and the twins, who were only eighteen months old, were killed instantly, Sally was quite badly injured with a lot of internal problems. He got off lightly and was not injured too badly. Their relationship was already going through a bad time and they split up a couple of months later, and I don't think they've seen each other since then."

"I'm sorry about that, I didn't know."

"Sally has never kept it a secret but the injuries in the car crash meant Sally would not be able to have any more children. Anyhow, about a month ago, my Mum and Dad started getting letters addressed to the twins, which were mainly loan and credit card problems. We believe that somebody has been using the twins' identity for fraud purposes and they would've got the address from the birth certificates. Naturally Sally is horrified and upset. I made some initial enquiries with the loan and credit card companies and soon found out that duplicate birth certificates had been issued by the General Register Office in Manchester. They said that they were issued to the father Ron Thomas and he had produced some sort of identity."

"I know that name, but it could be just a coincidence. There was a Ron Thomas involved with the Mitchell gangsters in Cheshire. The Mitchell's were both killed in Spain but he went to prison for three years, but that was only a few months ago. That Ron Thomas will still be in prison and he will not be out now. What else do you know about your Ron Thomas? How old is he? Do you have any other details?"

"He will be about forty years old. His full name was on their birth certificates, it's Ronald James Thomas. I haven't seen him for twenty years, so I can't give a description but he is just over six foot in height. He used to live in Manchester."

"The bloke who went to prison was forty one years old, and he is about six feet tall. I've got good contacts with the Police and I'll get in touch with Anne Graham from Cheshire Police. We should be able to confirm if it's the same Ron Thomas, but it sounds unlikely. Once I've spoken to Anne, I'll let you know but this sounds like another case of identity fraud. I'd be pleased to meet you and Sally, when do you want to meet?"

"Sally is away at the moment but she's back the day after tomorrow. How about meeting early next week at my office, say Tuesday, three o'clock?"

"That'll be fine; I'll see both you and Sally then."

Alisa had been sitting by David when he was on the phone.

"That sounded interesting. I presume you mean the Sally O'Brien who's often on the news. She's quite a well known reporter but she's also a Patron for a Children's Charity and was on television a couple of weeks ago trying to raise money for the children."

"That's right; we watched it when we were in the Lake District. Apparently, she had twin boys around twenty years ago, but they were killed in a road accident when they were only eighteen months old. She split up from the father, they weren't married, but he was a bit of a gangster and it looks possible that he asked for copies of the twins' birth certificates. They've now been used for identity fraud and Sally's parents are getting all sorts of letters. I didn't know that Sally was Darren's sister, but I know Darren from the travel fraud case."

"You mentioned the Mitchell brothers being killed in Spain. I thought I'd heard the last of them but I have to say I wasn't sorry that Steve Mitchell was killed, after all he had shot and crippled my cousin, Luiz. I gather that the Ron Thomas involved with the Mitchell gangsters was the father of the children?"

"We're not sure yet, but you wouldn't believe that somebody like Sally O'Brien was involved with Ron Thomas, although she was young at that time. These things happen."

"I know you'd never forget the death of your children but it must be agonising for Sally, having the memories brought back in this fashion, especially, as it looks as though the father, Ron Thomas, may be behind the frauds. He has got a background of fraudulent activity, having been involved with the Mitchells."

"Sally has turned her life round and she must have worked really hard to recover from that disaster, then study and achieve what she has done as a reporter. She's also a great fund raiser for children."

"Darren was telling me on the phone that the injuries that Sally sustained in the road accident have prevented her from having any more children."

"Oh that must be awful. You're seeing them next Tuesday?"

"Yes, I've arranged a meeting at Darren's office. I think I'll try and speak to Anne Graham now, I've got her mobile number."

David picked up the phone and dialled Anne's number which was quickly answered.

"Hello, Anne Graham."

"Hi Anne, its David Parish, how are you?"

"I'm fine David, unless you're going to give me some bad news."

"I don't think so. I want to pick your brain."

"You can try."

"I've been asked to look at an identity fraud. It might concern Ron Thomas, but as far as I know, he's still in prison, isn't he?"

"Yes, he got three years, as you know and he's currently in Walton Prison in Liverpool."

"I spoke to Darren O'Brien, a solicitor I know in London. He was involved in the Travel Fraud case that I was investigating. Apparently, his sister is Sally O'Brien, who is the news reporter on television."

"Oh yes, I know who you mean."

"Anyhow, his sister had twin boys about twenty years ago and they were killed in a car crash when they were two years old and the driver of the car was a man called Ron Thomas, full name Ronald James Thomas. I'm trying to find out if it's the same person."

"I remember the crash. I was a young recruit in uniform and had only been in the police about three months. It was tragic and that Ron Thomas is definitely the same Ron Thomas that we put in prison a few months ago. I'd forgotten about the children's mother, but she was a nice girl who got mixed up with the wrong bloke. I'm sure the name was Sally O'Brien but I never connected that with the Sally O'Brien on the television. She's also high profile for one of the charities, isn't she?"

"Yes. The identity fraud that I'm looking into concerns the use of the twins' names. Somebody got their birth certificates and has been using them for identity fraud. Darren spoke to the Births Registry Office in Manchester and they said that the person who asked for the certificates was the father, Ronald Thomas."

"Well, it wasn't our Ron Thomas, he's safely tucked away. Sounds like someone is pretending to be him but if this fraud is in Manchester, how come I haven't heard about it?"

"You will do shortly, but I haven't spoken to Sally O'Brien yet. I'll be speaking to her and Darren at his office next

Tuesday and I'll tell them you should be involved. I'll obviously give them my help and advice if they want it. They probably will."

"Keep me in touch David. I wonder why somebody is impersonating Ron Thomas, it makes me uneasy, and you wonder if he's involved in some way even though he's locked up."

"I've had the same thoughts myself."

"We had some concerns about his partner. He's been with her for about five years and they have a daughter who is two years old. We thought that she was involved as part of the gang working for the Mitchells and she has got some form for theft. She was also found guilty of an assault on another woman in a night club, who she thought was having an affair with Ron Thomas. That was about four years ago and she was sent to prison for six months. A nice lady is his partner, Lucy Tindall. You've got me thinking now David; I think I'll check to see if she's still visiting him in prison."

6

Later that morning David made his way to the Metropolitan Police Station for the meeting with Peter Daley and the interviews that were taking place later in the morning. He found Peter waiting at the front desk and they were both allowed to enter the Police Station and made their way to the staff canteen, where they purchased a couple of coffees.

Peter then asked David.

"Have we got any agenda for today?"

"I only know what I told you on the phone last night. The bloke, who is the friend of Wendy Carson's boyfriend, starting talking in the car. Ross just listened but told him anything he said would be mentioned on tape today. I gather the other three didn't say much but I suspect they know they've been caught and will just do what they have to do, and take the punishment. Ross wants us involved because we've got more background knowledge into the fraud. I'm in with Ross and you'll be with one of his colleagues interviewing a second person. I don't know who's interviewing the other two, it might be the police or we may be doing two interviews each."

"Do we know anymore about Wendy Carson?"

"No. I bet her daughter or mother has been speaking to her on the phone. I wonder if her boyfriend's mate knows anything."

"I presume if he talks, you'll let us know what's been said and it may help us in our interview."

"I'm sure Ross will have that sorted out."

A few minutes later, Jan Burgess a colleague of Ross walked over to David and Peter. Jan was known to both David and Peter.

"Good Morning. Our fraudsters are waiting for us and we'll complete the taped interviews. Ross is with you David, you're seeing Denis King. I'm with you Peter, we're seeing Chris Sugden. Four of our colleagues are interviewing the other two blokes, but not for a couple of hours, in case something crops up in our interviews. We might suspend the interviews if we feel we need to discuss what's been said during one of the interviews, but we'll play it by ear. We have given their solicitors copies of the bank statements and the account information, so they'll have had the chance to examine them."

They all left the canteen and headed towards the interview rooms where they met up with Ross. David and Ross then entered their interview room where they found Denis King sitting down with his solicitor, Phil Desmond. Phil stood up and shook hands with David saying.

"It's nice to meet you Mr Fraud. Your name is often mentioned in legal circles."

"Nicely, I hope."

"Well, most of the time."

Ross started the preliminary discussions with Denis and Phil.

"I just want to check that you understand what we are going to do. David will operate the tape machine and you will hear a loud noise before the start of the interview, this is normal. Has Phil explained what we are going to discuss and the procedures that will take place?"

"Yes, I do understand, thanks."

"Okay, David will you start the tape please?"

David started the tape and the noise appeared before Ross started the interview with the opening procedures.

"This Interview is being tape recorded, it is the twenty fifth of February, two thousand and eight and the time by my watch is ten thirty five a.m. I am Ross Edgar an Inspector with the Metropolitan Police. The other person present is."

"David Parish a Fraud Consultant representing the Euston General Hospital."

"I am interviewing, please state your full name, address and date of birth."

"Denis John King, Twenty three Glendale Road, Finsbury, London. Date of birth Twenty Ninth of September, nineteen sixty seven."

"Also present is."

"Philip Alan Desmond, Desmond and MacLaren Solicitors, London."

"We are in the Interview Room of the Metropolitan Police Station, London. At the end of the interview, I will give you a notice explaining the procedures for the dealing with the tapes and how you can have access to them. Before the interview begins I must caution you."

"You do not have to say anything, but it may harm your defence if you do not mention when questioned something which you later rely on in court, anything you do say may be given in evidence. Do you understand the caution?"

Denis understood this but was clearly quite startled.

"Yes I do."

"The reason for this interview is that we are investigating allegations that you were involved in the receipt of fraudulent salary claims at the Euston General Hospital between August, two thousand and five and September, two thousand and seven knowing that the receipt of the salaries was based on false claims, using false names and false documentation to open two bank accounts. The total number of salary claims paid into the two bank accounts is forty eight, and the cost of these salary credits totals one hundred and twenty one thousand and sixty two pounds. Do you understand the reason for this interview?"

"Yes."

"If at any time you wish to speak to your solicitor in private or if you wish me to stop the interview for any reason, then tell me and I will stop the interview."

"Okay."

"First of all, I would like to confirm, for the record, some of the information that you gave me last night, when you were being driven from your home in Glendale Road to the Police Station."

"That's fine with me, but if I do help you, will you stop me being sent to prison. I think it's only fair if I help the police then they should help me."

"It is not up to me what sentence you are given, that would be down to the Judge, but we will put in a good word and tell the Judge that you have helped us, that's if the information you give to us is helpful. Your solicitor will know that is all we can do."

Phil Desmond then turned to Denis.

"That is normal procedure, the Police will advise the Judge, but I would also arrange for the Judge to be informed of any assistance that you may have given."

Denis then looked at Ross and David and said.

"Okay, I'll tell you everything that I know."

Ross then started the questioning.

"You told me yesterday that Wendy Carson gave you the documentation and the names and addresses to be used when the accounts were opened. Is that correct and what actually did she give you?"

"She gave me passports, driving licences and some bills which had the name and addresses on them."

"Whose photos were on the passports and driving licences?"

"My photo was on them. I went to a photo booth a week before and got eight photos taken and gave them to Wendy. She put them in an envelope and I asked her for the eight pounds that I paid for the photos. She didn't have any money with her in the room and went next door to see Frank Sinclair.

There were four envelopes on the table, one had my name on it, and I made a note of the other three names."

"What were the names?"

Denis then put his hand in his pocket and took out a piece of paper.

"Chris Sugden, Jim Barrowcliffe and Tom Crouch. They've all been round to see Wendy and Frank at some time or other."

"Do you know them?"

"Not well, but I have met them a couple of times."

"You're saying that you gave photos to Wendy Carson and received false passports and driving licences a week later, with your photos but two different names."

"That's right."

"Do you know who forged those documents?"

"I imagine it was Frank Sinclair. He has served a spell in prison in the States for forgery and he was here at that time."

"Did you go to the banks and open the accounts?"

"Yes, there was no problem once I provided the documentation."

"You said that you went to the bank each month and withdrew the salary payments. You kept twenty five per cent and gave seventy five per cent to Wendy. Is that correct?"

"Yeah. She was quite fussy. If the salary was two thousand and twenty pounds, I'd have to give her one thousand five hundred and fifteen pounds. The first month, I gave her one thousand five hundred quid and she asked me for the other fifteen."

"What did she do with the cash?"

"She put it in a brown envelope in her shopping bag. I sometimes saw that there were other brown envelopes with money inside."

"What did you do with your money?"

"I spent it."

"How much money have you received since you became involved in this fraud?"

"I've kept records. Over the couple of years, around a hundred and twenty thousand has been credited to the two accounts and I've been able to keep about thirty thousand quid for myself. I imagine the other three would have been given around the same."

David then asked a question.

"If you four have received around a hundred and twenty thousand pounds, then you would have given Wendy, three hundred and sixty thousand pounds."

"That sounds about right."

"We understand that four bank statements were being sent to the address where you live, two that you have told us about. The other two were quoting female names, whom operated those two accounts?"

"Wendy Carson managed those two accounts herself. She wouldn't have had to share the proceeds of those, except with Frank. I've done my sums but if all the salary payments were similar then each bank account would've received about sixty thousand pounds, making six hundred thousand pounds. The four of us received a hundred and twenty thousand pounds, so she and Frank must've got four hundred and eighty thousand quid."

"You've no idea what they've done with all the money?"

"No, they've had a good time during the past couple of years, so they've probably spent a fair amount. I knew how much they were getting and asked her for an increase to forty per cent. She said she'd think about it, but a couple of days later she came back and threatened me. I thought she was joking but she said I'd end up in the Thames if I tried to be greedy, so I didn't ask for anymore again. I know she's a woman but she's into Jujitsu in a big way and I wouldn't fancy having an argument with her. I spent some time in the States and met Frank and we became mates, but once he met Wendy that was the end of it. He might think he's tough but I got the impression that Wendy pulled the strings."

"You're not American, what were you doing over there?"

"Travelling. I was left some money when my mother died and decided to travel to many parts of the world. I would get a few jobs now and then and that's were I met Frank. I was a waiter in a restaurant and Frank got a job doing the same a few weeks later. We got talking and I found out that he had artistic talents and when I asked him why he was working in a restaurant, he told me he'd been in prison and that was the only job he could get."

"How come he came to this country?"

"I returned home and we spoke on the phone a couple of times. He said he would like to come over and I invited him. You're probably going to find out anyway, but I was going out with Wendy Carson at that time but when he came over she fell for his American accent and charm."

"I suppose we might have broken up, but if he hadn't been on the scene we might have stayed together. Wendy can easily get round me, which is why I got conned into doing this. I've never been in trouble before and don't want to go to prison. I know you're going to say its jealousy and I want revenge but I've been stupid and I would hate the thought of being locked up. That's why I'm helping you."

"Have you got their contact details in America?"

"Oh yeah. I've got the address in New York and I've got his telephone number and mobile number. I've also got Wendy's mobile number but I imagine you've got that. Pass me a piece of paper."

Denis took out his diary and looked up the details. He then wrote them down and passed the piece of paper back to David.

"Frank has made threats that I'd be in trouble if I said anything to the police and he'll have threatened the others too. I don't really care but will I get some form of protection from the police?"

Ross replied to Denis.

"We'll try but he's in New York. We might have trouble getting him back but it should be easier with Wendy. If he stays in the States, I wouldn't go over there if I was you."

"I've got no intention of going there again. I'm happy with this country, but hopefully not in prison."

There was a knock on the door and Jan Burgess popped her head in and said to Ross.

"Can we have a word?"

Ross turned to Jan.

"I think we'll be finished in five minutes. Can it wait till then?"

"Yes sure. We'll be in the corridor."

Ross looked at David.

"I think we've got enough for now. Is there anything else you can think of?"

"No, we need to have a meeting with the others but I think we've finished for the moment."

Ross then asked Denis a further question.

"Do you wish to add anything further or clarify any point on anything you have told me?"

"I have told you everything and I can't help you with all the money that has been taken. You will have to ask Wendy and Frank, but hopefully I won't go to prison."

"I can't make any promises but your full co-operation will be reported when the case gets to court."

"Thanks."

"Here is the notice which explains your entitlement to a copy of the tape used in this interview. This interview is concluded at eleven twenty eight a.m. on the twenty fifth of February, two thousand and eight. Switch off the tape recorder."

Ross, Jan, David and Peter met after the interviews had taken place. Ross then spoke to Jan.

"Denis King has admitted everything but how did the interview go with Chris Sugden?"

"He hardly said a word and wouldn't admit or deny anything. I got the impression that he was too frightened to speak and thought he'd be in bigger trouble if he said something or admitted his part in the fraud. His solicitor's firm are acting for Barrowcliffe and Crouch and he told me on the way out that they would probably act the same way."

"Do our blokes know who are interviewing Barrowcliffe and Crouch?"

"Yes. I've told them."

"I think we should make searches of the mother and daughters houses now. I don't know if they'll hear that we have people in custody, but they may find out and tell Wendy. It's worth doing the searches now and we'll take two teams. Will you two join us?"

"Of course." replied David.

"Okay, you come with me, David and Peter will go with Jan."

7

Frank Sinclair sat quietly in his apartment in Manhattan thinking about what Wendy Carson had told him. He had spent nine months in a Federal Correctional Institution in New York, when he forged some documents to help a friend. It was the worst time of his life and he had never intended to get involved in any other criminal activity, but Wendy had persuaded him to forge some documents and he was infatuated with Wendy. He had no intention of going to a prison again, either in the States or in the United Kingdom and was thinking of his next step when Wendy returned to the apartment and walked straight over to him.

"I've been thinking. We've got about fifty thousand pounds, which is about a hundred thousand dollars in some American Banks. I think we'll have to draw that money out in cash straightaway or it might get frozen like they have done with my money."

"That's my money. You gave it to me for helping you out."

"That's right Frank, but it's no good to you if the accounts get blocked. You're best to go and draw the money out in cash. We'll go now and get hold of the money before somebody else gets it. I still have money hidden in England but I can't get that until we go back."

Frank was a bit startled and a little reluctant to let Wendy get near the hundred thousand dollars, but it did make sense to get hold of the money in cash.

"Okay, we'd better go now before the banks close. The money's in two different banks."

As they left the apartment, Frank turned to Wendy.

"What happened to your travellers cheques? Did you try to cash them in?"

"I went to one of the money exchange places and thought I'd try and cash a hundred dollars but when he pressed some buttons on the computer, he told me they'd been stopped by the bank. He didn't know why, but I told him my husband in England had blocked them, because I'd left him after meeting some nice American bloke. He was a bit thick and believed me, but it's not worth trying again to cash any traveller's cheques."

It was an hour later when they both returned to the apartment with a hundred and seven thousand dollars in cash. Frank had been thinking of what to do next and confronted Wendy as soon as they'd opened the doors and put the cash on the table.

"I haven't got a clue how much money you've made on this fraud Wendy, but I think it's a lot more than I first thought. My part in this is only small; I've forged a few passports and some other documents which were used to open bank accounts. I don't want to go to prison again and I certainly don't want to go back to England. I don't think they'd extradite me for my part in your fiddle. I've been thinking and I'll give you fifty thousand dollars and I'll keep the rest. You've still got some more hidden back in England."

"That's right but I can't get it over here. What are you planning to do with the money you say you're keeping?"

"I think we should split and go our own ways. We can't stay here and I don't want to go to jail, I'll disappear somewhere in the States. You can do what you want to."

"You want us to split up. I don't know anybody else in the States and I wouldn't know where to go."

"Do as your daughter says, return to England and take the wrap. Your mum and daughter need you, go back home, they'll soon catch you in this country. You won't go to prison for long if it's your first offence."

"I thought you loved me Frank Sinclair. Obviously I was mistaken, wasn't I?"

"I did love you but I don't think you love me."

Ross, David and Detective Constable Geoff Ricketts left the Police Station in one car and Jan Burgess and Peter left in another car with Detective Constable Sam Dixon. Ross headed towards Wendy Carson's house which is where her daughter, Pauline lived. Jan made their way to the house where Mary Longridge, Wendy's mother lived. They were both followed by Uniformed Officers in two police cars.

Ross knocked on the door, which was soon opened by Pauline Carson.

"Pauline Carson?"

"Yes, who are you?"

Ross pulled out his warrant card and showed it to Pauline.

"Detective Inspector Ross Edgar, Metropolitan Police. You know David Parish, a Fraud Consultant with the Health Service. We have a warrant to search these premises."

"What for?"

"David has spoken to you and you will be aware that we are undertaking a fraud investigation, which is linked to your mother, Wendy Carson."

The four police officers, led by Ross and David entered the premises and started a search of the property. The search took the best part of an hour, and they had found and confiscated a lap top computer belonging to Wendy. They also took away two mobile phones, diaries, bank statements, credit card statements, letters and a variety of other paperwork. Also hidden but located by one of the policemen were the passports used to open the bank accounts. They showed the photograph of Wendy but the names were the same as the two bank accounts. There was also a third passport showing the photograph of Wendy but using a name not known to Ross. There were photographs on the wall of Wendy receiving awards for her performances in Jujitsu. It was the first time that Ross had been made aware of the interest in Jujitsu. He turned to Pauline.

"I didn't know your mother was a Jujitsu star?"

"She's been doing that for a few years. Somebody she knew was mugged and attacked and she thought she would take up some type of defence to protect her. She picked Jujitsu because I'd had a boyfriend who was interested in it."

"Where is your mother now?"

"I think you know she's in America."

"Have you spoken to her?"

"No, I tried ringing her on her mobile, but got no reply. It was switched off, but I think the mobile I rang is the one that you've just taken."

"Do you have an address where she's staying?"

"No Frank would have arranged that and Mum was going to ring me once she was settled in"

"I think you know where she is or you've spoken to her. It'll do her no good trying to hide from us. We'll be contacting the New York Police to seek their assistance, its best if she comes home straight away."

"I know. That's what David Parish told me and I'll tell her when she gives me a ring."

Geoff Ricketts came into the room holding a large envelope.

"I've just found this hidden in some clothes, there's a couple of thousand pounds in cash."

Pauline turned to Geoff saying.

"That's the household emergency money in case something goes wrong. You can't take that, I might need it."

"I'm sorry, its evidence. We don't know where it came from and it's probably part of the proceeds from the fraud."

"You've blocked my bank account and I've got no money. What are you going to do about it?"

Ross glared at Pauline.

"Speak to your mother and ask her where the six hundred thousand pounds has gone from Euston General Hospital. She might slip you a few quid to keep you going."

"How much?"

"You heard."

"I don't believe it. She can't have taken that much money and I haven't got it apart from the twenty five thousand she transferred to my account and my Nan's account. We didn't even know the money had been transferred. I'm going to ring Nan."

"I wouldn't bother at the moment. Her house is being searched as well and a police officer will answer the phone if you ring her now."

"We've done nothing wrong."

"We will want you and your Nan to come to the Police Station in the next couple of days to be formally interviewed. I'll be in touch but you should both get a solicitor."

Ross left the house with the property they had taken as part of the search operation.

Jan Burgess, Peter and the team had completed the search at Mary Longridge's house and had found twenty thousand pounds in cash but little else of interest.

"Where did you get this cash from?"

"It's part of my life's savings. I don't always trust the banks and I'd rather have some cash in the house."

"There are a lot of the new twenty pound notes in this package. You haven't had those for years, how did you get hold of them."

"I know notes go out of date so I change them bit by bit"

"Have you spoken to your daughter?"

"No. I haven't spoken to Wendy since she had left to go to America, but I am expecting her to call shortly as she always has done in the past when she was away."

"You'd better tell her to come home immediately for her own good."

"I know. I'll tell her when she rings me."

"We will want you to come to the Police Station in the next couple of days to be formally interviewed. We'll be in touch but you should get a solicitor."

The cash was confiscated and taken back to the Police Station together with some paperwork and bank statements.

Pauline picked up the phone and rang her Nan.

"Hello."

"Hello Nan, its Pauline. Have the police been round to your place?"

"Yes. They've taken the package with twenty thousand pounds, which your Mum gave me a month or two ago."

"What package and what twenty thousand pounds?"

"She told me to mind it and use it as emergency money if we needed it, but the police have now taken it away."

"Didn't you ask where she got the money?"

"No, I thought it was none of my business. I hid the money but the police found it."

"They told me that we're going to be interviewed and I should get a solicitor."

"They said the same to me. Did you speak to your Mum?"

"Yes, but she said she would get back to me and she hasn't yet. I think I'll try again. I'll let you know if I speak to her. Bye for now."

"Bye Pauline."

Pauline thought she'd better not ring from the home phone in case the police were able to check on the line. They hadn't taken her mobile phone so she dialled Frank Sinclair's number in New York but there was no answer to her call. She then tried her Mum's mobile phone but that was switched off.

David, Peter, Ross and Jan met in Ross's office at the police station. Ross started the meeting.

"Jan, what happened in the interviews with Barrowcliffe and Crouch?"

"They didn't say a word, just like Chris Sugden"

"That's no surprise. We've searched the properties of both Wendy Carson where her daughter lives, and her mothers. There's a bit of paperwork, her laptop computer, forged passports and about twenty two thousand pounds in cash. We've found her boyfriend's address and phone number on the computer and I tried to ring the number and got no answer. We also found some mobile phone numbers but when we tried them they were was switched off, and I would guess that her daughter, Pauline's rang her, and she's made herself disappear for the moment. There's nothing much to add to the information that you've already provided David."

"We have got some of the cash."

"There was twenty thousand at Mary Longridge's house and a couple of thousand at Wendy's house. Mary knew about the money, saying it was her savings but I don't think that Pauline knew anything. I would guess that Wendy slipped her mother the money as an emergency and no questions were asked."

"When can we start asking for help from the New York Police?"

"I'll start the proceedings within the next couple of days, but I doubt if they'll rush into anything. It's not terrorism or murder, if it was they would move pretty quickly. I'm not convinced they'll help much with Frank Sinclair, he is an American and all we have, for his part, so far, is possible forgery on a small scale. We will charge the other four blokes today, and they'll appear in the Magistrates Court tomorrow and they'll be released on police bail. We've got their passports and they'll have to report to a local police station on a daily basis."

David nodded his head and then said.

"I'd like us to start proceedings to get the money back from the frozen bank accounts and returned to the Courts. They'll then get it sent back to the hospital. I know it'll take a while but we may as well start. If you mention it to the Court tomorrow, I'll make a start on the formal proceedings."

"That's fine David. We'll get all the paperwork together with what you've already given us and pass it to the Crown Prosecution Service and they'll work on it while we chase Wendy Carson and her boyfriend Frank Sinclair. We'll keep you in touch with what's going on and let us know if you find out any more."

"Okay Ross, is that all we need for now Peter?"

"Yes, there's nothing much doing until Wendy Carson is back on the scene."

David then turned and shook hands with Ross.

"Thanks Ross. We'll be in touch, hopefully it won't be too long."

David spoke with Peter as they made their way to the Tube Station before Peter returned home and David returned to Alisa's flat.

"I'll return home to Liverpool tomorrow morning and find out where Brian is up to with our dentist friend. There's not a lot that we can do at the moment with regards to Wendy Carson, it's a sit back and wait scenario. The legal processes will be completed by the Crown Prosecution Service but they will have a few queries, no doubt, but I'll let you know. I mightn't need to be in London while this is going on, you'll probably be able to keep it ticking over, but let me know if you need anything."

"Enjoy your trip home and I hope our dentist has not given us too bad a time. I wouldn't visit him if you have toothache."

"Thanks."

8

Alisa was home when David returned to the flat and greeted him with a big hug and a kiss.

"How was your day with the Police, Senor Fraudo?"

"It was fine, everything is proceeding but we don't know where our fraudster is. Well, we know she's in New York and it's a question of trying to get her back. We'll get her in the end if the American Police find her, it'll just take time. I've finished here for now and I'll have to return home early tomorrow and then drive to Lancashire for a meeting with Brian Lewis."

"In that case, we should have a night in and go to bed early."

"That sounds a wonderful idea to me."

They were finishing off their evening meal when the telephone rang and Alisa picked up the phone.

"Hello."

"Hola Alisa, its Felipe."

"Hola Felipe, and how are you and the family?"

"We're all fine. I thought that I'd let you know that Ben Alexander, the dentist that David is investigating has returned to Manchester with his family this afternoon. I've also found out that he's been looking at buying a boat in Espana, he might have bought one but I don't know yet. Will you tell David?"

"Yes Felipe, he is here at the moment but going home tomorrow. Do you know the price of the boats he was looking at?"

"I believe there were a couple in the region of a hundred and fifty thousand euros."

"It must be a nice boat."

"I would say so. Do you have any plans for a trip home to here in Murcia or your apartment in Seville?"

"I was thinking about that today. I'll have a chat with David but I could be free in about three weeks for a small break. I'll let you know, nice to speak to you. Bye for now."

"Bye Alisa."

David was looking a bit puzzled when Alisa put the phone down.

"Who's buying a boat?"

"Ben Alexander has been looking at boats costing a hundred and fifty thousand euros."

"He can afford it with the frauds that he has been undertaking."

The following morning, David made his way to Euston Station to catch the first train back to Liverpool, which departed at a quarter to seven but would arrive at half past nine.

When the announcement came that the shop was open, David got out of his seat and walked to the next carriage. The self-service shops on these trains were better than the old buffet cars and being a creature of habit, he collected his usual, Premium Bacon Roll and placed it on the counter before asking the assistant for.

"A Large Americano, please."

She filled the large coffee container and handed it to David.

David handed over a £5 note and collected the change.

"Thank you."

He then made his way back to his seat for the journey which would take about two and three quarter hours.

This early start allowed a visit home to check some paperwork and pick up his car and make the journey to Southport, where Brian Lewis had set up a base to work with the Dental Fraud team, checking into all the dental claims made by Ben Alexander.

It was early afternoon when David met Brian Lewis and was able to get an update on the fraud undertaken by the dentist.

"How are you getting on in the world of fraudulent dentistry?"

"I'm getting a lot of help from the Dental team, but we have to go back further than we thought. We're now going back eight years and it looks as though the fraud started in 1998. I've completed an interim report and it's probably better if you read this first and then we'll have a discussion afterwards."

"Thanks Brian. I'll have a look at it now."

David picked up the report and started reading in order to get a full picture of the fraud.

Benjamin John Alexander
Dental Practitioner

The above has maintained a one man Dental Practice in Lancashire for thirteen years. He obtained the Batchelor of Dental Surgery degree in 1992, having attended the five year course at Liverpool University and initially worked in a local hospital for two years, before the retirement of the previous Dental Practitioner left a thriving business opportunity. Benjamin Alexander took over the Practice which has remained successful and mainly treats National Health Service Patients.

He is thirty nine years of age, married, with three children, aged ten, eight and six years. His wife has a small upmarket clothing shop, but this is one of several ventures which appear not to have been successful and is reported to be having difficulties. Indications are that it will close shortly with considerable financial losses. All the children attend fee paying private schools.

The Dental Board and the Local Health Trust complete random checks on the claims made by Dental Practitioners, and have in the past year started taking a closer look at one man practices where the overall claims are above a certain level, especially for the more costly dental treatments. It was soon discovered that claims were being made, but no information was evident on the patient records. Treatment had not been carried out on existing patients and further checks showed that claims had been made for deceased patients, patients who were no longer linked to his practice and fictitious patients.

The initial checks were made over the past two years, before being referred to the Health Trust who informed the Fraud Consultant, David Parish. Following consultations, it was agreed that the checks should be made for a period of five years. This research showed similar fraudulent claims for the full period and checks were then backdated to 1998, a period of eight years. In the year 1998/1999 the total of fraudulent claims would appear to be in the region of fifty thousand pounds but there is no evidence of any false claims prior to the financial year 1998/1999.

The false claims have continued since 1998 and total five hundred and eighty six thousand, seven hundred pounds. Dental Practitioners are paid a fee for every item of treatment and they claim by completing documentation and then submitting computerised claims to the relevant Board. Details of the cost and number of fraudulent claims are as follows.

1998/99   £49800 250 claims
1999/00   £58500 290 claims
2000/01   £60600 306 claims
2001/02   £59300 294 claims
2002/03   £80250 401 claims
2003/04   £85350 423 claims

2004/05   £95200 476 claims
2005/06   £97600 486 claims
Total   £586700 2926 claims

Benjamin Alexander is due to return to work shortly. The Health Trust has concerns relating to the dental welfare of patients in the area. He is the only Dental Practitioner taking on new National Health Service Patients and has a full appointments diary for the next four weeks. He does leave a small allocated period for emergency treatment and the Health Trust are unable to provide another Practitioner for the area if the current dentist, Benjamin Alexander is not allowed to treat patients. This will leave the area without an available National Health Service Dentist for new patients and the existing patients would not have the facility of a Dental Practitioner. Both the Dental Board and the Health Trust have no complaints against the standard of dental treatment, which has always been to a high standard.

David then spoke to Brian.

"Did we find any specific dental treatment that he has claimed for?"

"No, he's claimed for all types of treatment. He's claimed for standard treatment such as check ups, fillings, extractions, false teeth as well as the more expensive treatment such as bridges. In most cases the actual claims have never been for more than two hundred pounds."

"I have spoken to Michael Fox, the Director of Finance, a couple of times, and he did mention the problems they may have if the Dental Practice was to close. I understand what he's trying to say, but personally, I wouldn't want a fraudster to carry on working for the Health Service. To be fair, there's no chance of Alexander getting away with any more fraudulent claims. We'd make sure every claim was double checked and we would be contacting patients as well. For all we know, he mightn't want to carry on working once he's found out that we know all about his fraudulent claims."

"When are you going to contact him?"

"I'll ring him on his first day back which is next Monday, and will, hopefully, get to see him later that day. If not, it will have to be later in the week, because I've got a meeting in London on Tuesday. I won't complete the formal taped interview, but I will let him know he can have a solicitor present if he feels it necessary. If he is going to bring a solicitor, I'll let you know and we'll go together. I will tell him that we know about the frauds and will arrange the formal taped interview with his solicitor. In the meantime, he has the option to carry on working at the Practice, but that's up to him. I suppose it depends on how loyal he feels for his patients, not that he has much loyalty to the Health Service."

"That's fine with me David. I imagine if he carries on at the Practice, and his Barrister tells the court that he carried on working, under great pressure, for the good of his patients, it might help him a little bit."

"I'm sure they'll try anything but he'll spend a fair amount of time in one of our prisons."

"How long do you reckon he would get for this?"

"My guess would be three years, maybe even four years. It will depend on what he can pay back to a certain extent."

9

The group of six boys left the hotel on Seventh Avenue, New York, and made their way to one of the local eating places within a couple of blocks from the hotel. There must have been over a hundred eating places within three blocks of their hotel.

They were on a five day break, having just completed their "A" level examinations at a school in Liverpool. It would not be long before they left school for the last time and headed to different universities across the country, but a couple were thinking of having a years break, travelling, before they started a university course. They had been friends since starting High School, seven years ago, and this trip seemed the ideal way to celebrate their friendships and the end of an era in their lives.

Over breakfast they discussed the trip they were about to take on the helicopter. It was one of the better rides and was called, not surprisingly, New York, New York. One of the boys father had some contacts in the travel business in New York, and he had managed to get them a deal on the trip, which cost them a hundred and twenty dollars each. They had a couple of brochures and passed them round, which gave them details of the journey.

The New York, New York - Helicopter Tour is the longest lasting of the four helicopter tours we offer and departs from two different locations depending on the day of the week. Your flight includes views of New York City's five Boroughs!
Your aerial tour begins as we head down the Hudson River

towards New York Harbor passing Ellis Island and giving you a birds-eye view of the Statue of Liberty.

You'll also have spectacular views of Governors Island, the Verrazano Bridge which joins Brooklyn and Staten Island and Manhattan's Financial District before returning up the Hudson past the Air Craft Carrier-USS Intrepid to view Midtown's famous skyscrapers: Empire State, Chrysler and Met Life (Pan Am) Buildings, along with Central park, Yankee Stadium-Home of the New York Yankees, St. John the Devine Cathedral, Columbia University, George Washington Bridge and the Palisades of New Jersey.

It departed from the Downtown Manhattan Heliport, Pier 6. The Heliport consists of 84,000 square feet, the pier 550 feet by 85 feet and the barge 90 feet by 300 feet. The barge accommodated 12 helicopters and 18 vehicles were allowed in the parking lot.

Their trip was due to start at eleven o'clock and they had to go to the subway and there was then a bit of a walk in order to reach the Heliport.

Mike tended to be the organiser and he looked at his watch before saying.

"We had better get going to give us plenty of time to get to the Heliport."

There were a few grumbles about leaving too early, but they all soon left the fast food restaurant and made their way to the subway.

They arrived at twenty five to eleven and soon met up with the pilot and they discovered that they were the only six people on the ride. He gave them all a type of belt to wear containing some type of float, not that they felt that they were going to need it. There were, however, a couple of the boys who were starting to look slightly concerned.

It only took a few minutes to climb on board the helicopter and the pilot started the engines with the loud whirring noise of the helicopter blades. They were soon airborne and they saw the first bridge which was Manhattan Bridge and the helicopter then made its way down the East River passing over Brooklyn Bridge.

Mike was looking down at the River and suddenly looked startled.

"There's a body in the water, just under the bridge."

By the time the others looked the helicopter crossed over the bridge and nobody else could see the body.

"We can't see any dead body in the water. You need new glasses or you had too much to drink last night," said Sam.

"I'm sure it was a dead body. We'll have another look when we return."

"Okay, we'll look then and see what it was that you have seen, probably a piece of wood."

The ride was wonderful and some tried to take photographs. The tour lasted nearly seventeen minutes and included views of New York City's five boroughs! The brochure was fairly accurate and the tour went down the Hudson River, Manhattan's Financial District, Woolworth Building and Ellis Island, allowing for a birds-eye view of the Statue of Liberty, Governors Island, Verrazano Bridge, which joins Brooklyn and Staten Island before returning up the Hudson passing the Air Craft Carrier-USS. You were able to view Midtown's famous skyscrapers, Empire State, Chrysler and Met Life (Pan Am) Buildings, along with Central Park, Yankee Stadium-Home of the New York Yankees, St. John the Devine Cathedral, Columbia University, George Washington Bridge and the Palisade of New Jersey.

As they passed over Brooklyn Bridge, they all looked out of the windows towards the river.

"There it is," yelled Mike and they all spotted a body floating just under the bridge.

The pilot had noticed the boys looking out of the windows and looked down himself. He also saw a floating body in the water.

He landed the helicopter safely and passed a message to the authorities that he believed there was a body in the water near Brooklyn Bridge. He then spoke to the six boys.

"I've told the police and river authority and they'll send a small boat out to see if it is a body and they'll bring it ashore. It's not that unusual, I've seen a couple of bodies in the river during the four years that I've been doing these trips. If you want to see what goes on, you can walk down to the bridge, it won't take too long. You can tell them that you saw the body and reported it to the pilot of the helicopter. If the local press get to know quickly, and they usually do, you might get your pictures in the paper or on television."

"Thanks for the ride, it was super" said John. "Shall we take a walk to see what's going on?"

There was a shout of "Yes" from most of the group and they all started walking towards Brooklyn Bridge. As they arrived, they could see a diver in the water by the small boat and they were putting a body on board the boat. The boat headed towards dry land but there were no signs of a reporter or a television crew. They then left the scene, a bit disappointed, and made their way to the subway to continue their sightseeing tour of New York.

The following morning a man approached the reception desk of the hotel where the boys were staying, and showed a card to the receptionist.

"Good morning, I'm Detective William Jackson, New York City Police Department. I understand that you have six boys from England staying in the hotel and they went on the New York, New York Helicopter ride yesterday. Do you know who they are if I give you their names?"

"We know all about the trip and the body that they saw under Brooklyn Bridge. They were disappointed that they weren't on the television last night. They are in the lounge now, if you go through you won't miss them."

"Thanks for your help."

"No problem."

Detective Jackson walked into the hotel lounge and saw six boys, who were clearly discussing the sights they wanted to see today. As he walked towards the group, a couple looked up and saw him ambling towards them.

"Hi, I'm Detective Jackson from the New York City Police Department. I believe you're the boys from Liverpool, England, who went on the helicopter trip yesterday?"

Mike and Sam both said "Yes" at the same time.

"I believe you saw the body under the bridge?"

Mike quickly replied.

"Yes. I saw it when we first went over the bridge, but this lot didn't believe me. It was only when we came back that we all saw the body again. Who was it?"

"I can't tell you that yet, but it was a male in his forties."

"Did he jump off the bridge?"

"We don't think so. It's being treated as a murder enquiry."

Sam then said.

"Where are the reporters and the television crews?"

"They're not here. Sorry about that, but I need to ask a few questions."

"Go ahead."

Detective Jackson pulled up another chair and sat down with the group of boys and looked at Mike.

"We've been told that the body was only in the water for about an hour. That means it must have only been put their just before you saw it. Taking into the account the time of the trip, the notification by the helicopter pilot and the time it took to get the body out of the water, we think he's been dumped around the time you noticed the body. When you saw the body, did you see anything else?"

Mike thought for a few seconds.

"No, I was looking into the river and just saw the body floating. There was nothing else nearby in the water"

"You didn't notice anything on land by the bridge?"

"No, once I saw the body, I kept staring but it was only a few seconds before the helicopter crossed the bridge and I lost sight of it."

Stuart then joined the conversation.

"I was looking by the side of the bridge and saw a car moving away."

"When you say moving away, what direction?"

"It was being driven away from the river."

"I don't suppose you have a description of the car?"

"Yes. It was a Ford Crown Vic, don't think it was new but they haven't changed that much over the years. I might be wrong but I think there was a fairly big dent in the back."

"Did you notice the colour of the car?"

"Oh sorry, I didn't say. It was brown."

"Anything else?"

"No, I couldn't see who was driving and I didn't notice anything else."

"That's very helpful. Did anybody else see anything?"

There was a shaking of heads from the rest of the group but Stuart then asked Detective Jackson.

"Can't you tell us anymore? We want to know all about it."

"I can tell you that the chap who is dead had a Brown Crown Vic with a dent in the back. The pathologist looked at the body yesterday and feels that it was a case of strangulation from behind, using your arms, possibly by an expert in martial arts."

Mike then raised his hand.

"Do you mean a Kung Fu chop just like this?"

He moved his hand down quickly and was greeted with a shout of "Rubbish, that's the worst Kung Fu, I've ever seen."

The group and Detective Jackson all started laughing.
"When do you all go back?"
Sam replied.
"The day after tomorrow."
"What are you going to see tomorrow?"
"We wanted to watch the New York Yankees Baseball match but we couldn't get any tickets, so we'll probably just have a walk around and we might do some shopping."
"Mike and Stuart, here's my card. If you think of anything else, let me know. I don't think I might need to take a statement but I'll be in touch if I need to. Does the hotel have all your home details and contact numbers in England?"
Mike nodded his head.
"Yes, we filled in all the forms when we arrived."
"Thanks guys."
Mike then added.
"If we're back in England and you need us, just send us the flight tickets and book a hotel and we'll come back, no problem."
"I don't think our budget goes that far, but there's no harm in trying. Cheers and if the local press boys are interested, shall I send them over?"
"Yeah, we'll be pleased to speak to them. Should we ask them for a fee?"
"You've got no chance but you might get your pictures in the paper."

Detective William Jackson returned to his office at the NYPD and was immediately approached by a colleague Detective John Reagan.
"Hi Will, you've been looking into the body that they discovered at Brooklyn Bridge, haven't you?"
"Yeah, I've just been talking to some lads from Liverpool, England, who saw the body on the helicopter trip."
"He's been identified as Frank Sinclair hasn't he?"

"That's right, we haven't had any formal identification yet, but it is Frank Sinclair."

"When you went to his apartment, was anybody there?"

"No, I spoke to a few of the neighbours and they said that his girlfriend was over from England. Her first name was Wendy, but that's all they know. They haven't seen her for a day or two. Why are you asking John?"

"We've had an enquiry from the Metropolitan Police in London. They are investigating a big fraud from a hospital and they are searching for a Wendy Carson and Frank Sinclair, who they reckon are responsible for this fraud. They want us to arrest both of them and they will then start extradition proceedings."

"Well they're not going to get Frank Sinclair. When I was chatting to the English lads, one of them saw a brown Crown Vic leaving the scene, he thought there was a dent in the back. When I was talking to Sinclair's neighbours, they told me he had a brown Crown Vic with a dent in the back. I haven't got the number yet but I'll check that out later. I wonder where this Wendy Carson is now."

"The Metropolitan Police have sent us a photo of her and you'll probably need to circulate it."

John then passed the photograph over to William who had a quick glance and looked at John.

"In this photo, she's getting an award. If you look at the writing on the certificate, it's South London Jujitsu Club. Maybe my brain's working overtime, but the feeling is that Sinclair was killed by a Martial Arts expert. Makes you wonder if this involves Wendy Carson. I reckon we should put out her name on our most wanted list for suspicion of murder. That takes priority over the extradition request from the Metropolitan Police. I'll contact them and let them know what's going on over here. Have you got the details?"

"Yes, you need to contact a Ross Edgar, here's the file. Saves me a job, thanks Will."

"I'm just too good for you. I'd better put a search out at all airports, I doubt if she'll want to stay over here if she's involved in the murder of Sinclair. She may have already fled the country for all we know."

William completed the necessary paperwork for all the airports and also informed the border staff at Canada and Mexico, asking them to keep a look out but to check for any flights that she may have caught over the past couple of days. He also found the registration of the Crown Vic and put the search requests out to the local and state police as well as the airports and border authorities.

It was only a few hours later when William's phone rang at the NYPD.

"Hello."

"Is that Detective Jackson?"

"Yes."

"Oh hi, it's Dan Hunt from JFK Airport Security. You asked us do some checks on a British subject, Wendy Carson and a search for a vehicle, a Crown Vic."

"Yes, that's quick, have you got something for us?"

"Yes, the vehicle is in the Airport Car Park at JFK and we've managed to find out where Wendy Carson has flown to."

"She's left the States?"

"She sure has. She flew on an Iberia flight from JFK to Madrid, Spain yesterday evening at nine o'clock and the flight landed in Madrid at a quarter past ten this morning."

"I can't say I'm surprised, she couldn't fly back to England. I suppose she picked the first available flight which is as near to the United Kingdom as possible."

"That makes sense because the flight was only paid for about two and a half hours before it departed."

"Do you know how she paid for the flight?"

"Yes. I checked that and she paid cash."

"No surprise there either. Have you secured the vehicle?"

"Yes, we've put a couple of clamps on the Crown Vic and put a cover over it. I presume you'll be collecting it as soon as possible?"

"I'll get our people to come and collect it and take it for forensic checks."

"That's okay, but tell them to ask for me when they come to the airport car park. I'll show them where it is and take off the clamps."

"Thanks for your help Dan."

"No problem."

As William put the phone down, John walked past his desk.

"John, you'll not be surprised to hear this woman Carson has left the country."

"Where's she gone?"

"She flew to Madrid, Spain, yesterday and arrived this morning."

"She's probably too frightened to go straight to England. Do you want me to inform the Spanish Police?"

"If you would John. She's probably well hidden now, but you never know."

"I'll get on to it straightaway and I'll give your name as the contact."

"Gee, thanks a lot John."

"I suppose I'd better get some brief statements off a couple of the lads from England. We can still get some free tickets to see the New York Yankees can't we?"

"We usually can, why who's going?"

"I thought I'd help international relations between us and the United Kingdom, by giving these lads six free tickets."

"You're best to give the Public Relations bloke a ring at the Stadium to see if he can arrange it for you."

"Yeah, I'll do that now."

The following morning, Detective Jackson walked into the hotel and spoke to the same receptionist that he had seen the last time he was there.

"Hi, are the six English lads around?"

"Yes, I think you'll find them in the restaurant having breakfast."

He walked into the restaurant and saw the group from England in the corner finishing breakfast and as he approached, Mike turned to him.

"Good morning Detective Jackson, do you need our help again?"

"Yes, I need a couple of short statements from you and Stuart."

"Anything to oblige."

"If you can do them now, I might have a little present for you."

"What type of present?"

"I've got you six free tickets in one of the guest boxes for the New York Yankees match."

There was a chorus of approval from all the group and Mike and Stuart quickly followed the detective to the reception where they completed the statements. They were also told to contact the Public Relations man at the Stadium and he would show them their seats for the match.

10

David picked up the phone at home and rang Ben Alexander's Dental Practice.

"Good morning, Alexander Dental Practice."

"Oh, Good morning, my name's David Parish from the local Health Trust, is it possible to speak to Mr Alexander?"

"He's just finishing with a patient, would you like to hold the line?"

"Yes, that's okay."

There was a wait of a couple of minutes before the telephone was picked up.

"Hello, Ben Alexander."

"Good morning Mr Alexander, my name is David Parish. I'm a Fraud Consultant with the National Health Service and I'm currently undertaking an investigation on behalf of the Health Trust and the Dental Board. It is an ongoing investigation but both myself and the Primary Care Trust feel that it would be appropriate to speak to you at the earliest opportunity concerning some of the findings that we have made to date."

"What are the findings you are talking about?"

"Like I said, it is an ongoing investigation, but we are talking about some of the claims that you have made for dental treatment over a number of years. It is my intention to complete a short fact finding meeting with you and I'll confirm some of the findings that we have made. I appreciate that you will have patients booked in today and probably for a couple of weeks ahead. It is not our intention to create problems with you and your patients, but I should put you in the picture and discuss the running of your Dental Practice."

"Will I need a solicitor?"

"I was just going to say that it might be appropriate for you to contact your solicitor, but it is not our intention to complete a formal interview today. That would take place at some future date."

"I'm not sure that I would like to meet you during the day at this Dental Practice."

"We can see you after you've finished with your patients for the day. What is the last appointment that you have today?"

"I'll just check. I've been on holiday."

"Yes, we know that."

"My last appointment is at four, forty five and I should be finished by five o'clock. How about a quarter past five?"

"That's fine, I'll have a colleague Brian Lewis with me and I'll give you this number if you need to contact me. Zero, eight, five, two, six, three, seven, seven, nine, two, eight. Thanks for your co-operation and I'll see you at a quarter past five."

David then phoned Brian Lewis on his mobile.

Brian recognised the telephone number on his ringing mobile.

"Good morning David, have you spoken to Ben Alexander?"

"Yes, we're seeing him at his Dental Practice at a quarter past five. I'll meet you in Southport at three o'clock and we'll have a chat before making our way over to his place. I can't see us being in there for more than fifteen minutes. He was going to contact a solicitor and arrange for him to be there. I've given him my phone number in case there's any problem but my intention is to give him a briefing, without going into full detail, into the investigation that we're undertaking. I know Michael Fox, the Director of Finance has some concerns and he and the Dental Board want the Practice to continue until they can sort something out. That's probably up to Ben Alexander, but we'll have a chat this afternoon."

"Okay David, I'll see you here around three o'clock."

One of David's passions was walking and he made several walks each week, some brisk to help improve his fitness levels and cardiovascular activity. He would often take a walk from his own home through some of the lovely parks in Liverpool. After speaking to Brian, he put on his walking shoes and placed his mobile phone in his pocket. He always found that he could think about his investigations when on a good walk, it often cleared his mind and allowed him to organise and make sense of some of the difficult investigations.

He was just watching the grey squirrels clamber up the tree when his mobile rang.

"Hello, David Parish."

"Good morning Mr Fraud, it's Mark Weston from AGK Solicitors in Manchester."

"Hello Mark, what can I do for you?"

"I've just had Ben Alexander on the phone. I believe you've spoken to him about an investigation that you're undertaking and you want to see him today."

"That's right Mark. I didn't realize that you were his solicitor."

"What can you tell me about this investigation?"

"You'll understand that I can't give you all the details at this stage, but I'll give you a little background. I don't know what he's told you but we've had reason to check some of the claims that he's been making for dental work and we have some doubts as to the authenticity of many claims going back several years. That's all I was going to tell you today, but I was going to arrange a date for possibly next week in order to complete a formal taped interview. The concerns of the local Health Trust, the Dental Board and probably Ben Alexander are for the welfare of his patients. We don't want patients left without a dentist and I would imagine that Ben has a good relationship with his patients and he doesn't want them left standing outside the Practice because he is the only dentist in his Practice and works alone. I believe he's a good dentist and he's the only dentist in the area who's still taking on NHS patients but it's up to him what he wants to do. Once he knows about our investigation and I imagine that he is fully aware of what's going on now, he mightn't want to carry on, but that will be his choice for the time being."

"Off the record, he's told me he might be in trouble with regards to some claims that he's made. I don't know to what extent."

"Obviously, I've got some ideas Mark, but I can't give you more accurate details until we hold the formal taped interview. We'll then be able to give you the disclosure pack before the meeting, which will give you a fuller picture. As I said before, that's not the intention of today's meeting which is more about the immediate running of the Dental Practice. I suppose if he carries on and announces at some future date that he did this for the welfare of his patients, it might look good for him, but you're the expert in that field Mark."

"You might have a point David, but it depends on what mental state he is in, once you tell him what you've found."

"I think he should expect to know what our findings will be, after all it's him who has made all the claims."

"I get the picture David and I'll see you at his place at a quarter past five."

"Cheers Mark."

David had only just arrived home from his walk when the house phone started ringing.

"Hello."

"Hi David, its Peter Daley."

"Morning Peter."

"I've got some gossip."

"Go on, tell me more."

"I've just been to the Magistrates Court concerning one of the cases that I'm working on. As I was leaving I bumped into Ross Edgar from the Metropolitan Police and he gave me some news. He's just had an email from the New York City Police Department concerning Wendy Carson and Frank Sinclair. Apparently Frank Sinclair's body has been found in a river in New York and they believe that he was murdered. It looks like a case of strangulation from behind using your arms. It was very quick and tidy and their Pathologist believes that it may have been the result of somebody with Martial Arts knowledge. They've put out an international warrant for the arrest of Wendy Carson because they know that she has left the States and flown to Madrid. They think that she might be headed back here but know that the Police here want to arrest her. They've no idea if there's any connection in Spain but they're seeking the help of our police and the Spanish police."

"Lovely woman. When we interviewed Denis King, he told us he used to go out with Wendy Carson and he was a bit frightened of her because of her prowess in Martial Arts. We still want to arrest her and might end up having to fight with the Americans to get first choice but their crime is more serious than ours. I suppose it depends on whether they've got enough to arrest and charge her for murder."

"Ross did say that he was going to give you a ring and let you know what's going on but he's tied up in Court today and will probably have to wait until tomorrow. He knows that you have connections with the Spanish police and might seek your help."

"That would be easier if she was back in Spain. Alisa's still in London but I'll see her tomorrow when I go down there. We might give her brother Felipe a ring but I'll confirm this with Ross Edgar first."

"I thought you'd like a bit of gossip."

"I'm not sure if it's good news for us. It certainly isn't good news for Frank Sinclair though. I wonder what went on over there to cause that, I'd put bets on it being about money since all hers has been frozen over here. Thanks for letting me know Peter."

"Bye for now."

David left his house just before two o'clock for the hours drive to Southport. He arrived for his meeting with Brian Lewis at three o'clock and they made a couple of cups of coffee, before they sat down to discuss the forthcoming meeting with Ben Alexander and his solicitor, Mark Weston. He then started to discuss the progress to date.

"Have you or the Dental Board people made any changes to the figures that you gave me last time. There were just under three thousand claims totalling five hundred and eighty six thousand pounds."

"No, we went back eight years to nineteen ninety nine but we couldn't find anything before that. We probably need to sort the disclosure pack and go through that with you, but I presume we're not going to discuss this today?"

"No, I'll tell them there have been many occasions of fraudulent practice going back eight years, but I'm not going to go into that much detail today. It really is a question of what's going to happen to the Dental Practice in the interim period. Personally, like I've said before, I don't like the idea of a fraudster carrying on working in the Health Service, but the authorities above all want him to carry on seeing his patients until they feel they can find somebody else, or some temporary interim measures are put in place. I suppose it's in the interests of the patients that there is a dentist available to see them when they've got some problems with their teeth. At the moment, we're still investigating but once we've carried out the formal interview on tape, I don't see how he can carry on working."

"When are you going to have the formal interview?"

"I told Mark Weston it might be in a week's time, but I'd better have a word with Michael Fox. He will probably want to talk to the Dental Board and see how soon they can get another dentist or make some other arrangements. I'd better not make any definite date today. What are your thoughts?"

"I'm like you, but we are fraud investigators. I just want him out of the way, but we can't throw him out of the building because he owns the premises. We're going to have to go along with the Health Trust."

"It makes sense for him to carry on treating his patients. Okay, there won't be any fraudulent claims made any more, but the longer he stays, there is the chance that he could sell the Dental Practice as a going concern. If somebody else arrived on the scene wanting to take over the Practice, it would be worth some money to him. If he did sell and received a lump sum, we would then sue him and get our hands on the money he'd get for selling the business. If it was closed and the business went elsewhere he'd get a lot less money if he then sold the property."

"We've got to go along with it haven't we?"

"I think so. I'd better have a look at the paperwork, I think I know everything but I'll just refresh my memory."

"Have you got any good investigations going on?"

"I've got this case and a few small investigations. The usual type of fraud, working somewhere else, when she was off sick from her job in the Local Authority. A couple of timesheet fiddles but not a lot of money involved. I'm doing a lot of proactive work, making presentation to staff and how to prevent fraud and what they should be looking for."

"I think presentations are good and do help prevent fraud. It's surprising how many follow up phone calls we get, or they approach you a day or two later with some suspicions that they may have."

David read through the documentation before he and Brian got into David's car and made their way to Ben Alexander's Dental Practice. They parked the car before ringing the bell on the door of the building, which was opened by Ben Alexander.

There was no greeting but David remarked.

"This is my colleague, Brian Lewis."

There was no shake of the hands and both David and Brian followed the dentist into the waiting room where Mark Weston was waiting. There were no other staff around and David presumed they had all left the building.

"Hi Mark, you know Brian, don't you?"

"Yes, Brian was working with you on the Pension Fraud case. My client went down for eighteen months and did you know he agreed to sell his house and give the profits back to the Pension Funds?"

"Yes, they did tell us after they received the money."

"I've told Ben the details of our telephone conversation, perhaps you could tell us a bit more?"

"Yes, Brian has been doing a lot of the research investigations alongside the Dental Board. I'm not in a position to give you the total figures, which we believe to be fraudulent claims, but I can say it is several hundred thousand pounds and the false claims go back up to eight years. We will provide the full details when we have a formal interview but that will not be before next week and it might be longer than that. I'll let you know, of course, when we're ready to proceed."

"It won't be next week then, but you want my client to carry on with the Dental Practice in the meantime."

"I'm not going to state my personal view, but I would have thought Mr Alexander would want to carry on for the benefit of his patients. He wouldn't want them left stranded without a dentist."

Ben Alexander then joined the conversation.

"What do you think it would be like to have to continue working, knowing you have something like this hanging over you?"

Mark interrupted Ben.

"Be careful what you say at this stage Ben."

David then continued.

"We know what we believe has been going on, and we believe that you know, but save that for the formal interview as Mark says. At this stage, you haven't been charged with anything and we haven't given you the full details of our research. The Health Trust and the Dental Board feel it would be in the best interests of your patients if you continued to treat them. It's none of my business, but Mark will have told you that there may be some future benefits to you, if you carried on. We will, naturally, be examining all claims very closely and I've no idea of what the financial arrangements would be between you and the authorities."

Ben then asked the question.

"Does that mean they won't pay me anything for this period?"

"This has nothing to do with us, we're the Investigating Officers, and financial matters would be for future discussion."

Mark again interrupted.

"I think we should forget the financial arrangements for the time being. I have spoken to Ben and we both feel that he should carry on with the Dental Practice for the time being, but these thoughts may change when we've had the formal taped interview. Will you give me plenty of notice for this David?"

"Yes, I'll give you a week's notice."

Mark turned to Ben.

"Is that okay with you Ben?"

"I suppose so and I am concerned about leaving my patients without a dentist and I am a sole practitioner. There are no other dentists taking NHS patients in the immediate area."

David and Brian then got to their feet and walked towards the door as David said to Mark.

"I'll be in touch as soon as possible Mark."

"Thanks David."

David and Brian walked to David's car and were chatting about the brief meeting with Ben Alexander and Mark Weston during the journey back to Brian's car. Brian remarked.

"Do you think he'll carry on working?"

"I'm not sure. He looked a bit shell shocked to me. He obviously knows what he's done, I've never met him before but he mightn't have the will power or self control to carry on. The only reason that he'll continue working is that it might look good when he appears in court. Mark will probably tell him to keep working, at least, until we formally interview him."

"I wonder if he knows how much he has defrauded over the years."

"Probably not. He might have started keeping records when he started the fiddle but he may have stopped after a couple of years."

"I suppose it's best if we warn Michael Fox at the Health Trust that it's his intention to carry on, but we wouldn't guarantee it."

"Yes, will you give him a ring tomorrow?"

"I'll ring him first thing. Where are you tomorrow?"

"I've got a meeting in London. I think I'll get the train down tonight, there's one that leaves at a quarter to eight and gets into Euston at eleven o'clock. I'll drive straight to Runcorn and catch the train there at eight o'clock and I'll stay over at Alisa's flat. She's down there at the moment."

"She's on a secondment isn't she?"

"Yeah, she's working on some of the day to day problems involved in extradition issues between Spain and the United Kingdom."

"When is the work going to finish and is she due to return?"

"I don't know, but I don't think it will be too long. She has been doing a few other jobs recently but they've nearly finished as well."

David dropped Brian off at his car and made the journey to Runcorn Station in order to catch the London train. He had packed a small bag but he had a change of clothes at Alisa's flat in London.

He parked the car at the station, obtained his tickets from the booking office and gave Alisa a ring on his mobile.

"Hola."

"Hi Alisa, I'm catching a train tonight rather than first thing in the morning. It should arrive in London about eleven o'clock and I'll jump a taxi, and should be at the flat by half past eleven."

"That's fine David. Do you want anything to eat?"

"I'll get a snack on the train, but I'll have a little supper and a couple of glasses of Rioja when I arrive."

"Okay David, I'll see you later."

"Bye for now."

The train arrived on time and David found his way to an empty seat. He put the luggage on the rack but kept his laptop alongside him for use on the journey. The train had only been going about ten minutes when David made his way to the self service shop coach, carrying his laptop as he always did, and obtained a cheese ploughman's on a multigrain roll and a coffee.

The journey was uneventful with his carriage only about half full, but the train arrived about five minutes early and he soon found his way out of the station and jumped in the cab for the relatively short journey to Alisa's flat near Regents Park.

He was greeted by a smiling Alisa, who immediately poured out a couple of glasses of wine.

"How was the train journey?"

"Fine, on time, but they usually are nowadays."

"Did you have something to eat?"

"Yeah, I had a cheese ploughman's. It has kept me going."

"Do you want anything else to eat yet?"

"No, we'll have a drink and a little gossip first."

"Mui bueno."

"I was talking to Brian Lewis earlier, we had a meeting with a dentist and his solicitor, but Brian mentioned, funny enough, when your secondment was coming to an end. We spoke about it a couple of weeks ago and thought it might be soon. Have you heard anymore?"

"I think so, well, I have got a meeting tomorrow afternoon and I think the subject may be raised. When are you going back to Liverpool?"

"I've got the meeting with Sally O'Brien and it depends on how that goes."

"Come back here, and I'll give you an update. I will probably get the train back with you, either tomorrow or the day after. Do you fancy a trip up to your cottage in the Lake District?"

"That would be great. I should be able to make a couple of days holiday once I've had the meeting tomorrow. I think I need a couple of good walks."

"You always think when you walk, you solve all your cases and any problems that you've got. I mightn't have a job after tomorrow."

"We'll sort that out on the walk."

Alisa laughed at David's comment.

"I'll give you a slice of my Spanish Tortilla. It might help you sleep."

"I don't think so. I've got something else on my mind when we go to bed."

"Have you now, Senor Fraudo?"

They both had another glass of wine with the tortilla before making their way to the bedroom.

The following morning, both David and Alisa had a light breakfast and a couple of cups of coffee before they were ready to make their journeys in different directions on the Tube. David's mobile rang and he noticed the caller was Brian Lewis.

"Good morning Brian, it's nice and early."

"Hi David, I've just heard some information which might be interesting."

"Go on."

"The bloke from the Dental Board who's been helping with the case concerning Ben Alexander has just rung me. He knows somebody who knows Ben Alexander a little bit. Apparently, Ben Alexander and his family went to Spain on holiday recently."

"That's right, they went to Madrid."

"The story is that their marriage is on the rocks and they were trying to sort something out. He is supposed to be having an affair with a receptionist who used to work for him and it looks as though they are going to split up. I'm not sure how stable that may make him and will he try to disappear?"

"Good question, Brian. I think that I'll have a word with Anne Graham in Cheshire Police. We don't want him leaving the country, thanks Brian, I'll be in touch."

"See you David."

11

David made the fairly short journey of three stations on the Tube for the meeting with Darren O'Brien and his sister Sally. He walked out of the station and soon found the offices of Howarth & Davies Solicitors, where Darren worked.

He made his way to the reception area and spoke to the rather attractive, slim, dark haired lady.

"Good morning, my name is David Parish. I've got a meeting with Darren O'Brien."

"Yes, he is expecting you, I'll let him know that you're here."

She picked up the phone and dialled the number.

"Hello Darren, I've got David Parish in reception. Shall I bring him through to your office?"

"If you would please Linda."

David followed the receptionist to Darren's office, where he was met by Darren and Sally O'Brien.

"Morning David, this is my sister Sally."

"Hello David."

"Hello Sally, it's nice to meet you."

They all sat down and Darren turned to Linda, the receptionist, who was waiting by the door.

"We'd like some drinks please Linda. What will you have David?"

"White coffee please."

"That'll be three white coffees please Linda."

Darren then started the meeting by talking to David.

"Sally knows that I've spoken to you and given you the background on this identity fraud. I know you said you've had some dealings with Ron Thomas and you've probably made some initial enquiries."

"Yes that's right. I was involved with some Cheshire gangsters last year who were responsible for frauds involving faked car crashes. They were also using machines to obtain details of peoples credit cards which they then copied and used the false cards to obtain goods and cash. The head of the gangsters was a Steve Mitchell who worked with his brother and Ron Thomas. It all came to an end but as far as Ron Thomas was concerned, he was sent to jail for three years and he is still in Walton Prison in Liverpool. Whoever obtained the copies of the twins' birth certificates was definitely not Ron Thomas but they must've had some good knowledge to know about the twins."

Sally then joined in the conversation.

"Obviously, I know Ron Thomas well, at least I used to, but that was eighteen years ago. I have only seen him the once since then, and that was when I bumped into him in a shopping arcade in Manchester about ten years ago. We only spoke for a couple of minutes but I don't think he would have used the twins' identities for a fraud. Okay, he's in prison and I know that he's a bad one and from what you say, he hasn't mended his ways over the years, but I don't think it's him, nor do I think he will have arranged this identity fraud from his prison cell. He knows he was driving too fast when the twins were killed and he was really distraught afterwards. It was his fault but it was an accident, and he regrets that and he apologized again when I spoke to him. No case was ever brought against him."

"It might not be him Sally. This type of identity fraud has been known to occur when somebody has been walking around a cemetery and looking at gravestones. When they see a youngster's gravestone, they'll take the details and go searching the local press for the dates they have obtained and this is the start of their research and subsequent frauds. I didn't ask Darren, were the twins buried?"

"No, they were cremated, but I know that people have been known to search newspaper records and the internet to obtain information. We were talking about this type of thing in work a couple of months ago when one of my colleagues was completing research on a fraud. I didn't think it would involve me."

"It can happen to anybody."

"I know. The death of my twin boys is not a secret, I don't talk about it much, but in my position, it's probably best not to have secrets. Somebody will always find out that you've a relationship with a bad guy who's been to prison and you've had twins when you were single and not married. I've often mentioned the twins when I've been involved with the children's charities and it's not worth keeping something hidden when you're working to help children."

"I think you're right, you're involved in the media and you'll know the lengths that they have to go to and the research required to obtain a news story. What role do you want me to play in this; you can go to the police and seek their help if you want. It won't cost you anything then."

"If I have to go to the police or if you have to go to the police, that's fine with me but I would appreciate it if you made some initial enquiries, see what you can find out and we'll take it from there. This has come at quite a funny time really, what I mean by that is, I've been approached to be the new face on Criminals Captured and I'll be taking over in a couple of weeks. They will be promoting the new series within a matter of days and you'll soon be seeing me more often on the television screen. I don't want to start the first programme by talking about a fraud involving myself. Anyhow, I had heard about the famous Mr Fraud and when I mentioned your name to Darren, he told me that he'd had some dealings in a fraud case last year. The lady committed suicide the day before the trial didn't she? Sad wasn't it?"

"Yes, it was a shame. I must say that I'm quite a fan of Criminals Captured. It certainly gets to the public and the responses you get to crime is excellent, even crimes that have occurred many years ago. Mind you, it is shown at peak time on television."

"Nice to know you're a fan, I hope I don't put you off when I join the programme. I do want to employ you as a Consultant and I'm not bothered about any costs."

"I'll be even more interested, now that I've met you. I know that your parents received information about credit cards and loans in the twins' names. Who's been in touch with the financial organisations?"

Darren then spoke.

"I have spoken to them all. They seem quite happy that it is nothing to do with us and they have blocked the cards, but there were a few loans taken out and all credit cards were at their limit. I understand that there is sixty-five thousand pounds outstanding, but they feel they may take some more hits. I was put in touch with one of the Bank's Fraud Investigators and I told him that we were going to get you to help us. He then told us that he knew you and had only spoken to you about a week ago."

"You don't mean Eric Page do you?"

"Yes, that's the bloke."

"I'll have a chat with Eric. You mentioned last time that you had spoken to the General Register Office in Manchester."

"That's right."

"Did they give you any details of the person who applied for the copies of the birth certificates?"

"No, only that he said he was the father and produced some form of identification but I don't know what that was."

They were interrupted when Linda came in with the three coffees and a plate of biscuits.

"I'll have a talk to the Register Office in Manchester and see if they remember anything. He will have paid cash, I think they only cost about seven pounds each, but I'm not sure."

Sally then asked.

"Will you contact Ron Thomas?"

"I might do, but I'll have a word with the police. My contact in Cheshire raised some concerns about his partner and she was going to make a couple of enquiries with Walton Prison to see if Ron was getting visits. They do have a two year old daughter."

"Does he? She won't be seeing her Dad for a couple of years."

"What paperwork have you got to give me?"

Darren then handed David a blue file.

"You'll find all details of what we've done so far and there is a copy of all the letters that have been received. There are the contact details of Sally, and mine are also there, but you probably know them already."

"Thanks. I'll be in touch but give me a week to see what I can find out. If anything else crops up, let me know as soon as possible. I will try and keep it fairly low key, but if things are getting out, I will keep you updated."

"We will do. Thanks David."

David then left the offices of Howarth & Davies and made his way back to the tube station for the start of the return journey to Alisa's flat.

As soon as David entered the flat he decided to make a couple of phone calls. He first looked up the direct number of Eric Page, the Bank Investigator and made contact.

"Hello, Eric Page."

"Hi Eric, its David Parish. Its not about Wendy Carson, I need to ask you a few questions about something else."

"You're going to mention Sally O'Brien and her twin boys who died in a car crash."

"That's right, Darren did tell me he had spoken to you on the phone."

"Who are you acting for on this David?"

"I am acting as a private consultant for the O'Brien's. I did inform Sally that she could use the Police but she knew about me, and I have dealt with Darren on a previous case. I think they want to find out who is involved and I thought that you would be looking at the case with some other Bank Investigators. I can use the police if necessary, but do you have any more information?"

"Not much to be honest. We have made some enquiries and we think it might only be the one bloke who is involved, and is using both of the twin boys' names. The description is vague, a man in his forties, dark haired with a beard and moustache. About six foot tall but he does speak with a Geordie accent. That's been confirmed by the one person who saw him and a couple of phone calls he made asking when his credit cards would arrive."

"Okay, thanks for that Eric, I'll make a few enquiries and if anything crops up, I'll let you know."

"Have you heard anymore about the payroll fraud and our friend Wendy Carson?"

"We know she went to New York where her boyfriend lives and, apparently, the boyfriend has been found dead and looks as though he was murdered."

"Who did it?"

"The American Police have put out a search for Wendy Carson but believe she is somewhere in Europe. She did fly to Madrid but we don't know if she's still there, they'll be asking the Spanish Police to have a look but they mind find it difficult to trace her as she's moving around."

"Cheers David. I'll let you know if we find anything, but I'm not too hopeful."

David then made a second telephone call to Anne Graham in Cheshire Police.

"Hello Anne Graham."

"Hello Anne, its David Parish."

"Hi David."

"Did you find out anymore about Lucy Tindall, Ron Thomas's partner?"

"Yes, we made a couple of enquiries. She visits him at Walton Prison at every opportunity and it certainly looks as though she's standing by him. We even made some discreet enquiries and there is no evidence of any other bloke. One of our plain clothes men saw her going into a bar in Manchester with three other ladies. He followed them in and sat near them when they got their drinks. He said all he could hear was Lucy going on about how much she was missing Ron and couldn't wait for him to be released, but that's not going to be for another year at least. She also said that she's had to get a job because money was tight and she's working in some clothes shop in the City Centre. Apparently, he's been no trouble in prison and there's no sign of him being up to anything dodgy."

"I spoke to Sally O'Brien and she admits that Ron Thomas is a career criminal, she's only seen him once in the past twenty years, and that was about ten years ago when she bumped into him when she was out shopping. She knows he's a rogue but doesn't think that he would use his twin boys' identities for fraudulent purposes. He was pretty upset at the time and Sally could tell he was still upset when he saw her. It was as though seeing Sally had brought it all back."

"It could be just a co-incidence. We do have fraudsters who search graveyards and scour the local press for background information, but when we're talking about a fraudster, this seems a bit unlikely to me."

"It does to me as well. I can't help feeling that he will know something. If it's not him that's operating this fraud, he might help if he finds out that it's his twins identity that has been stolen, and Sally O'Brien has asked for help in trying to find out who's involved. I think that I might visit him in Walton Prison. I will probably need to get clearance for a special visit. Will it be better if you get this for me or shall I contact the Prison direct?"

"It's probably better if we arrange clearance. I'll get one of my staff to contact the prison and let them know that you'll be contacting them shortly. We'll do this today and you'll be able to contact them tomorrow."

"Thanks Anne, I'll let you know what I've found out as soon as I've made the visit. One other thing while I'm talking to you. I am involved in a fraud investigation concerning a dentist named Ben Alexander. It is the early stages and we haven't completed a formal interview at this stage but we have met him and told him an investigation is taking place. He has agreed to carry on working for the time being but I've heard through the grapevine that he may be splitting from his wife and is having an affair with a receptionist who used to work in his Practice. I'm a bit concerned that he might try and leave the country, any chance of blocking him?"

"Yes, I'll arrange that but will you send me an email with his full details then I'll warn the appropriate people."

"Thanks Anne, I'll send you the details as soon as possible."

12

Ben Alexander had to rearrange appointments for the last couple of patients because he wanted to finish work early to meet his girlfriend Sue Patterson. He parked the car in the driveway and even though he had a set of keys, he rang the doorbell, which was soon answered by Sue and their one year old daughter, Mandy. Sue was first to speak.

"This must be important Ben, if you've had to cancel a couple of appointments."

"It is. I needed to speak to you. A lot of things have happened over the past few days."

They both walked into the kitchen where Sue made a couple of mugs of tea, whilst Mandy sat in the lounge playing with her favourite dolls.

"I've had a visit from two Health Service Fraud Specialists. They know all about the false claims that we've been making over the past few years."

"What do you mean when you say we've been making. Do they know about me?"

"No, I don't think so, they have presumed that I made all the claims and I haven't said anything about them yet. It was only a preliminary meeting, but as soon as he rang me, I contacted my solicitor, Mark Weston, and he was there when they made the visit. They are going to make a formal appointment, when I will be interviewed on tape, under caution. Until then, they wanted to know if I would carry on working and I agreed that I would. I think Mark agrees that it might go in my favour when things start to go badly. They will probably have all the details of the fraudulent claims when we meet next time and I don't

95

intend to tell them that you were involved from the beginning, but they may know that somebody else could have been involved."

"You're not going to tell them about me. All I did was to enter the claims on the computer, you knew all about it."

"But it was your idea to start it Sue. Don't worry, I won't tell them that, I've got you and Mandy to worry about."

"How about your wife and your other two children?"

"I told Lynn yesterday all about the fraud and that I might end up going to prison. She wasn't very happy, to put it mildly, and then she asked what's happened to all the money, because she hasn't seen it. She then said it must have gone to my girlfriend; she's suspected I was having an affair for a long time but didn't mention it because of the children. She was hoping that the holiday would have put an end to it but I then told her the affair had gone on for a few years and I had another daughter. I also told her that I was having the affair with you and she didn't really sound surprised."

"What did she say when you told her all about us and the fraud?"

"She said nothing to begin with and then took the children around to her parents' house and came back a couple of hours later. She'd left the children there and been to talk to a friend. Anyhow, she said she wanted me out of the house and I should go and stay with my girlfriend, so here I am."

"Did she think that I was involved in the fraud?"

"I think that she did, she wondered how you were able to afford such a nice house on your own and assumed it was with the help of a boyfriend, but didn't think it was me. She thought she was stupid not realizing that it was me but she probably didn't want to think about it."

"I haven't worked at the practice since I went on maternity which was over a year ago. Have you carried on claiming for the treatment that you haven't done?"

"No, even though I've had to in order to pay the bills and take care of you and Mandy. I've bought this house, all the furniture, your car and paid all the bills, but all I want to do now is move in with you and Mandy. My marriage is over and I want to start afresh with you."

"How can you start a new life with us when you will probably end up going to jail for a few years?"

"I love you Sue and I love our daughter."

"I need to think about this Ben. I can't help but worry that I might end up getting involved in this fraud. I did put the claims through on the computer system but only on your authorisation. I can just say that I did not know the claims were false, you just handed them to me, and I did what I always did."

"I've already said that I won't get you involved Sue. Don't you believe me?"

"I don't know what to believe. I think that you only came here because your wife threw you out. I'm sure that you'll go back and end up staying there. You've told me many times you were going to leave your wife but you never have. If she hadn't thrown you out now, you wouldn't be here today."

"That's not true Sue."

"It is Ben and you know it. I want time to think but I don't think there is going to be any future between us."

"I'll go for now but think about what you are going to do. I can easily tell the Fraud bloke that you were involved."

"And where will that leave your daughter Mandy?"

"I bought this house for nearly two hundred thousand pounds and it is in your name. Anybody can have a look around and see that all the furniture, televisions, computers and music centres must have cost thousands. Your car that's parked outside cost another ten thousand pounds. How will you explain where you got the money to pay for it all? I would have a good think about this Sue, you're going to need my help if you want to stay out of trouble."

Ben Alexander stormed out of the house banging the doors as he left. Sue turned around to look at Mandy who had tears in her eyes. She immediately walked over and gave Mandy a big hug and started playing with games with her daughter. It did not take Sue long to decide that she and her daughter did not want a future with a man who had defrauded the Heath Service. She had put a fair amount of money to one side, which had been given to her, over the years, by Ben Alexander. She had to hope and think of ways how she could avoid being involved with this fraud investigation. She didn't want to go to prison.

Ben was not the main man in her life. He provided her with a lovely lifestyle but he was always the second man and he was not the father of Mandy. He didn't know that, and she had no intention of telling him, but it now looked as though her main source of money was coming to an end.

13

David was in the flat when Alisa returned from work and her meeting to discuss her future role in the Spanish Police, now that her secondment to the United Kingdom was nearing an end.

David could tell from Alisa's face that she was deep in thought and looked a little worried and had to ask.

"How did your day go?"

"Oh, it was okay."

"And how about the meeting you had this afternoon?"

"I think I'll get changed first and we'll need a drink."

"What would you like?"

"It had better be a long drink. A gin and tonic would be lovely."

David prepared two large gin and tonics as Alisa was getting changed. He knew that they were going to discuss their future but they had talked about this a few times without reaching any final decision.

Alisa and David have never married, but have had a longstanding on and off relationship for the past seven years, Alisa is a senior officer in the Guardia Civil based in the Andalucia region of Spain, although for the past nine months she has been on a secondment looking at extradition issues between Spain and the United Kingdom. Alisa has an apartment in Seville but did live with David for three years in a villa on the Costa del Sol. At that time, David was employed by U.K. insurance companies investigating fraudsters who were active in both Spain and the United Kingdom. These investigations, would, however, involve visits to many European countries and occasionally the United States. It also necessitated him to return to England on many occasions and they decided that their work required them to live in their own countries and David returned to England. Since his return, they have still remained very close and neither has looked for any other partner or romance. They make frequent trips between Spain and England and the increasing introduction of the budget airlines make this an easy journey. Frequent flights are available between Seville and Liverpool and they have taken advantage of this mode of transport.

The work secondment to this country for Alisa has allowed their relationship to flourish but both David and Alisa knew this was not a permanent move.

Alisa walked into the lounge and David gave her a gin and tonic, with the necessary ice and lemon.

"Thank you very much Senor Fraudo. Cheers."

"Cheers."

They both sat down and David then spoke quietly to Alisa.

"Tell me what's been said. I can see that you're troubled."

"I went into the meeting and was told that they were very happy with my work on the problems involved with extradition issues between the two countries. They thought my findings were very useful but did feel the work had nearly come to an end. I have been given another month but then I would have to return to Spain. I presumed that I would be going back to my old job in Seville but they offered me a promotion. They want me to take on the role of Chief Inspector with the Guardia Civil, not in Seville, but to be based in Murcia."

"What would this job involve?"

"It's with the UEI that's the Unidad Especial de Intervention. A Special Intervention Unit."

"What have you said to them?"

"Nothing really, I told them that I wanted to think about it, and they gave me a week before I have to make a decision. I needed to talk to you first. There's no possibility of another job in this country which is what I was hoping for, but if I took the new promotion, it would also mean that I would have to move house in Spain from Seville to Murcia. I like Seville and if I turned down the promotion, I could return to my old job in Seville, but I'd never be offered a promotion again, at least not for a few years. I suppose my brother Felipe and his family live in Murcia so I would be nearer them. I don't know what to do David."

David had known this moment was going to arise but had tried not to think about, in the hope that some solution may have arisen or Alisa's job in the U.K. may have been extended.

"I suppose we both knew that the job here was not permanent but we thought you would probably be offered your job back in Seville. This promotion is a bit of a surprise but you deserve it for the work that you've done over the past few years. If we weren't a couple and you were on your own, what job would you take? I mean would you want to return to Seville or would you take the promotion in Murcia with the Special Intervention Unit?"

"I think we're more important than any job but if I was asked to choose a job, I'd probably take the promotion and move to Murcia. I must say that I've enjoyed the work over the past year in England but as far as a job is concerned, I prefer working in Spain."

"I know that Alisa. I do think that travel is much easier between here and Spain, and there are direct flights from Liverpool to Murcia which only take just over two hours. I can't think straight at the moment because I've got used to you being near me and I think we're closer than we've ever been but you love your work in Spain like I do here in England. I've tried working in Spain but it didn't really work out."

"I've thought about this for weeks, I mean I didn't know about the promotion in Murcia but I thought that I may have to go back to Seville. On the other hand, I think we could cope with the jobs in two countries but still remain together. Let's face it, I've been based in London, especially over the past three months, and I've returned to Liverpool on Friday evenings and returned to London on Monday morning, or I've stayed here and you've come down on Friday and left for Liverpool on Monday mornings. I know that you've worked down here a few times and stayed with me in the flat, but I think we can commute between Liverpool and Murcia. We should be able to meet most weekends either in Murcia or Liverpool, and we can both have six weeks holiday from work."

"That's true. We've managed to stay together for years even after I returned to this country after working in Spain but we didn't see each other enough after I came back."

"I know, and that was mainly down to the hours that I worked. I had to work different shifts which often included weekend work, but the promotion is mainly weekdays and not Saturday and Sunday, at least that's what they've made me believe."

"We'll sort something out. Let's go out for a meal and we'll have a good chat. Where do you fancy going?"

"I've already booked a table in the Spanish Restaurant. We'd better get a move on, we've only got an hour."

"You know me too well Alisa Garcia."

"I should do after all these years."

"Do you want a glass of Rioja while we get ready?"

"That sounds like a wonderful idea."

David walked over to Alisa and gave her a kiss and a big hug. He had no intention of this relationship ever finishing.

They had a lovely meal in the Spanish Restaurant and returned to Alisa's flat when Alisa suddenly remarked.

"We've been talking all evening, but we haven't mentioned tomorrow. Are we going to the Lake District for a couple of days?"

"Most definitely, but we'll have to go home to Liverpool first, and then we'll drive up in the afternoon. I've got to make some phone calls tomorrow but everything else can wait until we get back from the Lake District."

"I love your cottage and I'm looking forward to some good walks. Hopefully, the weather is not too bad."

"I can't promise that in the Lake District."

David waked over to Alisa and they kissed passionately before making their way to the bedroom.

The following morning they caught an early train from Euston Station arriving at Liverpool just before midday. They then caught a taxi back to David's house where he made two telephone calls.

He first called Anne Graham at Cheshire Police.

"Hello, Anne Graham."

"Good morning Anne, it's David Parish."

"Hi David, I presume you're ringing about visiting Ron Thomas at Walton Prison?"

"Yes, any luck?"

"Yes, it's all arranged. You have to give Jocelyn Ward a ring at the prison. She is the Personal Assistant to the Governor and her direct number is four, nine, seven, three, two, nine, four. That's if you're ringing from Liverpool, otherwise add the code. She will arrange a private visit for you, assuming Ron Thomas will talk to you."

"I think he'll talk. If I wanted to have a brief chat with the Prison Warden in charge, would Jocelyn be able to arrange that?"

"Yes, I mentioned that to her. It'll be no problem."

"Thanks Anne, I'll give her a ring now and go and see Ron Thomas early next week."

"Let me know how you get on."

"Sure. I'll give you a ring after I've spoken to him."

David then rang Jocelyn Ward.

"Hello."

"Could I speak to Jocelyn Ward?"

"Speaking."

"Oh Hello Jocelyn, my name is David Parish. I understand that Anne Graham from Cheshire Police spoke to you about me visiting one of your prisoners, Ron Thomas?"

"That's right. When would you like to come and see him?"

"How about next Monday?"

"That will be fine. Can you make it eleven o'clock in the morning?"

"Yes, I'll be there then."

"If you go to the reception area, they will know that you're coming and will take you to the visiting area. I will arrange for someone to let Ron Thomas know that you're coming to visit."

"Thanks Jocelyn. Is it possible to speak to the Warden in charge, before I speak to Ron Thomas, it will only be a few minutes. I'd also like to know what visitors he's had?"

"Yes, I'll arrange that, his name is Roy McKenzie."

"Thanks, once again, bye."

A little more than half an hour later, David and Alisa were in the car making their way to the Lake District.

They stayed at the cottage for three nights and completed two of the popular walks. They had a stroll around Penrith when they arrived late afternoon. The first walk was the next day when they took in the Place Fell walk starting at Sandwick, taking in Place Fell and then heading for Lake Ullswater and then returning to Sandwick alongside the Lake. That walk was just over seven miles, but with stops, drinks and a boat trip, they were out for nearly five hours.

The second walk started at Cow Bridge and passed Angle Tarn and Thornthwaite Crag, a distance of ten miles which took David and Alisa four and a half hours. The beauty of the Lake District was evident and the source of much discussion.

Each evening was spent in a local inn, where they chose the specialities of the house from the menu. They had friendly chats with the locals who they had got to know quite well during their many times spent at the cottage.

They also talked in great depth about their future and the promotion being offered to Alisa in Murcia. They agreed that Alisa should accept the promotion with the Unidad Especial de Intervention and move from Seville to Murcia. Promises were made with each other that David would go to Murcia for a minimum of three days each month and Alisa would spend a minimum of three days with David in Liverpool. Holidays would be spent together and their relationship would continue, their feelings for each other were too strong. Alisa would find a new home within half an hour of Murcia, San Javier Airport to allow ease of travel. There were Ryanair flights direct between Liverpool and San Javier. The flight was only just over two hours and David lived only fifteen minutes from Liverpool Airport.

They returned to Liverpool on Sunday afternoon, leaving the cottage late in the morning after getting out of bed late, in order to allow Alisa to catch the Monday morning train to London. David also had his meeting arranged with Ron Thomas at Walton Prison at eleven o'clock on Monday morning.

The following morning David dropped Alisa off at Lime Street Station to catch the ten fifteen train to London. He parked in the short stay parking area and walked with Alisa to the platform for the London train.

"Have a nice journey, I'll give you a ring this evening and you can give me an update on the new job in Murcia."

"That's if they let you out of Walton Prison."

They both laughed as David made his way back to his car for the relatively short journey to Walton Prison.

It was about twenty minutes later when David parked his car in the visitor's area of Walton Prison. He was a little early for his eleven o'clock appointment, but made his way to the reception area of the prison for his meeting with Ron Thomas and the Prison Warden, Roy McKenzie.

14

David was greeted by a young lady and he then asked.

"My name is David Parish, Jocelyn Ward has arranged for me to meet one of your wardens, Roy McKenzie and prisoner Ron Thomas."

The lady looked at the book on reception and then said.

"Yes, it has been cleared. I will arrange for someone to escort you to the interview room."

She then picked up the telephone saying.

"David Parish in the reception area for a meeting with Roy McKenzie and prisoner Ron Thomas."

"Somebody will be with you in a minute."

David was soon called by one of the prison staff and went through the usual security checks before he was allowed to enter the prison. He followed the officer and was soon escorted into an interview room where Roy McKenzie was already sitting down waiting.

"It's Mr Fraud, I presume?"

"Yes, I see my name is known on the inside. Who knows me?"

"Actually, it was Ron Thomas who told me you were called Mr Fraud. Apparently you were involved in the investigation that got him locked up and saw the end of the Mitchell boys."

"That's right but I don't suppose that Ron Thomas will be too pleased to see me?"

"Not really. He didn't want to see you when I first mentioned it, but he's got no choice in the matter. He'll do what we tell him to do. When he calmed down, he was curious what you wanted to see him about, and then he thought that it'll give him a break from his prison cell, so he thought it mightn't be a bad idea. I presume it's nothing to do with what he's in prison for?"

"No, it's another fraud investigation."

"Anyhow, you wanted to see me?"

"That's right. I have been asked to investigate a case of identity fraud. Briefly, Ron Thomas had twins with a previous girlfriend, but this was twenty years ago. When the twins were two years old, they were killed in a car crash and he was driving the car. It was an accident and no charges were brought, but he and his girlfriend split up soon afterwards and they went their own ways. She's quite a prominent and successful lady these days and it's her that has asked me to undertake an investigation. In the past few weeks, letters have been arriving at her parents' address, where she used to live when she was with Ron Thomas. The letters are addressed to the twins and relate to unpaid loans and credit cards over the limit. Somebody has obviously copied their identity, got birth certificates and is now fraudulently obtaining money in their names. My client does not think that Ron Thomas is involved but I've got an open mind as far as he's concerned. Once a fraudster always a fraudster, but maybe not."

"He's probably had birth certificates since they were born. Somebody might be using them on his behalf."

"No, we know copies were given out at Manchester Register Office only a couple of months ago. The person told them he was the father and had lost the certificates, but clearly, it wasn't Ron Thomas because he's locked up in here."

"He might have arranged that."

"The staff member in the Register Office seemed to think that the bloke who applied seemed to know an awful lot about the children and Ron Thomas. I'm wondering what visitors he's had since he's been here?"

"Jocelyn did ask me to check, but apart from a couple of visits early on from his solicitor, he's only ever had the one visitor and that's his partner, Lucy Tindall. Oh make that two visitors, sometimes she has brought in their daughter. She comes at every opportunity and to be fair, they seem quite close. Do you think that she's got anything to do with it?"

"I'll never say no, but from what I've heard and what you say, I have my doubts. We don't think there is another bloke on the scene and it was a bloke that went into Manchester Register Office. He had a Geordie accent, aged about forty and was about six foot tall, dark haired with a beard and moustache."

"No he's had no visitors like that."

"Never mind it was a long shot, can I speak to him now?"

"Yes, I'll bring him in."

Roy started walking towards the door, when he suddenly turned around.

"I've just thought of something. When he first came into the prison, he was sharing a cell with another prisoner. They were quite friendly and seemed to get on quite well, and he was a Geordie. He would be about forty years old and was dark haired, he didn't have a beard or moustache. Yes, Geordie Jack, his name is Jack Inglis. It might be nothing but it's a possibility and he was released a couple of months ago."

"Thanks Roy, I'll bring that up when I speak to Ron Thomas."

About five minutes later, Roy returned with the prisoner, Ron Thomas, and commented.

"This is David Parish, a Fraud Specialist. The visit has been approved by the Governor and we'd like you to help him with his investigation."

Ron Thomas turned to Roy.

"I don't need an introduction, I know who he is. Mr Fraud and you're partly responsible for me being here and for the end of the Mitchell family, at least Steve and Alan, who were shot and killed in Spain."

David looked at Ron Thomas, who didn't appear to look any the worse for his time spent in prison.

"I hardly think I've got anything to do with Steve Mitchell setting off to kill members of his family."

"Probably not, but why do you want to see me? If it's anything to do with the Mitchell's, it's all over and I'm serving my sentence here."

"No, it's nothing to do with the Mitchell family and it's got nothing to do with your activities with them."

"Go on. I'll listen to you, I've got plenty of time but I doubt if I'm going to help you in any way."

"My role covers all areas of fraud, mainly working for the Health Authority, other parts of the Public Sector and Insurance Companies. In this case, I've been hired on a consultancy basis, to investigate a case of identity fraud."

"I can't see how I can help."

"Hear me out. The person who has asked me to investigate this identity fraud is a lady named Sally O'Brien."

"Sally?"

"Yes, I thought you might be interested when I mentioned that name."

"I presume you know all about me and Sally, we go back a long time and I imagine you know that we had twin boys."

"Yes, Sally and her brother Darren, he's a solicitor, have told me everything. I know about the boys and that they were killed in a road accident. Obviously, I know that you were driving the car, but be assured Ron, this has nothing to do with what happened to your twin boys."

"Why has Sally contacted you then?"

"The identity fraud has occurred using the names of your twin boys, Paul and John O'Brien."

"They've been dead for about eighteen years."

"I am aware of that, but somebody obtained copies of their birth certificates and started applying for loans and credit cards in their names. At the last count, the amount involved was over sixty thousand pounds. It only came to light when all sorts of correspondence was sent to Sally's old address but her parents still live there and they, naturally, contacted Sally."

"You don't think that I've had anything to do with this do you. Why would I want copies of their birth certificates, I've got original copies at home with their death certificates. Sally doesn't think it was me does she? She knows that I felt terrible about the twins and I wouldn't do anything that would harm their name. Has Sally sent you here?"

"No, it's just part of the investigation and for your information, Sally does not think you would get yourself involved in any type of fraud using the boys. She knows that you are in prison for an involvement in fraudulent activities but has stressed to me that using the boys' names isn't the type of thing that you would do. If you ask me for a personal view of my own, I'm not too sure, but I'll go along with Sally for the time being."

"I've only seen Sally in person, once in the last eighteen years, that was in a shopping arcade in Manchester. I've seen her on television many times, and I'm glad that she's done well for herself. I'm not proud of my past, but I'm telling you now, I've had nothing to do with any fraud involving my twin boys. You don't have to believe me, but that's the truth."

"Okay, I'll accept that, at least for the time being unless I find some evidence to the contrary."

"Try as hard as you want, Mr Fraud, but there's nothing there to find involving me."

Both men looked at each other and shrugged their shoulders before David carried on with the meeting.

"Let's get on with this anyway. The man who obtained the copies of the birth certificates went into the Register Office in

Manchester and informed the staff member that he was the father of the twin boys."

"It wasn't me."

"I know that because it was only a couple of months ago and you were in here."

"That should be a good alibi if it ends up in court."

"I agree with you on that. The bloke who was getting the birth certificates did know a lot about you. He actually told the clerk that the mother was Sally O'Brien and that she was a famous reporter on television. He also said that you had split up, but the boys often spent time with you, by that I mean he said the boys spent time with Ron Thomas. He was told that you had destroyed the original certificates by accident, which is why he wanted copies. Interestingly, the man was also talking about his new relationship and that you had a two year old daughter."

"I'm trying to think who would know all that about me. I don't really talk about my past with Sally, you wouldn't make it known to everybody that you drove a car that killed your twin boys would you?"

"No, but somebody knows you or knows all about you."

"Do you know anything else about this bloke, any description, age, who was he with? I need a bit more if you think that I can help and I will help you. If somebody has used my twin boys to commit some identity fraud, I'd like to find out who it is. I know you're thinking that I'm a fraudster serving time and why should I want to identify another fraudster. There are some loyalties in the criminal world, but that doesn't stretch to somebody using my boys' names."

"All I know is the following. The man in his early forties, a similar age to you. He was about six foot tall, dark haired with a beard and moustache but he spoke with a Geordie accent."

Ron Thomas sat back, clearly thinking very hard and then his expression changed and he suddenly remarked.

"A six foot Geordie, my age. That could be Geordie Jack."

"Go on, tell me a bit more."

"When I came into this prison, I shared a cell with Geordie Jack Inglis. He seemed a nice enough bloke and was serving time for benefit fraud. He'd been claiming all types of benefit saying he was unfit for work, but was working in the building trade. There was nothing wrong with him and he got away with about fifty thousand pounds. He was sent down for nine months. We got talking quite a lot in the prison cell and we spoke about our past sometimes, but we were watching television one time and Sally came on the screen reporting about something. When we got back to the cell, I told him about us and the fact that we'd had twin boys. I also told him about the car accident and that I'd been driving when the twins were killed. He would also know about my relationship now with Lucy and our daughter, Jayne. I say that I can't believe it was Jack but I can't think of anybody else that I've talked to. He is a Geordie and the right age but it could be somebody else. Anybody can do the research and people can examine all the local papers over a certain period and look for deaths or accidents. Some people will walk in churchyards looking at gravestones but the boys were cremated. You should know all about that anyhow, Mr Fraud, it's your job to know how people commit fraud."

"Thanks, I'll take that as a compliment."

"It wasn't meant to be one."

"Thanks for your help. I'll start a search for Jack Inglis, hopefully he shouldn't be too difficult to find. His details will be on record here or with the police."

"I don't know what address is on file, but I've got his address and mobile phone number."

"Where are they?"

"They're in the cell, I'll give them to Roy here when I get back to the cell."

Roy McKenzie was standing at the back of the room, not really interested, but did make a move when his name was mentioned.

"I'll wait here for the information but it might be on file anyway."

"Will you do me a favour?"

"It depends on what it is that you're after."

"Will you tell Sally that this has got nothing to do with me. I wouldn't do anything to damage the name of our twins."

"I'll tell her that."

Ron Thomas put out his hand and shook hands with David.

"I'd never thought that I'd shake hands with Mr Fraud in view of our past history, but there's always a first time. Maybe I'm getting soft in my old age."

Ron Thomas then left the room followed by Roy McKenzie who spoke to David.

"Wait here, I'll only be about ten minutes. I'll make a quick phone call and check what details we have on file."

David sat in the interview room for fifteen minutes when Ron returned with a piece of paper.

"The address is the same as we have on file, it's his mother's address. We don't have that mobile number on file and he probably didn't tell us he had a mobile phone. He used to have fairly regular visits from his girlfriend. I've written down her details on the sheet of paper. I don't think Thomas is involved but it's only a gut feeling. My money's on Jack Inglis."

"I'm tempted to agree with you but I'll keep an open mind. Thanks for your help Roy."

"That's okay. I'll take you back to reception."

15

Detective William Jackson sat back on his chair at his office in the New York Police Department. He had been examining the contents on the file relating to the death of Frank Sinclair and the search for Wendy Carson. A thorough search had been made on the apartment belonging to Frank Sinclair and his colleague, John Regan, had found some forged passports showing the photographs of Sinclair and Carson but they were in different names.

The result of the search had got him thinking about the travel arrangements concerning Wendy Carson who had, supposedly, travelled from JFK to Madrid with Iberia Airways. John Regan had contacted the Spanish Police Authorities who had been quite helpful and had made contact with Iberia and the security staff in charge at Madrid Airport. He had sent them a photo of Wendy Carson in the hope that they may be able to locate her, but the response was not what he expected.

Airport security had shown the photo to the crew of the flight but they did not recognize her but they were able to obtain the details of the passengers who sat next to Wendy Carson. The police made a visit to these passengers, who lived locally in Madrid, and it turned out that one of the passengers is an officer of La Policia in Spain. They did recall an English lady sitting next to them on the journey from New York, mainly because she hardly spoke to them and was quite ignorant at times. When shown the picture of Wendy Carson, they were most definite that the picture was not the lady sitting next to them. The question was now who flew from New York to Madrid. The flight records said Wendy Carson but she had not made that flight, and where was Wendy Carson. She may still be in New York or somewhere else in the United States, but he felt it more likely that she had flown out of the country using a passport in another name.

He turned to John Regan.

"I think I'd better let the Metropolitan Police in London know about our friend, Wendy Carson. She's not in Spain, I doubt if she's still in this country. My bet would be that she's back in England. I'll give Inspector Ross Edgar a ring, its half past two here, the time difference is five hours, so it'll be half past nine in the morning over there. That's okay, I'll give him a ring now"

He looked up the phone number for Ross Edgar and picked up the phone. It was only a matter of seconds before he obtained a response.

"Hello, Ross Edgar."

"Hi Ross. It's Detective William Jackson, New York Police Department."

"Good morning William, or is it afternoon over there?"

"It's half past two in the afternoon. I'm just ringing about our mutual friend, Wendy Carson. You were probably aware that we thought she had flown from New York to Madrid."

"That's right William."

"Well, that's not the case. A lady did fly from New York to Madrid, using the name Wendy Carson, but our Spanish colleagues have done some investigations, and they say that it was not our Wendy Carson. We sent them a photo and they got the cabin crew and the passengers sitting next to her to have a look. I know the crew will see hundreds of faces and might have forgotten what she looked like, but the passengers said it definitely was not the lady sitting next to them. One of the passengers is a Spanish Police official, so we can probably take it as being correct. They've got her details on file, but don't think she's there, I doubt if she's here with a murder charge hanging over her. If I was to guess, I'd say she might be back with you, better facing a fraud charge than a murder wrap, don't you think?"

"Thanks a lot William. I'd better put this on file and start search proceedings over here. She could be anywhere, but she'd probably feel more comfortable over here, especially if she thinks we're looking for her in Spain."

"Couldn't agree more Ross, have a nice day."

"Cheers William."

Ross walked out of his office and walked over to Jan Burgess.

"I've just had William Jackson from the New York Police Department on the phone. They've found out that the lady who travelled under the name of Wendy Carson from New York to Madrid was not the real Wendy Carson. They've no idea where Carson is now, but there's a possibility she might be back in this country and came home under a different name. I wonder if she's been in touch with her mother, Mary Longridge or her daughter, Pauline. I think it's worth paying them another visit. We'll try and avoid them talking to each other, so I'll go with Sam, you go with Geoff and take Lynn Baxter from Scenes of Crime to see what she can find to help identify Wendy. They live pretty close together, so we'll arrange to see them this evening at say six o'clock. Pauline should be home from work then."

"I don't think Pauline knows that much but I'm sure that Mrs Longridge knows more than she's been saying."

"I tend to agree. She's had plenty of money off Wendy and she must know it's not all from honest living."

It was six o'clock on the dot when Ross Edgar and Sam Dixon called at the house of Mary Longridge. Ross rang the doorbell and waited until she opened the door.

"Good evening Mrs Longridge, I'm Inspector Ross Edgar from the Metropolitan Police, I believe you've met Sam Dixon."

"He came last time, what do you want? I haven't heard from Wendy."

"May we come in and we'll talk about it."

"Oh come in."

They both followed Mary Longridge into the kitchen and all sat around the table.

Ross then started the meeting.

"Have you seen your daughter Wendy?"

"She's in New York and you know that."

"We're not sure she is, we think she may have left the States and returned to this country."

"It's new to me, why would she come back here, she's with her boyfriend Frank."

"Not anymore she isn't. He was found dead in a river in New York and there was no sign of Wendy."

"How do you mean dead, what did he die of?"

"He was murdered and the New York Police Department are looking for Wendy and they're seeking our assistance."

"Murdered, Wendy wouldn't kill anybody. Don't be so stupid."

"Well the quicker we find her the better."

Mary Longridge then broke down in tears and sobbed.

"Wendy wouldn't murder Frank, he was her boyfriend."

"We don't know what's happened but we do need to speak to her urgently. Have you spoken to her on the phone?"

"No, I haven't seen or heard from her since she went to New York. I don't know if she's spoken to Pauline. Should I ask Pauline?"

"There's no need, two of my officers are around there at the moment. Look, I know how upset you must be Mrs Longridge, but it is better if we do speak to Wendy. Will you let us know if she makes contact with you, or better still, get Wendy to contact me. Here's my card."

"Pauline will be worried sick if she thinks her Mum's wanted for murdering somebody. It can't be true."

Jan Burgess and Geoff Ricketts called at Wendy Carson's house where her daughter Pauline lived. She took one look at Geoff and said.

"What do you want, you've already searched the house."

Jan then spoke.

"I'm Sergeant Jan Burgess from the Metropolitan Police. You know Geoff Ricketts and this is Lynn Baxter, who will want to have a look around and she may take some of your Mum's belongings."

"I couldn't forget him, you'd better come in, I suppose."

Jan and Geoff sat in the lounge and Jan then spoke to Pauline.

"Lynn needs to have a look in your Mum's room. Do you want to go with her?"

"No, but show me what you're going to take away. Mum's room is upstairs, first on the right."

"Have you seen your Mum, Pauline?"

"Of course not, she's in America."

"Have you spoken to her on the phone?"

Pauline hesitated but then replied.

"No, I've tried to get her on the phone but I've not been able to get through."

"I've got some news from New York. Her boyfriend, Frank Sinclair, has been found murdered in New York. His body was dumped in a river, and the New York Police have put out a warrant for your mother."

"A warrant, what for?"

"The murder of Frank Sinclair, I'm sorry Pauline."

"You must be joking. Mum wouldn't do that."

"It's important that we speak to your mother. It's for her own good."

"Look, I don't know where she is, I'm worried sick. She must still be in America but I know that she wouldn't do what you're saying."

"We're not saying anything, we just want to speak to her, but we do think that she might be heading back to England."

"Why do you think that?"

"We don't think she would want to stay in America and we know somebody else used a passport in her name to travel to Spain."

"How could somebody else use her passport, the photo would be different?"

"It's a forged passport. Your mother may be travelling in a different name."

Pauline then looked shocked.

"Something may have happened to Mum, somebody may have stole her passport. She might have been killed as well."

"We don't know anymore Pauline, but its better all round if this is sorted out as quickly as possible, don't you think?"

"I don't know what to think. Mum isn't a big criminal. You wanted her for a fraud to begin with and you now want her for murder. I just don't believe what I've been hearing. She might be hiding in fear for her life."

"Let us know if you speak to her, at least we'll know she's alive."

Lynn came downstairs with a bag containing a hair brush, some make up containers, lipstick and a drinking glass. She showed them to Pauline saying.

"I'll arrange for you to be given an official receipt."

Pauline looked at the bag and then waved her hand as a gesture of acknowledgement.

Jan left her card as they left the house. As they were returning to the car, Jan had a word with Geoff.

"Do you think she's spoken to Wendy?"

"I think she might have spoken to her before the body was found, possibly, but not afterwards."

"You could be right. We'll head back to the Station but I don't want to give Ross a ring at the moment in case he's still with Mary Longridge. We'll discuss what they've found out later."

Denis King, who was on police bail for his part in the Hospital payroll fraud returned to his house, having had a few drinks in the pub just around the corner from where he lived. He opened the front door and walked into the lounge and was startled to see a lady with short dark hair sitting on the settee.

"What are you doing here, who are you?"

"Hello Denis."

"Wendy, I thought you were in New York with Frank, where is he?"

"We've split up Denis, so I've returned home and left Frank in New York."

"You've changed your hair, it's a different colour, I hardly recognised you?"

"That's the idea. I imagine the police are looking for me?"

"You're not surprised are you? They caught up with me, Chris, Jim and Tom. We all got arrested and interviewed, and we've now been charged with fraud and we're all on police bail."

"What did you tell them?"

"Not a lot. They already knew about you and Frank."

"They were on to us very quick in New York. I was out on my own and returning to Frank's place when I saw a police car outside. The police were talking to the neighbours so I didn't bother to go back there. Frank wasn't in and I rang him and warned him not to go back. I met him later in a bar and we had an argument and eventually decided to go our own ways. I don't know where he is now, have you heard from him?"

"No, I haven't tried to contact him. Our friendship has been a bit strained since you left me to go with him."

"I'm sorry about that, I shouldn't have fallen out with you, it was a mistake and I regret it."

"Are you saying you want us to get back together?"

"If you'll have me?"

Denis was in a state of shock. He was still in love with Wendy, but he had told the police all about her involvement in the fraud. She would find out if the police caught up with her, but if he could help her escape, she might never find out what he'd told the police.

"I need to think. You'll soon be caught if you're found with me. How did you get back here from America?"

"I got on the plane, stupid. Did you think I'd walked?"

"Well no, but they would have had your name listed at the airports when you arrived back in this country."

"I didn't travel in my own name. I've got a passport in a different name. My name is now Colette Brady."

"How did you manage to do that?"

"It was quite easy really. I got some birth certificates and then changed the name by deed poll in order to cover my tracks better. You can change your name by deed poll over the internet, I think it only cost about ten pounds. I was then able to get the documents together to get a new passport, I actually did it a few times, but I had to leave some of the passports in New York. They don't know about this name though and Frank doesn't know either."

"Where are you going to go?"

"I'll find a place to hide, I've got a new name and my appearance is different."

"Can you get me a new identity and we'll escape together?"

"That might be possible. Is there any chance of a drink in this house?"

"Sorry Wendy, I mean Colette, what do you want?"

"Have you got any red wine?"

"Yes, I've been to the supermarket today and bought a couple of bottles of Australian Cabernet Sauvignon."

"That would be nice."

Denis walked over to the cupboard in order to get the bottle of red wine and was immediately followed by Wendy. As he bent down, Wendy pounced, grabbed his neck from behind and within a matter of seconds, the dead body of Denis King lay on the floor alongside the drinks cabinet.

Wendy looked at the dead body and spoke to the corpse.

"You must think I'm stupid, Denis King. I know that you told the police all about me, they couldn't have got that address in New York from anybody else apart from you. Frank's dead as well, he couldn't be relied on. The others didn't know about the New York address and I rang Chris Sugden, Jim Barrowcliffe and Tom Crouch from New York. They were adamant that they didn't tell the police anything, they just kept saying no comment to all the questions, just like I'd told them to. They know what's good for them, not like you, who was probably trying to do a deal with the police. Silly man."

Wendy picked up the bottle of red wine, unscrewed the top and poured herself a glass. A few drinks later, she made her way to the bedroom leaving the body of Denis King, where she had killed him.

Wendy left the house the following morning, and eventually found a public phone box. She dialled her mother, Mary Longridge, making sure that there was no trace of where the call was coming from.

"Hello"

"Hello Mum, its Wendy."

There were tears on the other end of the phone line.

"Where are you Wendy, I've had the police round and so has Pauline. They're looking for you about this fraud from the hospital and now they're saying that Frank's been murdered in New York."

"Frank's death had nothing to do with me Mum. He had some enemies, they must have killed him."

"Where are you?"

"I can't tell you at the moment, I just want to tell you and Pauline that I'm okay and not to worry. When I get myself sorted out, I'll be in touch, will you tell Pauline?"

"She's your daughter Wendy, you should speak to her yourself."

"I can't at the moment, she'd get too upset."

"I'm upset and I want to know what's going on?"

"I'll come and see you and Pauline as soon as I've sorted myself out."

"What country are you in Wendy. Are you in America or are you back here?"

"I can't say Mum. I'll have to go, but I'll be in touch and I'll take care of you both. Bye for now Mum."

Mary Longridge rang 1471 on the phone, but the message came back saying the caller had withheld the number.

She then rang her granddaughter, Pauline.

"Hello"

"Hello Pauline, its Nan. I've just had your Mum on the phone. She wouldn't give me her phone number or tell me where she was, but she said that she was okay and had nothing to do with the murder of Frank. She told me to tell you and I told her that she should ring you, she hasn't has she?"

"No, I haven't heard anything. Try ringing one, four, seven, one on the phone and see if you can get her number."

"I thought of that and did ring, one, four, seven, one, but the message came back saying the caller had withheld the number."

"I don't think you can withhold the number unless you're ringing from this country. It's a B.T. service, I think. She must be in this country, is she hiding from the police or is she hiding from somebody else?"

"I don't know Pauline."

"Should we tell the Police?"

"No, I think we'd better keep it quiet for the time being. I think she'll contact us again sometime."

"Okay. Thanks Nan."

Ross Edgar had called a meeting with Jan to see if anything had come out of their meetings.

"How did you get on Jan?"

"Nothing came of it. She said she hadn't heard or met with her mother but we felt that she might have spoken to her at some time but possibly not since the murder. I mentioned that somebody had travelled from New York to Spain on a passport in the name of Wendy Carson and she then wondered if something had happened to her mother. I don't think she knows anything."

"I don't think Mary Longridge knows anything either but I think we might have to keep in touch with both of them."

They were interrupted by a phone call which Ross took, listened and then said.

"Strange, will you send somebody round to his address and see if he's there?"

"That was the front desk. Denis King did not turn up today. Its part of his bail condition that he presents himself at two o'clock in the afternoon. He's normally quite efficient and turns up five minutes early. I've told them to send somebody round to check."

About half an hour later, Ross and Jan were packing up for the day and about to return to their homes, when his phone rang again. He again listened before telling the caller.

"Tell them we're on the way and get Scene of Crimes Team there as quick as possible."

He put the phone down and looked at Jan.

"They've just made a visit to Denis King's address and found him dead. There's no obvious cause of death, he might have been strangled, but Scene of Crime will be on their way. We'd better have a quick look before we go home. Sorry about that."

16

The phone rang in David's house and he picked it up expecting it to be Alisa.

"Hello."

"Hi David, its Ross Edgar. I've got some news for you."

"Go on."

"We've just discovered the body of Denis King. He didn't turn up at the Police Station which was part of his bail condition. A couple of officers went round to his place and they found the body inside, no signs of disturbance, it was all very tidy inside. There was no sign of forced entry and it looks as though he may have known his attacker. It looks as though he might have been strangled, there were marks on his neck, but it wasn't very clear to me. Scenes of Crime are there now and we should get a pathology report tomorrow. The problem is it might be a similar death to that of Frank Sinclair in New York, which brings us back to Wendy Carson. It's not the usual type of murder committed by a female but we know that she was into martial arts. We don't know if she's involved and we don't know where she is, but she's going to go on our wanted list straight away. I didn't want you searching for her and finding her without knowing what she might have done."

"Thanks Ross, I don't want to end up as number three if that's the case."

"Where are you tomorrow, because there will be a meeting with Scenes of Crime, Murder Squad and ourselves. You're welcome to come if you are around, the meeting will be late morning?"

"I can travel down tomorrow morning, that's no problem."
"Okay, I'll say eleven o'clock at this Station."
"See you tomorrow Ross."

David then picked up the phone to call Alisa.
"Hello."
"Hello Alisa darling, guess where I'm coming tomorrow?"
"That sounds as if Senor Fraudo is coming here?"
"That's right. I've got a meeting with Ross Edgar at eleven o'clock. One of the blokes involved in the payroll fraud has been found murdered and it looks similar to the murder of Frank Sinclair in New York. Ross feels that it could be the work of Wendy Carson and she's top of their wanted list. He told me to be careful if I was closely on her trail, but I haven't got a clue where she is."
"You must watch out for dangerous ladies, especially me if you upset me."
"I'd be too frightened to do that."
"I had another meeting today about returning to Spain, but we'll talk about it tomorrow. I've confirmed that I'll go to Murcia probably in about three weeks, but I'll be winding down here in the next week or so."
"Okay Alisa, my meeting should be finished mid-afternoon, I'll see you after you've finished work tomorrow evening. My mobiles ringing, I'd better answer it."
"Bye for now David."

David picked up the mobile and saw that it was Eric Page, the Bank Investigator who was calling.
"Hello Eric, what can I do for you, or have you got news for me. I was going to ring you?"
"We've uncovered several cases of identity fraud over the past few days and made some initial enquiries. We've come up with a bloke in his forties, about six feet tall and talks with a Geordie accent. He didn't have a beard this time but it sounds

very much like your Geordie and he's using other identities besides the O'Brien twins. All the cases have been in respect of people who have died and their identity is being used. The local police are now involved and I understand that Anne Graham is heading the investigation."

"It definitely sounds like the Geordie. I did go and see Ron Thomas at Walton Prison and I don't think it is down to him. He did seem a bit shocked when I told him I was working for Sally O'Brien and looking at identity fraud relating to his twin sons. Would you believe that he shared a cell with a Geordie called Jack Inglis who was released a few months ago? He is forty years old, six feet tall and Ron Thomas did tell him all sorts of things when they were locked in a cell."

"Do you know where he is?"

"Not at the moment, but if I'm searching for him, so are you, Anne Graham will be searching for him when I give her the details in a few minutes. He might have bigger problems if Ron Thomas has put word out that he wants him found."

"I think he'd be better if we found him before Ron Thomas."

"I couldn't agree more, Eric. I'll give Anne Graham a ring now."

"Cheers David."

David made the next phone call.

"Hello, Anne Graham."

"Hello Anne, its David Parish."

"Have you been to see Ron Thomas?"

"Yes, I saw him and got the impression that he's got nothing to do with the identity fraud. I know that you've been speaking to Eric Page about an increase in identity fraud and you're looking for a Geordie, about forty years old, six feet tall."

"That's right, have you got anything for me?"

"I think so. Ron Thomas shared a cell with a bloke called Jack Inglis who was released a few months ago. It turns out he is a Geordie with the same description and Ron admitted telling him about his past and the death of the twin boys. I'd put him top of your list but it wouldn't surprise me if Ron Thomas had put out a search as well."

"I'm sure he will. I'll be able to get more information on this Jack Inglis. Thanks for that David."

"If you have any luck, will you let me know?"

"No problem David. Speak to you again."

David put the phone down and decided that he deserved a reward for the days work. He headed for the drinks cabinet and made himself a large gin and tonic.

17

David made his way to Lime Street Station in Liverpool for the train trip to London. It was a regular journey but he was getting an earlier train this morning, leaving just after seven o'clock and arriving at London Euston around a quarter past nine. The next direct train would not be arriving until after half past ten, which would be too late for the meeting with Ross Edgar and the Metropolitan Police.

The journey was uneventful, he managed to grab a cup of coffee but spent most of the time examining paperwork and updating documents on his laptop. He sent an email to Brian Lewis suggesting that they arrange a date to complete a formal interview with Ben Alexander and what dates was Brian available to assist in the interview. He received a reply just before they arrived at Euston Station with Brian stating he had a couple of days leave early the following week but there would be no problem later in the week, or the week after.

The train arrived on time, which allowed David to have a bite to eat before making his way across London to the meeting with Ross. He walked to the station concourse and made his way to the French Deli outlet and bought a couple of croissants and a coffee. The croissants were quite pleasant and David then went downstairs to catch the Tube across London.

The meeting was held in Ross Edgar's office and there were seven people present. David only knew Ross Edgar and Jan Burgess.

They were all presented with a folder and Ross opened the meeting.

"I think we all know each other with the exception of David Parish."

David waved his hand and smiled.

"David is a Fraud Consultant and has earned the nickname of Mr Fraud. He started the initial investigation into Wendy Carson, when he was informed about a big payroll fraud in a London Hospital. It was worth six hundred thousand pounds and it was soon discovered that the fraud was instigated by Wendy Carson. She was helped by her boyfriend, Frank Sinclair, who you will know was found murdered in New York. We know Wendy Carson went to New York and we did arrest four accomplices to the fraud, one of whom was Denis King who was found dead yesterday. The New York Police Department did put out a warrant for Wendy Carson but she had disappeared. They did find out that a Wendy Carson travelled from New York to Madrid and assumed, initially, that she had fled to Spain. The Spanish Police then started doing some research and they found out that the person who flew from New York to Madrid was not the real Wendy Carson and a forged passport showing a false name had been used. Anyway, I decided to invite David because of his knowledge and contacts in the fraud world. She will probably go underground, but David's contacts may be able to locate her. David, you know Jan and myself, we also have Lynn Baxter and Paul Richmond from Scenes of Crime together with Kevin Donnelly and Roger Christian from the Murder Squad. Let's start with you Lynn, do we know how he was murdered?"

"It seems as though he was attacked from behind and he was strangled by use of the arms being tightened round his neck. It's a normal type of strangulation from behind but what is unusual is that it's not a murder normally carried out by a woman. You would not expect a woman to have the strength to carry out such a murder, but she was well trained in martial arts and this would, therefore, be quite possible according to a couple of experts that I've spoken to today. We do know that it was the same type of murder carried out on Frank Sinclair in New York, so we have to consider that it may have been carried out by the same person, in this case Wendy Carson. We took some fingerprints from the house and collected a few articles including an opened bottle of red wine and a drinking glass. The fingerprints are being examined as we talk now and compared with some that I took from her house when I went with Jan to see her daughter. We have got Wendy Carson's DNA from some of the stuff I collected and I know that you would expect to find her fingerprints or DNA at the murder scene, because she was certainly there a week or two ago before she went to New York. Hopefully, I've collected prints or DNA from a visit yesterday."

"Kevin, have you managed to get the murder enquiry under way?"

"Yes, we've started and I managed to speak to Detective William Jackson in New York last night. I've told him there has been a murder in this country and our main suspect is Wendy Carson. He thought that she's probably back in this country and this now makes it even more certain in his opinion. She is still listed at all airports but he doesn't think she'll return and I have to agree with him. We agreed to keep in contact and decide what to do once we find her, he's confident that she can't hide forever, but think she's quite a talented fraudster. They are going to send over the findings of their enquiry to date."

David then remarked.

"Do we know if the other three accomplices, Chris Sugden, Jim Barrowcliffe and Tom Crouch are all okay?"

Jan Burgess was able to reply.

"Yes, I was going to mention that in a moment, but I made early morning visits to all three and they've not seen her at all since she left for New York. I did mention that Frank Sinclair and Denis King had been murdered and it was in their own interests that they should tell me everything. Chris and Jim didn't make any comments but Tom Crouch went pale and I thought that he was going to pass out. He then said that Wendy had phoned him from New York asking what I'd said at the police interview. He told her that he'd said no comment to everything like he'd been told to. I pushed him a bit further and he said that he knew that Chris and Jim had said nothing, but he guessed from talking to Denis King that he'd told the police more than he was supposed to. He hadn't seen her and he didn't think Chris and Jim had seen her either. I did tell them to be careful if they saw Wendy and they all said that they'd make certain they didn't follow the paths of Frank and Denis."

David then came out with a few more comments.

"Wendy Carson committed a payroll fraud. This would be a one off fraud and highly unlikely that she would be able to commit this type of fraud again. She has been involved in identity fraud as part of the payroll and was probably given a lot of advice by Frank Sinclair. We have to accept that she might have acquired some knowledge in this area and if she needed money badly, she might look at this area again. In the fraud game, we often say, once a fraudster always a fraudster. It's sad to say but identity fraud is still a big area and it wouldn't take a lot for her to get involved in this area. She's committed two murders, or at least it looks like, she's got a taste for money and will want to live that lifestyle, at least that's what I think."

Roger Christian then told the meeting.

"I think she'll go underground and stay hidden. She'll probably change her appearance but she's wanted for two murders, a payroll fraud of six hundred thousand pounds and several cases of identity fraud. We don't know where she is, she is probably still in this country but we can't be sure. I think we might have to consider making this case high profile and it might be worth considering seeking public help by going live on television. It could be a case of approaching the television programme, Criminals Captured and I know it's going to start again next week. There is a new presenter, I've seen it advertised on television. Can't remember her name."

David then gave the answer.

"Sally O'Brien is the new face for the programme. I've met Sally and her brother Darren, he's a solicitor in London"

Ross replied.

"I know Darren O'Brien but I didn't realize he was related to Sally."

"Yes, I'm helping Sally with an identity fraud case, but it's nothing to do with Wendy Carson."

Roger continued with his thoughts.

"If we want to go live on television, we'll have to get permission from our big boss. I think I'll have a word and see what he thinks. We could have a joint plea for a fraudster and a murderer, it might be worth thinking of David joining one of us on the programme, but we need to seek further thoughts on that. What do you think Ross, should we try for Criminals Captured?"

"To be honest, I think it's quite a good idea. We could do with all the help we can get."

The meeting was interrupted by Lynn's mobile ringing. She looked at the mobile and said to the rest of the group.

"I think I should take this, it's going to be an update on the fingerprints that are being checked for Wendy Carson."

"Hello, Lynn Baxter."

The group watched while Lynn listened to what was being told to her on the phone.

She then said.

"Thanks very much," and put the mobile phone off.

"I've just got the results of the fingerprint tests. They have checked the fingerprints that I got from Wendy's house and compared them to prints at the murder scene. There were no prints on the wine glass, it had been rubbed clean. There were no prints on the screw top of the wine bottle but her prints have been found on the side of the bottle. She got careless, and before you ask, we found a receipt, dated yesterday, from the supermarket which showed the purchase of two bottles of cabernet sauvignon. There were only two bottles in the house, one opened and one unopened. They were not old bottles from when she was last at the house. They've also found a set of prints on the toilet handle and they were the most recent prints. I think that confirms what we all think, Wendy Carson is in this country and was at the house of Denis King and probably murdered him."

Kevin was first to make the comment.

"Thanks for that Lynn, that gives us more to go on, but we still need to find her as quick as possible. I'm going to see the boss and get his approval for Criminals Captured. Are you happy to go on live television David?"

"I'll do anything to help. I still want to get her for the fraud of six hundred thousand pounds. I know it's a lower priority than the two murders but I want to finish my job."

Ross closed the meeting.

"You've all got the files and we've now had a verbal update from Lynn concerning the fingerprints. We have circulated all Police Forces with the details of Wendy Carson and the computer details will be updated. Kevin and Roger will start checking on Criminals Captured and they will let you know David. It'll be nice to see two of you on television, it'll fear the life out of Wendy Carson. Hopefully, we should get some information from any calls that are taken on the programme."

They all left Ross's office in search of Wendy Carson.

David made his way to Alisa's flat near Regents Park and updated his records concerning the now famous Wendy

Carson. Her fame would increase if he would be joining the police on the Criminals Captured television programme.

He decided to write to Ben Alexander and formally invite him to attend the taped interview in a couple of weeks' time. The dates had been cleared by Brian Lewis, who would again be assisting David. He arranged for the letter to go to his Dental Surgery and he would send it by Special Delivery, in order that it would be signed as received at the surgery. It would then be possible to confirm proof of delivery by checking the Royal Mail site on the internet.

David picked up his mobile phone and rang Ben Alexander's solicitor, Mark Weston. A female voice answered the phone.

"Good afternoon, AGK Solicitors."

"Hello, may I speak to Mark Weston?"

"Who is it speaking please?"

"David Parish."

There was a short delay before Mark spoke to David.

"Hello David, I presume you are going to tell me about the interview with Ben Alexander?"

"That's right. I'll be sending him a letter by Special Delivery inviting him to an interview in two weeks' time. I thought I'd let you know but you should hear from Ben within a couple of days, once he's received the letter."

"Where are you going to hold the meeting?"

"I've suggested that the meeting is held at the local Health Trust headquarters in Southport."

"I know where that is. I'll see you then, all going well."

"I hope so, bye for now."

David then left the flat and had a gentle stroll to the Post Office to arrange delivery of the letter.

18

Wendy Carson sent a letter to her daughter, Pauline, and gave a mobile phone number for Pauline to contact her. She also told Pauline to use a phone booth in the road, rather than use the phone at home or her mobile phone. Pauline left the house, went to phone booth and rang the number. There was a short delay before the phone was answered.

Wendy looked at the number on her mobile phone, and knew it was from the phone booth and it must be Pauline.

"Hello Pauline."

"Mum, I've been sick with worry. What's going on? The police are looking for you and say that you're wanted for murder. Frank has been killed in New York."

"I don't want to discuss what I've done. I just wanted to talk to you before I move on because I'm not sure when I'll see you or Nan again."

"I want to see you Mum."

"I'm sorry but you can't see me at the moment Pauline, it wouldn't be safe for you or me."

"What do you mean safe?"

"The police might be following you."

"I won't tell the police, you must know that?"

"I do, my love, but you mightn't know if they were following you."

"You can't just go like this."

"I will be in touch when I feel it is safe, but you won't be able to call me on this mobile number as I'll be destroying it later."

"How can I contact you Mum, if I don't have a number?"

"The police can locate where a person is using a mobile phone and they might be tracing this call as we speak. They have been known to tap into people's phone lines. I will be in touch, that's a promise but take care of yourself Pauline and give my love to Nan."

There were tears at the end of the phone line but Pauline managed to splutter out the words.

"I love you Mum. I don't know what you've done but don't disappear. Keep in touch."

"I will Pauline, that's a promise. I'll get you some money to take care of the house and you can have the car. Bye, speak to you soon."

The phone went dead as it was disconnected.

Wendy was in her new car when the phone rang. She took the SIM card out of the phone and destroyed it and then broke the phone beyond repair and took a short walk and threw it in a bin.

She had purchased the four year old blue Fiat Punto the day before at a garage in North London. It had cost her four thousand pounds which she paid in cash, they had taxed the car for twelve months and she had produced a driving licence and a forged insurance certificate in the name of Colette Brady.

Money was not an immediate problem, she had some of her own cash which had been hidden and still had secretive bank accounts, which she was sure had not been discovered. She also had brought the dollars from Frank Sinclair's apartment in New York, most of which had been changed to pounds sterling and it would not take too long to change the rest. She had been to several places to get the money changed. She also had twenty six thousand pounds in cash which she had found in Denis King's house after she had killed him. He had obviously not declared this to the police when he had been interviewed. It was his little nest egg.

The use of false identities may be a useful way to earn money in the future. She knew how to obtain birth certificates, driving licences and passports in false names and already had a collection ready for sale. She had discovered, about six months previously, that there was a good market for foreign nationals who were in the country illegally. Some contacts had already been made and a steady sale of forged documents had been made. Sensibly she had not used the names of Wendy Carson or Colette Brady when making these sales and she was also known as Amanda Jeffers and had the driving licence, birth certificate and passport in that name.

Wendy made her way across London and took the M25 motorway, before leaving and taking the M40 towards the Midlands. She stopped at a Service Station before the M42 and then drove along that motorway before joining the M6, heading north, leaving at Junction 10A and taking the next motorway, the M54 towards Shrewsbury. She then joined the A5 and made her way through Wales, stopping briefly at Llangollen. The remainder of the journey took her through Wales across the Britannia Bridge into the island of Anglesey, and she then made her way to Llangefni, where she had rented a cottage for the next three months. The cottage was isolated, which is just what Wendy wanted.

Anglesey had always been a favourite of Wendys when she was a child and had spent several holidays on the island. She had also brought Pauline, when she was a child, with her ex husband when they were married. She had not been for a few years but still knew the island quite well. She had located the cottage when searching the internet and contacted the owners who now spent most of their time in Spain. Wendy had agreed a rental fee and deposited the cash into the owner's bank account. The key was hidden but they had told Wendy where she would be able to locate it.

Wendy drove down the country lane and was soon able to locate the cottage and find the key to the front door. She walked in and was more than happy with the cottage which would be an ideal place to stay for a few months while she decided what to do next. It would be a nice place to bring Pauline, but she knew that would be impossible at this period of time.

There was a note on the table addressed to Colette Brady.

Colette,

We hope you enjoy your stay at the cottage. If you have any problems, you can see Mr Jones in the cottage next door. He does have a spare key and our contact number. There is a phone number for the gas supplier when you run out. The canisters are outside and you should be okay for three or four weeks. We have left a few provisions in the fridge and there is a bottle of red wine on the kitchen table. Hope you like red wine, sorry there is no white.

Regards

Lloyd & Hilary

Wendy walked out of the cottage to take out all the luggage from her car and looked out at the wonderful views you could see from the cottage gardens. She had brought some food but some had also been left in the fridge. She would be fine for a couple of days but she was looking forwards to touring the island and visiting some of the places that she been to many years ago.

Wendy had made herself a meal and was enjoying her second glass of the red wine when the phone in the cottage rang. She stood still and was undecided on whether to answer the phone. She decided to pick up the phone.

"Hello."

"Is that Colette?"

"Yes."

"Hi Colette, its Hilary. I was just checking that you have arrived okay and managed to find the key for the cottage?"

"Oh yes, everything is fine and the cottage is lovely."

"One thing we forgot to tell you. The phone in the cottage, it will be cut off tonight until we return, I hope that doesn't give you a problem."

"No, that's okay and I wouldn't have used it anyway."

"Have you got a contact number for your mobile phone?"

"My mobile packed in yesterday, but I'll buy a new one tomorrow. Thanks for the food and red wine. I'm drinking a glass at the moment, it's very nice."

"I'm glad you've settled in. Enjoy your stay."

"I will, bye for now."

Wendy put the phone down and spoke to herself.

"Nosy cow, what does she want with my mobile phone number?"

She went back to the kitchen and poured herself a third glass of the red wine.

Pauline Carson rang her Nan, Mary Longridge later that evening.

"Hello."

"Hi Nan, its Pauline. I thought that you should know I rang Mum earlier today. She's okay but wouldn't tell me where she was or where she was going. She wouldn't talk about Frank or the Police."

"Do you have a phone number?"

"I received a note from her through the post, telling me to ring a number, but when I rang her, she told me the number would be no good in the future. I tried ringing it again about an hour ago but the line was dead."

"I've had something from her as well."

"What have you had?"

"A parcel came by special delivery, not the Royal Mail but one of those delivery men. When I opened it, there was money inside, five thousand pounds. There was also a note saying give half of the money to you and keep half for myself."

"She said that she would see me okay for money. What shall we do?"

"Keep quiet, I'll give you three thousand pounds and keep the rest. I won't need any more money but you will. Come over as soon as you can and collect the money but keep it hidden from the police."

"I'm worried about all this Nan, I don't want to get into trouble with the police, I'm frightened."

"This is cash, they'll never know where it came from, and I'll just say that I don't like banks and I've always put some cash to one side, but they'll never find out anyway."

"Okay Nan, I'll come round tomorrow and see you and we'll have a chat about what to do next. We can't contact Mum anyway and I've no idea where she is."

"Take care, don't worry too much and I'll see you tomorrow Pauline."

19

David returned to Alisa's flat to find she had returned from work.

"There is a message on your mobile, David. I haven't looked at it but it rang about five minutes ago."

He looked at the message and saw that it was from John Kingsley, a manager at a Benefits Agency. David had known John for many years and he used to be a member of the same Squash team about ten years ago. They had met at a few business meetings over the year and the odd social occasion.

The message informed David that the Investigators at his Agency were examining a benefits fraud which covered a variety of areas and covered several different authorities in the Public Sector. John had asked David to give him a ring to discuss the case but a meeting would probably be necessary within the next few days if that was possible.

He decided to return the call immediately and he rang John.

"Hello, John Kingsley."

"Hello John, its David Parish. I'm returning your call, sorry I missed you but I popped out and forgot to take the mobile with me. Anyhow, how are you?"

"I'm fine David, but we have been looking at a case of Benefit fraud. It's quite complex which is why we will probably need to arrange a meeting. Briefly, it relates to a man and his partner. He has been claiming invalidity benefits, stating he is unfit to work, when we believe he has been working as a builder and surprise, he has not declared these earnings. He has also supposed to have entered to run in a marathon shortly and has been in training for weeks. His partner is claiming unemployment benefits but we did receive an anonymous call on the helpline, saying she is working at a hospital under a different name. There is some other information, but we need to meet to discuss this. When are you available?"

"I'm in London today and will need to be back here next week, but it may be possible to meet in between. If I return to Liverpool tomorrow, I will then be able to drive across tomorrow afternoon. Is that too soon?"

"No that's fine David. What time do you reckon you will get here?"

"I'd better make it late afternoon, how about three o'clock?"

"Super, I'll see you then. Bye for now David."

"See you tomorrow John."

Alisa had been given the official notification of her new job in Murcia. David looked at the letter which informed Alisa that she would be starting in six weeks time. They had allowed a two week period to clear up any outstanding work in Seville, but in view of the secondment in England, there would only be a few loose ends to tidy up. She would, however, have to put her apartment up for sale and arrange the transport of her furniture and belongings to Murcia. Details of an appropriate removal company had been supplied but this would not be necessary for perhaps a couple of months, as temporary furnished accommodation was being made available in Murcia. It was Alisa's intention to purchase property nearer San Javier Airport, but this would only be a short journey to Murcia. There was also a nice little pay rise with this promotion. David finished reading the information and remarked.

"This looks fine, Alisa. Does it cover everything?"

"Yes, I have discussed it and everything is in order."

"I'm going back to Liverpool tomorrow, are you tied up here or can you come back with me?"

"I've already arranged a few days off, with holidays that are due. I'll travel back with you. I presume you are catching the train in the morning?"

"Yes, an early start I'm afraid. I've got a meeting in the afternoon and it'll take me three quarters of an hour to drive there. The meeting is at three o'clock."

"I'll make us a nice meal and we'll have to have an early night."

"Sounds a good idea to me."

They arrived back at David's Liverpool home just before midday the following day. It was just before two o'clock when David started on the journey to the Benefits Agency where John Kingsley was the Manager. A little less than an hour later he walked into the Agency and approached a lady on the reception desk.

"Hello, my name if David Parish, I have a three o'clock appointment with John Kingsley."

"John did inform me that you were coming, I'll take you through to his office now."

David followed and was taken to meet John and as he entered the office, John walked over and shook hands.

"Nice to see you David, would you like a drink?"

"A coffee with milk would be nice."

John turned to the receptionist.

"Would you arrange two coffees for us please?"

"Yes, no problem."

John then started the discussions.

"I gave you some brief details on the phone yesterday but rather than tell you the whole saga, I've got a couple of reports for you and it's probably easier if you take some time to read the reports. We'll then have a chat afterwards."

John handed David the paperwork and turned to him.

"You may as well carry on working until I've digested the contents of these reports. It'll probably take me a little time."
"Sorry about that David."
He opened the first report.

Michael Davis
17 Crossland Street
Chester
Date of Birth 26/4/75
Michael Davis has been receiving invalidity benefits for the past three years and has informed the Agency that he is unable to work. He claims to be in constant back pain and is unable to walk more than a few hundred yards and requires the use of a walking stick for most of the time. He also states that he has great difficulty walking the stairs at home and often has to sleep downstairs where there is a single bed. Sick notes have been received on a regular basis from his Doctor, confirming his inability to work due to back problems. He also claims to be living alone in his rented property and receives housing benefits and council tax reductions.

A month ago, he was in the Agency collecting his benefits and walking with the use of a walking stick. Another gentleman was in the queue, who we know is a legitimate claimant, and when he was collecting his benefits he remarked to the member of staff. "Don't quote me and I'll deny that I ever said this, but Mike Davis is no cripple, he works for a building bloke and gets paid cash in hand. I've seen him climbing a ladder and working on a roof. He also does a lot of running and has entered marathons, he's due to enter another one next month. It's not round here, it's somewhere in Yorkshire. The girl he lives with is probably just as bad, she's foreign and always seems to have plenty of money. I think they've got another house somewhere."
We have to take this information as anonymous and there was no proof that the allegations were correct. There are

occasions when information is provided in a vindictive manner and may be found to be incorrect.

The details were passed to our Investigations Department and they have made preliminary enquiries. Several visits were made to Crossland Street, where Inspectors stayed in the car and maintained a view on his address. It was noted that a female appeared to be living at the address and photographs were taken and her identity was later discovered that to be Agnieszka Kowalski, a Polish immigrant. It was noted that Miss Kowalski would arrive in the evening wearing a nursing uniform, presumably returning from work. Michael Davis was seen walking with the use of a walking stick on occasions but also without the stick when accompanying Miss Kowalski. He was seen on one occasion, walking with the use of a stick away from his house when he was picked up by a white van, with the name, Harris Builders and Roofers on the side. The investigator followed the van to an address in Chester but felt it advisable to leave the property at this stage and call back at a later time. The Investigators passed the house an hour later, and took a photograph of Michael Davis climbing a ladder carrying some slates.

A check on any marathons which were being run in Yorkshire was undertaken by our investigators in Leeds. A marathon was held last Sunday and they were able to confirm that a Michael Davis was listed as a runner. They were given his number and attended the marathon on Sunday, where the organisers were able to provide further information and his expected finish time. Three and a half hours after the start of the marathon, our investigators took a photograph of him crossing the finishing line.

No action is to be taken at this time until an investigation is completed into Agnieszka Kowalski.

David placed this report on the desk and looked at the second report.

Agnieszka Kowalski
9 Hayes Avenue
Chester
Date of Birth 10/10/77
Agnieszka Kowalski has been receiving unemployment benefits for two years and is now receiving job seekers allowance and also receives council tax rebate and housing benefits.

An anonymous telephone call was received on our hotline, four days ago, suggesting that Miss Kowalski was working at a hospital in Chester and known to be claiming unemployment benefits. The female caller was asked the address of Miss Kowalski and reported that she had two addresses. She was further asked who else lived at her address and was informed that a Michael Davis lived with her and there were no children.

Preliminary investigations were made with hospitals in the Chester area who reported that they had no record of an Agnieszka Kowalski in their employment.

Immigration were also asked to examine if they had any records of Agnieszka Kowalski and confirmed that she had entered the country legally in 2002 but were under the impression that she had returned to her native Poland two years ago.

No action to be taken until further enquiries are initiated at the Health Service and Immigration and discussions held with David Parish, Fraud Consultant, Public and Private Sectors.

David placed this second report with the Michael Davis report and turned to see John Kingsley smiling at him, who then commented.

"Did you enjoy reading about our couple from Chester?"

"They seem to be into everything."

"That's why I rang you David. If this was a simple Benefits Agency fraud, I could have dealt with this myself, without the need to contact you, but this seems to cover the Health Authority, Immigration and there looks like a possibility of identity fraud. We didn't want to go in head first and possibly damage an investigation into the other areas, which is why I decided to call Mr Fraud, David Parish."

"Thanks John, you're such a good friend, but you're right. This does look like it's crossed over a few boundaries and will interest different Fraud Investigators from other bodies. I'll make contact with them, and act as a lead for the investigation."

"I thought that is what you'd say. They're your copies of the reports and here are some photographs of both Michael Davis and Agnieszka Kowalski. Immigration should have photographs of her and it'll be interesting to see if she is the real Agnieszka Kowalski."

"I think I'll start with the local hospital. She seems to be working as a nurse, I've got a photograph and there can't be that many Polish ladies working there, hopefully somebody in Human Resources might be able to help me. I'll keep you up to date but appreciate that we may have to move quickly and you don't want to keep paying benefits to them."

"I look forward to hearing from you and I'll let you know if I get any more information."

"Thanks John."

David then left the Benefits Agency and made his way to his car but decided to call in at the local hospital before returning home. He had worked on a case there a year ago and knew the Director of Resources, Sue Smithers and a few of the Managers in Human Resources.

He made his way to Human Resources and the reception area, where he saw the receptionist talking to one of the Managers, Jan Burrows.

Jan saw David approaching and said.

"Hello David, do we have a problem again?"

"I don't think so, but I'm hoping one of your Managers may be able to help me."

"How can we help Mr Fraud?"

"I've got a photo of a lady who we understand is from Poland and works in a hospital. I don't know if it is this hospital but she may be working under a different name. If I show the photograph will somebody recognise her?"

"I don't know, let me have a look at the photo."

David passed the photo to Jan, and she and the receptionist both had a look, but both shook their heads.

"Follow me David and we'll show the photo to the other girls in Human Resources. We might as well go to Pat Jones first, because she has more involvement in dealing with foreign staff and nurses who come to this country."

They approached Pat Jones's desk who again asked David.

"Am I in trouble David?"

"No, I'm trying to trace a lady in this photograph. She is from Poland and I know her as Agnieszka Kowalski, but that may be the wrong name. I do know that you do not have a Agnieszka Kowalski working for you because an investigator from the Benefits Agency did speak to someone from this hospital and they checked their records."

"That's right, it was me that he spoke to. Let me have a look at the photo."

Pat looked closely at the photograph and turned to David.

"That looks very much like Felicja Jankowski. She's not a nurse but she is a Healthcare Assistant. Let me get her personal file."

Pat went over to the metal cabinets and opened one of the drawers and came back with a personnel file, which she opened and sorted out a passport photograph for Felicja Jankowski, which did look very similar to the photo David had for Agnieszka Kowalski.

David then asked.

"What address do you have for this lady?"

Jan looked in the file and replied.

"Nine Hayes Avenue, Chester."

"That's the address I've got for Agnieszka Kowalski."

"We do a lot of checks when a foreign immigrant starts work in the hospital. We obtain the passport, immigration information which contains a photograph, birth certificate and we complete a criminal check. This was all done on Felicja Jankowski. I'm sure that is her name."

"To be honest Pat, I think she is Felicja Jankowski, and your records are up-to-date. I don't think that she has done anything wrong as far as her work with you is concerned. There may be some problems for the Benefits Agency though, if she is claiming benefits under a different name."

"Do you want us to do anything?"

"No, she is working okay for you. Does she work full time and would you know if she is in work?"

"She works full time and I saw her yesterday in the staff canteen."

"Leave it with me Pat, but if you hear that she's off sick or leaving her job, will you let me know as soon as possible."

"Yes, that's no problem and we've got your contact details on file."

"Who is her next of kin and do we have any emergency contact phone numbers?"

Pat again looked at the file.

"Her next of kin is given as her father in Warsaw, Poland, but there is also a phone number of her boyfriend who lives local. A man named Michael Davis and his address is seventeen Crossland Street, Chester. Is that any help?"

"It certainly is. Thanks for your help ladies. I'll be in touch as soon as I know more."

David made his way out of the hospital to his car for the return trip to Liverpool.

20

Jack Inglis was sitting at the table in his Manchester home, checking all his records and confirming the amount of money he had received from his identity fraud scam. The discussions he had had with Ron Thomas in their prison cell at Walton Jail had become very useful and his contacts in London had been perfect when they suggested he contacted a couple who were able to produce false passports, birth certificates and driving licences.

He had travelled down to London a couple of months ago and met the pair who were using this scam in the London area. It had cost him ten thousand pounds and they provided half a dozen lots of documentation with the false identity, which he could then use to open bank accounts, obtain credit cards and loans. More importantly, they showed him how to obtain the information himself to arrange false documentation. The use of deceased people was a good method and his use of Ron Thomas's deceased twins was his first practise and had become extremely lucrative. He had wanted to thank Frank Sinclair and Wendy Carson but also talk to them about illegal immigrants, but all efforts to contact them had failed over the past few days. Messages had been left on her mobile but she had not responded until today, when she rang him to say that she might be able to help him with what he required. He had discovered that they were supplying false documents to the gangsters involved in human trafficking, especially women from Eastern Europe. That was in the London area but he knew that trafficking was taking place in the North West and thought this could be a lucrative area to be involved.

The front door bell rang and he opened the door to be confronted by two men who forced their way into his house.

"Who the hell are you, get out of my house?"

The taller man looked at Jack and said.

"We are here on behalf of a friend of yours. He thought he was a friend but now you have been destroying that friendship by betraying a private conversation that you had."

"I've got no idea what you are talking about and which friend is this?"

"Have you heard of the names Paul and John O'Brien?"

Jack knew immediately who they were talking about. It was Ron Thomas and he must have found out that he had used the names of his twin boys.

"They are dead."

"We know, but you used their names in an identity fraud and obtained lots of cash. You shouldn't have used those names and he doesn't like their names being used. They were his children, their mother isn't very happy, but she doesn't know that we are here. If she knew, she'd have the police around immediately. Our employer isn't with their mother anymore, but that's irrelevant, and people thought that he was involved in this fiddle but he wouldn't use his own children's name in this way. Only scum would use them and that's you."

"Tell Ron that I made a mistake and I'll give him the money that I got. I just obtained the birth certificates but somebody else gave me the other documents. I thought it would be okay and I'm sorry about that."

"It's a bit too late to be sorry."

The blows came hard and fast and it must have been some time before Jack woke up from his unconsciousness. He managed to get to his front door and was seen by one of his neighbours who must have asked for an ambulance. Jack recalled the ambulance arriving and being taken to Manchester Hospital before passing out again.

Jack was in his hospital bed when he awoke to see a broken leg in plaster and the pain from what must be broken ribs was excruciating. A nurse walked over to his bed when she saw that he was now awake.

"How are you Mr Inglis?"

"I'm in agony. What happened?"

"I thought you'd tell us what happened. Don't you know?"

"I can't remember a thing. My ribs are killing me and my leg looks as thought it's broken."

"The painkillers must be wearing off, I'll get you some more. Your face doesn't look too good either. There's a policeman outside to see you."

"I don't want to see a policeman."

"You haven't got much choice, he wants to see you. I'll let him know that you're awake."

The nurse returned with the painkilling tablets and was accompanied by a uniformed policeman who approached him.

"I'm Police Constable Bill Finnan from Manchester Police. I believe you've been attacked Mr Inglis?"

"That's very clever of you to notice."

"Don't try and be funny with me Jack. We know who you are and have recently been released from prison. Who attacked you and why did they do this?"

"I don't know. A couple of heavies burst into my house and gave me a good beating. I don't know who they were and I didn't get chance to have a look at them. I don't want to press any charges and just want to get better and forget this ever happened. It'll save you lot the trouble of investigating, just pretend it never happened. I know the cops are always busy but don't even bother setting up a file."

"We don't care if we don't investigate but we don't want to see any reprisals by you or anybody else."

"I can guarantee that I won't be taking this any further. I know what's good for me and I know when to shut up and say nothing. Goodbye officer."

"It's a pleasure meeting you Jack, I'll let my bosses know that you don't want it taken any further and the matter is closed. It couldn't have happened to a nicer bloke."

Police Constable Finnan returned to his station and noted the file and looked up the name of Jack Inglis. He was surprised to see a circular asking any officer to contact Inspector Anne Graham from Cheshire Police if anybody had dealings with Jack Inglis.

He immediately dialled Inspector Graham.

"Hello, Anne Graham."

"Hello Inspector, its Police Constable Bill Finnan from Manchester Police. I've just been to Manchester Hospital to see a man who had been attacked quite badly. He's got broken ribs, a broken leg and his face is in a bit of a mess. He didn't want us to take any action but I knew he was known to us. His name is Jack Inglis and we aren't going to take it any further apart from warning him from trying to get his own back. He said there was no chance of that but I could tell that he knew who arranged it and he wasn't going to try and get vengeance. His file said contact you if we had any dealings with him and I thought that I'd better let you know."

"Thanks P.C. Finnan, I could have a very good guess who arranged to have him beaten up. He won't take it any further but there are some Fraud Investigators who are looking into him. You needn't take it any further but I'll take it from here and I might even pay him a visit myself with David Parish."

"Mr Fraud. Is he involved in this?"

"Yes, he's been asked to investigate by a famous personality."

"Who's that?"

"I can't say at the moment but it may come out in the fullness of time."

"Okay, I'll mark the file that I've spoken to you and you may make a visit."

"Thanks a lot."

David picked up his mobile phone when it started ringing and saw that it was Anne Graham at the other end.

"Hello Anne, how are you?"

"I'm fine David. I've got some news for you. Jack Inglis is in Manchester Hospital and he's been given a good beating up. He wouldn't tell our officer anything about it but told him to forget all about it. He doesn't want any action taken."

"Sounds like the work of Ron Thomas, not him personally seeing as he's in Walton Jail, but I bet he's arranged this"

"I couldn't agree more."

"I've just had an email from one of my colleagues, Brian Lewis, who has been to the Register Office with a photo of Jack Inglis. Their staff member confirms he was the person who was given copies of birth certificates in the names of Paul and John O'Brien, the twins of Sally O'Brien and Ron Thomas."

"That's interesting. I think we might arrange for him to be transferred from his hospital bed to one of the prison hospitals, but we'll have words with him first. Do you want to come and see him tomorrow morning?"

"It'll be a pleasure, how about ten o'clock?"

"I'll see you at hospital reception at ten o'clock David. Bye for now."

Alisa was sitting in the lounge listening to David before he put the phone down. He turned to Alisa and shrugged his shoulders.

"Sorry, I've got a meeting tomorrow morning in Manchester. You can come with me if you like, I've got to meet Anne Graham in Manchester Hospital and we are going to see Jack Inglis, who we think is responsible for identity fraud involving the Sally O'Brien twins. Apparently, he's had a good hiding but won't say who's responsible. I'll only be an hour at most and then we can have a wander around Manchester."

"That sounds like a good idea. I suppose you know who beat him up?"

"It will have been arranged by his prison cell amigo, Ron Thomas."

"That's what I would have said."

The following morning David left Alisa in the hospital restaurant while he went back to the reception area where he was soon joined by Anne Graham.

"Good Morning David. I have spoken to the ward staff, they know we are coming and they did speak to Jack Inglis, who wasn't keen to see us. He tried to tell them he was too ill, but they told him that was a load of rubbish and they weren't going to stop us visiting him. I also asked them if there would be any problem getting him moved if necessary and they said that would be okay in a couple of days."

David followed Anne into the ward where they approached the Sister in charge.

"Hello Sister, I'm Inspector Anne Graham from Cheshire Police, this is David Parish. We're here to see one of your patients, Jack Inglis."

"I have been informed that you would be arriving. Mr Inglis does know but he's not very happy about it."

"I'm sure he's not but we might be moving him away for you."

"That's okay, we always need the beds."

The Sister led Anne and David to Jack Inglis's bed and told him.

"Visitors for you Jack."

"I don't want any visitors."

The Sister smiled as she walked away.

"Hello Jack. I'm Inspector Graham, this is David Parish, and he's a Fraud Consultant."

"I know who he is. It's the famous Mr Fraud."

David joined in the conversation.

"It's nice to be famous even to the infamous Geordie Jack Inglis. How did you like Walton Prison and your cell mate? I hear you were good friends but maybe not so good now?"

"What's this got to do with you Parish?"

"Your injuries and the attack have got nothing to do with me, and you've told the police that you don't want this to go any further. That's correct isn't it Inspector Graham?"

"That's right David, but what do you know about identity fraud, Jack?"

"Nothing. I don't know what you mean by identity fraud."

"It's using somebody else's name to commit a fraud such as twin boys called Paul and John O'Brien. I'm sure you know who they are?"

"I've never heard of them before."

"That's funny because they are the sons of your ex cellmate at Walton Prison, Ron Thomas, and we know that he spoke about them to you."

"I know he had twin boys who died but I can't remember their names."

"He told you the mother was a famous television presenter didn't he?"

"He might of, but I've forgotten who it was."

"Have you ever been to Manchester Register Office to get copies of their birth certificates?"

"No"

"That's not what we've heard. People seem to have recognised your photo as the man who collected the birth certificates. They also said that he had a Geordie accent."

"I'm not saying anymore unless I have a solicitor present."

"That's your right Jack, but I'll arrange for you to be transferred to a Prison Hospital, perhaps Walton would be a good idea."

"You can't send me there. I'll be a dead man. Send me somewhere else and I'll speak to me solicitor and we'll do a deal. In the meantime, I'm saying nothing."

"I need more than that Jack. What type of deal are you talking about?"

"I'll tell you what I've done and who helped me arrange it. That's it for now and I'm not saying another word."

Anne smiled at David and turned to Jack Inglis.

"I'll get you transferred to Manchester Prison Hospital the day after tomorrow and I'll then arrange a formal interview with your solicitor present. In the meantime, don't think about running away."

"Funny woman, how am I going to run with a broken leg, broken ribs and a face full of stitches?"

"Enjoy your stay."

David then looked at Jack Inglis.

"I think you're safer here or in Manchester Prison. If Ron Thomas knows you're trying to escape from us, I'm sure he'll help us find you."

"Get out Parish or is it Mr Fraud, stupid name that."

"I don't know. I quite like it."

As they walked away, Anne spoke to David.

"He'll be moved to Manchester Prison and we'll interview him in a few days time. There's no big rush, we'll have to arrange to get him remanded and I don't think he'll object, but his solicitor might make a plea to the court to stop him being remanded in custody. He'd be too frightened of being sent to Walton Prison and he's not going anywhere, but I'd like to hear who he's going to implicate, unless he changes his mind."

"I get the impression he'll give us names if it'll be easier for him."

As they approached the Ward Sister, Anne then said.

"All going well, I'll arrange for him to be moved to Manchester Prison the day after tomorrow. Will we need to arrange to have a police officer here to keep guard?"

"There's no need, he's not going anywhere, and he hasn't even got walking sticks."

"Thanks, we'll be in touch."

David found Alisa in the restaurant drinking a coffee and reading a magazine. They soon left the restaurant and headed for the car park and drove to the city centre, parking in a multi storey. Alisa was soon involved in a shopping spree, which could be her last in this country for some time.

21

On their return to Liverpool, David discovered that an email message had been received from Kevin Donnelly of the Metropolitan Murder Squad, who had attended the meeting at Ross Edgar's office. He had been in contact with Criminals Captured, and the search for Wendy Carson in respect of the murders of Frank Sinclair in New York and Denis King in London would be shown on the programme. It would go out, live, on the next programme, in a couple of days' time, and the broadcasting would take place in the television studios in Manchester. Even though it was an evening showing, the television programme had asked for Kevin and David to arrive in the morning to prepare for the showing and to meet up with the presenter, Sally O'Brien.

Kevin had provided details of the location of the television studio and asked David to confirm his availability. David did a quick reply and confirmed that he would be able to attend for the early morning meeting with Sally O'Brien. He also informed Kevin that he did know Sally and he would be briefing her on another matter, nothing to do with Wendy Carson and the murders.

David spent the next day with Alisa, when they spent some time walking through some of the lovely Parks in Liverpool. He did manage to spend some time updating his knowledge on the Wendy Carson case and the various frauds that were involved. They then had a nice stroll to a local Mexican Restaurant, where a starter of Nachos was followed by Tacos for David and Burritos for Alisa, not to mention a bottle of the house red wine. Alisa would return to London the following day, when David would be appearing on the programme, Criminals Captured. She would be sitting in front of the television in the evening to see how David coped with live television and had no doubts that he would be the envy of many ladies who would be watching the programme.

The following morning, David caught the train to Manchester and soon found his way to the television studios, where he met up with Kevin Donnelly. They were then shown into the studio where the show was to be filmed and met up with Sally O'Brien.

"Hello Sally, nice to see you again. This is Kevin Donnelly from the Murder Squad."

"Nice to meet you Kevin, so this is a case of murder and fraud."

"It would certainly appear to be. I'll be talking about the murders and David will mention the fraudulent elements, but I'm sure you and your team will guide us through."

"That's right Kevin and we'll sort out most of the questions beforehand so the pair of you won't be taken by surprise. It'll be about a half an hour before we get started so we may as well grab a drink in the canteen. Do you have any news on the identity fraud that you're helping me with David?"

"Yes, things have happened over the past couple of days."

Kevin then interrupted.

"Do you want me around when you talk about this Sally or shall I hide in a corner?"

"No, you can join us Kevin, it's no secret what has happened and David has been having the assistance of the local police down here."

They all obtained mugs of coffee before sitting in the corner of the staff canteen, when Sally then spoke to Kevin.

"David's been helping me with an identity fraud case. It concerns the use of my twins' names but they were killed in a road accident twenty years ago. Letters were received at my parent's house where I used to live, relating to unpaid loans in the twins names and credit card debts. My boyfriend at the time, Ron Thomas, was the driver of the car but we split up soon afterwards. I've only seen him once since and that was when I bumped into him when I was shopping in Manchester. It turns out he has been involved in criminal activities over the past few years and is currently in Walton Prison. We discovered that the person undertaking the identity fraud had a lot of inside knowledge, which could only have come from Ron or me. It wasn't me so it must have been Ron. We did consider that he might have been committing the crime but I didn't think so. It turned out that it couldn't have been him because he was in prison, so David was going to see him in prison. What's happened then David?"

"I found out that the bloke responsible for the identity fraud was a Geordie and I did have some type of description. I was talking to the prison warden before I met Ron Thomas and he told me Ron used to share a cell with a Geordie called Jack Inglis. When I told Ron about the identity fraud using the twins' names, he was horrified and visibly upset. I know it could have been an act but I didn't think so and when I mentioned a Geordie, he immediately pinpointed Jack Inglis. He had told Jack all about his past, what happened to the twins and their mother was a television star. He also knew that Jack had been involved in different types of fraudulent activities. I did tell Ron to take no action but leave it to us, but a few days ago, Jack Inglis was taken to Manchester Hospital. He had taken a good beating and had a broken leg, broken ribs and his face was a bit of a mess. I went to see him with Anne Graham from Cheshire Police and even though he didn't say, it was obvious that Ron Thomas had arranged the punishment. When Anne indicated that she would try and have him remanded to

Walton Prison, he nearly went berserk. He said his life wouldn't be worth living if he ended up in Walton, but offered assistance in providing names involved in the frauds if we made sure he wouldn't end up in Walton. He was clearly frightened to be near Ron Thomas. Anyhow, we haven't spoken to Jack formally, but I think we'll get him to agree that he was responsible for the identity frauds involving the names of your twins."

"I wouldn't want Ron Thomas to be involved but if it meant that you've caught the person responsible, then I can't say that I'm sorry. I'm probably not too upset that somebody has beaten him up, but that's off the record and I don't agree with that sort of thing. When are you going to interview him formally?"

"It'll probably be some time next week. I'll let you know as soon as we find something out."

"Thanks David."

Kevin Donnelly was listening quietly during the conversation and then remarked.

"I know that name Ron Thomas and I'm trying to think how I know him. Was he involved with the Mitchells who were killed in Spain?"

David replied.

"Yes, he was a member of the gang but was not involved in the family feud that took place in Spain."

"I was on holiday in Spain and it was in the news and I looked them up when I returned home, which is where I must have seen the name Ron Thomas. There was a murder in Manchester when one of his gang was killed for helping himself to some of the money. Small world isn't it"

"True. It was Steve Mitchell who killed his gang member. We don't know of any involvement of Ron Thomas in the murder, but he was a main player in the fraudulent activities undertaken by the gang, which is why he is currently in Walton Prison."

They then left the canteen to make their way to the studio for the evening filming of Criminals Captured.

Alisa Garcia sat in front of the television watching the start of Criminals Captured. The programme started with Sally O'Brien highlighting a few of the cases they were going to show to the public for their assistance. They would also show a rogue's gallery of faces relating to the most wanted of criminals and would ask the public to telephone if they knew the whereabouts of the most wanted, and if they could be of assistance to the Police.

She did not have to wait long before Sally introduced Kevin Donnelly and David. Sally explained that this was an unusual case because it involved murders in both New York and London but also different types of fraud. A picture of Wendy Carson was shown with her long blond hair before Sally introduced David to the television viewers.

David explained quite eloquently and professionally how he had been asked to investigate a payroll fraud in a London Hospital. The fraud was on the payroll of the hospital and the value of the fraud was six hundred thousand pounds. He explained that Wendy Carson was a manager, with responsibility for paying certain sections of staff in the hospital. Their initial enquiries had soon highlighted Wendy Carson as the person responsible but she had left her job and had fled to The United States of America and was believed to be in New York, with her American boyfriend who was also a party to the fraud. It was believed that she may now be using a different name and they had forged many documents to help with the payroll fraud. They had used four accomplices who, with the use of forged passports, driving licences and false birth certificates had opened bank accounts to receive the fraudulent payroll monies. All four accomplices used in the fraud had been arrested by the police. David made no mention of the murders and was leaving this to Kevin.

Kevin then continued with the report and explained how the body of her boyfriend, Frank Sinclair had been found under Brooklyn Bridge in New York. He also told the viewers that the body had been seen initially, and reported to the police by a group of boys from Liverpool, who were on a trip to New York, and had seen the body when on a helicopter flight. The New York Police Department were looking for Wendy Carson to help with their investigation into the murder, but believed she had fled back to England. Kevin then mentioned the second murder of Denis King in London, who was one of the four accomplices. There were similarities in both murders and the Metropolitan Police were seeking Wendy Carson in relation to this murder.

Sally O'Brien then asked the television viewers for their assistance as well as the criminal world. Many fraudsters would commit different aspects of fraud but would not believe in murder, and Sally thought she may aim at their consciences. The general public were asked to think if they had any contacts with Wendy Carson and had they seen her. She could be anywhere and she might have changed her appearance. The public were also warned not to approach her as she is regarded as dangerous.

The audience for this programme was expected to be in the region of ten million and it was hoped that somebody, somewhere, may have the information that David and Kevin were seeking.

There were some viewers who had been alerted to the face of Wendy Carson on the television screen.

Jack Inglis was sitting in his hospital bed when Wendy appeared on the television and knew immediately that she and Frank Sinclair had provided him with forged documentation to help him with his identity fraud. He had intended to give David Parish and Inspector Anne Graham information that may help him to avoid being sent to Walton Prison but did not realize that Wendy was one of the most wanted criminals. He had been visited in hospital earlier that day by his solicitor, and the solicitor had already advised Jack to fight the application to remand him to prison. The threat to have him sent to Walton Prison was only a ploy to get more information from him and his solicitor felt there was every chance to avoid being remanded. After all, Jack was in no fit position to be able to escape anywhere, any assistance he gave to them about Wendy Carson might stop him being remanded to prison, and could lessen his sentence when his case got to court. He turned to one of the nurses and asked.

"I want to make a phone call please, can you get the phone sent to my bed as I can't get to it."

"Okay, I'll go and get it now."

She returned within a couple of minutes and plugged the phone into the socket near Jack's bed. When the programme finished, he got some change and used that to make a call to Criminals Captured.

"Hello, Criminals Captured, can I help you?"

"I'd like to speak to David Parish about the missing killer, Wendy Carson."

"Who is it speaking?"

"I'm not prepared to give a name but he'll speak to me."

"I'll get him for you."

"David, there's a man on the phone asking for you, but is not prepared to give his name. He just said it is about Wendy Carson."

David picked up the phone.

"Hello, David Parish."

"Hello David, its Jack Inglis. I've just been watching you on television. I might have some information for you about Wendy Carson, but I'll only tell you if you make sure that I don't get remanded. I think you should talk to Inspector

Graham and then come and see me. I'll have my solicitor with me."

"I can't promise anything, but I will talk to Inspector Graham and she'll let you know when we're coming. How do you know Wendy Carson?"

"That's my secret for now, and you can tell Sally O'Brien that I'm sorry I used her children's names. I should have picked on somebody else and I wouldn't have got beaten up and ended up in hospital. Bye for now."

The phone then went dead.

Kevin and Sally were sitting at the desk when David put the phone down and turned to Sally.

"That was the bloke who has committed the identity fraud using your twins' names. He says he can help with the Wendy Carson case. I'll speak with Anne Graham and we'll go and see him. He's after a deal to avoid being remanded to prison and he said he's sorry he used your twins' names, only because he got a beating for using their names."

"I wonder what he knows."

"I don't know but we'll find out."

In Chester, Felicja Jankowski was sitting with her boyfriend Michael Davis, watching the programme. When the photograph of Wendy Carson appeared on the screen, she turned to Michael.

"That's the horrible lady who sold me the forged documents in the name of Agnieska Kowalski. She did have an American boyfriend and I moved here from London, to escape her. My sister Danuta also tried to buy some forged documents; she was encouraged by that lady, but couldn't find the money. She was found murdered in London and that lady is a murderer, she must have murdered Danuta. I can't go to the police because they will find out about the benefits that I am claiming, but I want to help Danuta."

Michael listened but didn't want to get involved because of the frauds that he was committing.

"Don't get involved. Keep out of it."

"No. I think she murdered my younger sister. I'm going to ring them but I won't tell them who I am and I'll make sure they can't trace the number."

Felicja phoned Criminals Captured making sure that their phone number could not be traced.

"Hello, Criminals Captured, can I help you?"

"I've just seen the lady Wendy Carson on television. I don't know where she is but I am sure she murdered Danuta Jankowski in London a few months ago."

"I'd like to put the Policeman, Kevin Donnelly on the phone. He is from the Metropolitan Murder Squad. What's your name?"

"I can't tell you that, but I will speak to him."

Kevin came to the phone.

"Hello Kevin Donnelly, can I help you?"

"That lady, Wendy Carson, murdered Danuta Jankowski in London a few months ago."

"I remember the case, she was a Polish girl wasn't she?"

"Yes"

"What else can you tell me, are you related or a friend of Danuta?"

"I can't tell you, but she was selling Danuta some forged documents and telling Danuta how to use them to give her some money. She wanted extra money to help with her studies but didn't have it. She couldn't pay for the documents and she was murdered. It must have been Wendy Carson. In the programme, you said there were similarities in the two murders. Check how Danuta was murdered. Danuta was a lovely girl and she wouldn't harm anybody. I've got to go now."

Kevin then spoke to David.

"That was a phone call accusing Wendy Carson of another murder. It was a Polish lady who was murdered and the caller was probably Polish. I remember the case, the murdered lady was called Danuta Jankowski. The caller mentioned the similarities in the two murders and suggested that I look to see how Danuta was murdered. I remember the murder and how she died. I didn't realize there was any connection but it was similar to that of the other two."

"Did you say Jankowski?"

"Yes, why?"

"I'm helping with a benefits fraud in Chester against a couple of people. One of the names is Felicja Jankowski."

"That's strange. I'll have a look at our files and will you let me know how you are getting on with this other Jankowski."

"That's no problem Kevin. This might be a third murder, are there anymore?"

"I hope not."

Sally then remarked.

"We will be giving an update in half an hour, should we mention this third murder?"

Kevin thought for a second and then said.

"Why not, but don't give the name of the person who was murdered. We'll just say that we had a phone call and have been asked to refer to an unsolved murder, and we are investigating to see if there is a connection to the other two."

Pauline Carson was also watching the television at her grandmother, Mary Longridge's house. They had been warned that her mother, Wendy, would be highlighted on the programme. She was in tears as her grandmother tried to console her.

"My mum hasn't done all these things Nan; they're talking a load of rubbish."

"I know dear, but it'll all be sorted out when your Mum turns up."

Mary was too upset to discuss what she was thinking. Wendy has gone missing, she did get a lot of money from somewhere, and her boyfriend, Frank Sinclair, has been murdered. Her ex boyfriend Denis King has also been murdered. She is hiding from the police and maybe she has done something really bad. When they both watched the follow up to the programme after the news, and the mention of the third murder in a telephone call, she thought, why have you done these things Wendy?

Wendy was in the cottage in Anglesey, also watching the television. She listened and looked at the photo they had shown of her, with long blond hair. She then looked at herself in the mirror, with her dark short hair. When she used the makeup, she did feel that her appearance was different to what they were showing and she was confident that she would not be recognised. She was taken back when she saw David Parish on the screen and he was talking about the fraud in the hospital and the identity fraud. He had been in the hospital a few months ago investigating a travel fraud and she thought he was rather nice. She recalled examining the hospital payroll to see if he worked for the hospital and noticed he was a consultant, and had been paid for the investigative work that he had undertaken. It was just curiosity to see where he lived but that was not local and he lived in Liverpool, but she remembered the address. A few members of staff in the canteen were talking about the fraud one day and somebody said he had a girlfriend who lived in Spain, but they travelled between the two countries on a regular basis.

She had the cottage for a few months and would then decide if she needed to leave the country. There would be no trouble in creating the false documentation.

Enjoying a glass of red wine, she watched the update on the Criminals Captured programme. Sally O'Brien said they had some interesting phone calls and the police, based on an interesting phone call to Criminals Captured, were now looking into a third murder.

Wendy smiled and thought to herself. That's taken them a long time, I'm too smart for them, and they'll never be fast enough to capture me. The bottle of red wine had been bought from a local shop in a small village in Anglesey. They sold food, newspapers, alcohol and a large variety of products. The lady who owned the shop was also watching the programme and sat, thinking to herself, the English lady, with the London accent. She popped into the shop to buy a few things and she has short dark hair, but she does look very familiar to that Wendy Carson. I must be imaging it, but I'll have a closer look next time she comes into the shop. She put the tape machine on to record the update later in the evening, and thought I'll be able to examine the photo more closely.

Alisa had enjoyed watching David on the television and was very pleased the way he had handled himself on the show. She again contemplated her move to Murcia, and how would she cope without David Parish, even though they would still be travelling to see each other at regular intervals. It wouldn't be quite the same as coming home from work into the hands of the man that she loved.

Sally, David, Kevin, other police presenters and the rest of the Criminals Captured team were having the usual meeting after the programme and the update had been watched by the millions of viewers. There had been several cases mentioned on the show with varying levels of success. When they were all discussing the Wendy Carson search, several of them had to smile. The idea of the show was to help capture criminals, not to have the number of murders they were being sought for to be increased. The phone calls to the reporting line did, however, provide information on other crimes concerning the criminals being chased, and Wendy Carson was no different.

There had been twenty-one phone calls relating to the search for Wendy Carson. They would all be investigated but the majority would probably come to nothing but some might be very useful. There was one from a retired policeman in Llangollen, who is definite that he saw a lady with dark short hair, and she was driving a blue Fiat Punto. He didn't have the car number but thought it was about four or five years old. He sounded very positive to Kevin who spoke to him on the phone and ex police tended to be very accurate with what they have seen.

22

The following morning Kevin Donnelly looked at the murder files relating to Danuta Jankowski, and was not surprised to see that details of her sister had been recorded. Her name was Felicja Jankowski and she lived in Chester. Whilst he did not know if she had made the phone call to Criminals Captured, he knew that David was going to speak to John Kingsley from the Benefits Agency Investigation Department. He gave David a quick ring.

David picked up the mobile and saw who was ringing.

"Hello Kevin."

"Hi David, I just thought that I'd let you know that Felicja Jankowski is the sister of the murdered girl, Danuta. We did check their immigration status at that time and they were both legally in this country. We do know that Felicja lived in Chester."

"The hospital records showed that Felicja was here legally and there has been no problem with her employment. I will probably leave the investigation surrounding the claims made to the Benefits Agency to John Kingsley. He wants to speak to Felicja and her boyfriend, Michael Davis, fairly quickly. Are you going to speak to Felicja about the murder of her sister?"

"We did speak to her at the time and she said she didn't know anything and hadn't seen her sister for a couple of months. I don't mind if John Kingsley mentions this when he's finished his formal interview, but I think it would be a good idea if you were involved and sat in the interview. You would then be able to bring up the murder and the identity fraud business."

"I don't see any problem with that. I'll talk to John and let him know."

"Thanks David."

David then rang John Kingsley.

"Hello, John Kingsley."

"Hello John, its David Parish."

"Morning David, what news have you got on our Polish friend?"

"Her real name is Felicja Jankowski, and she works under that name at the Hospital. The Human Resources Department at the hospital did check her status when she applied for the job and everything was in order including passport and birth certificate. They did contact the Immigration Department and were able to confirm that Felicja is allowed to work in this country. They've had no problems with her work and her emergency contact is Michael Davis. It looks as though you'll have to deal with this yourself, John, it would appear the only frauds they have committed is against the Benefits Agency, and there's no real need for me to get involved in that part of the investigation."

"That's okay David, I'm quite happy to deal with this and we'll make contact immediately and arrange for them to be formally interviewed."

"This is your case, John, but I've discussed other matters with Kevin Donnelly, and we thought it would be a good idea if I joined you with the interview. Did you see Criminals Captured last night?"

"I did watch Criminals Captured last night. You're becoming even more famous now but they didn't call you Mr Fraud last night."

"I wanted to talk to you about something that happened during the programme. I don't know if you saw the update which came on about half an hour later."

"Yes, I did."

"There was an anonymous phone call received which suggested there might be a third murder linked to Wendy Carson, who is also involved in identity fraud in a big way. This third murder relates to a Polish lady in London called Danuta Jankowski."

"Jankowski?"

"Yes, she was Felicja's sister. The Metropolitan Police did speak to Felicja but know that she's had no involvement with the murder, but there might be a connection between the fraudulent documents that they have, and Wendy Carson and her deceased boyfriend Frank Sinclair. We don't know who made the phone call, which Kevin Donnelly took, but he did say she had an eastern European accent and he thought it was Polish. He also thought the person ringing might have been a close relative but that is only a possibility. It might have been Felicja and John thought it might be worth bringing up at the end of the interview."

"That's fine with me David. I'll deal with the benefits fraud and lead you into the other matters. It's probably better if we interview Felicja first and then Michael Davis afterwards."

"That makes sense. Once you've finished with the main business, I'll pretend to be a bit sorry for her and say that I know about her sister. I'd take the view that I'd be quite happy to help her and find out who murdered her sister. She might be a bit shocked after the first part of the interview and won't say anything, but if she felt that we were trying to help, she might open up."

"There's no harm in trying to find out but if she does open up a lot, I've no doubt that Kevin Donnelly may want to come and see her. Do you want me to move fast on this one?"

"I think so John, how quick will you be able to move?"

"Everything has been prepared. We'll contact them tomorrow and interview in two or three days if that's okay with you."

"That's excellent and I'll be available."

"I'll give you a ring once I've got the interview dates and let you know if anything else has turned up."

"Thanks John, I'll speak to you again."

Jack Inglis was appearing at Manchester Magistrates Court and his solicitor, Andrew Young, had informed Jack that they should fight the police wish to have him remanded to prison, especially if the intention was to transfer him to Walton Prison. Anne Graham had discussed this with the Police Prosecution Solicitor, Jane Hitchin, but she was not hopeful of getting the remand. She felt that the medical condition of Jack Inglis, having a broken leg and broken ribs would act in his favour, and she knew that Andrew Young would make the most of this. He would be telling the magistrates that his client could not go anywhere with his injuries and had only been released from hospital that morning. Despite his injuries, Jack Inglis seemed quite confident that his solicitor would be able to prevent him being remanded.

A couple of hours later, Anne Graham had returned to her Police Station and telephoned David Parish.

"Hello Anne, how did today go?"

"Jack Inglis has not been remanded to prison, and to be honest, I'm not really surprised. We made our pleas but his solicitor was on the ball. He played on the injuries that Inglis has and that he would not be able to go anywhere easily. It was only fraudulent charges that his client would face, he was no danger to anybody, and he would be cooperating with the police and may have some information that would assist the police into three murder enquiries. Once Jane Hitchin heard this statement, she asked the magistrates if she could have a quick word with me. They agreed to a ten minute break and Jane suggested to me that we withdraw our opposition to bail, providing Jack Inglis spoke to me immediately regarding these three murders. We went back into the court and informed them that we would agree to bail providing Jack spoke to us immediately. He got bail and was told that he must report to the local police station daily and hand in his passport. His solicitor then tried to say he might have difficulties, with his injuries, to get to the police station daily. The magistrates then said if it was too difficult he would not allow bail, so they agreed. I spoke to Jack Inglis, informally, and he informed me that he had purchased fraudulent documents in London for ten thousand pounds, and the people he had purchased the documentation from were Wendy Carson and Frank Sinclair. All he had to get were the birth certificates and they did the rest. He said that he had tried to contact them again and had left messages, but had not received any replies. I'm not sure if he was telling the truth but I checked the numbers he had used to contact them. We had them on file, and they were no longer active. One thing he did say was that they were involved with a group involved in Human Trafficking and thought that they were providing them with fraudulent documents."

"Do you think that he'll plead guilty to the identity frauds?"

"Yes, he indicated that he would be pleading guilty, but is, obviously, hoping to do a deal and get his sentence reduced. He also felt that Wendy Carson might still get in touch with him because he thought that she had received his messages. He knew they were going to New York the same day that he rang and their mobiles would have been active. They were probably on the flight to New York when he tried to contact them."

"He might think so, but I would have thought that Wendy Carson is keeping well hidden for the moment."

"He also said that he had got a message to Ron Thomas and had spoken to Ron on the phone, and apologised for using the twins' names. He said he told Ron that he only got the birth certificates and paid for the fraudulent documents. According to Jack, Ron said he had finished with the matter and it was now closed."

"I suppose Ron Thomas was responsible for the beating and that might be the end of the matter. We'll see, thanks for letting me know what's happened, Anne. I'll be in touch."

"Bye for now David."

David updated all his paperwork and computer records with what had happened over the past couple of days and then started examining the files relating to the dentist, Ben Alexander. He had received more information from Brian Lewis and the Dental Board surrounding the fraudulent claims that had been made. Brian had highlighted several fraudulent claims but Ben Alexander had been on holiday abroad and couldn't have made the claims himself. His password and entry details had been made but not by Ben and it was now becoming clear that a second person was involved.

23

David was at home later that day, and spoke to Alisa about how the investigations were proceeding.

"I'm involved with a few investigations at the moment, but it's a bit of a coincidence that there are some links between them. It all started with the payroll fraud at the London Hospital, which was clearly the work of Wendy Carson. In order to complete this fraud, she and her boyfriend were involved in identity fraud. The next thing is the two murders of her boyfriend, Frank Sinclair and their accomplice Denis King. I was then asked by Sally O'Brien to look at the identity fraud concerning her twin boys who died twenty years ago, and it transpires the identity fraud was the responsibility of Jack Inglis, but he had to obtain forged documents and he got them from Frank Sinclair and Wendy Carson. The next case is the benefits fraud, in which I was helping John Kingsley from the Benefits Agency. It transpires that the lady involved, Felicja Jankowski, had a sister, Danuta, who was murdered in London, when she was probably involved in some type of identity fraud. There have now been accusations that she was murdered by Wendy Carson. At least the investigation concerning Ben Alexander, the dentist, does not involve Wendy Carson, at least I hope so. It does seem, if you upset Wendy Carson, your days are numbered."

"I think you have to be careful David. She will have seen the Criminals Captured television programme, and will know that you are involved in the investigation. There was a case in Spain, about ten years ago, when a lady had committed a couple of murders, and when she realised that she was being hunted by a member of our police, she got into her car, ran him down and killed him. When she was caught, she did not seem concerned as she had committed two murders and thought a third wouldn't make much difference and she thought he deserved it for catching up with her. This Wendy Carson won't stop at three murders if she thinks she can get away from you. She'll become one of your country's famous female murderers and she won't care less. Take care if you are getting close."

"Don't worry, I won't be going in alone if I know she's around. It'll be a job for the police and they'll probably go in armed, if they feel she's that dangerous."

"What formal interviews have you got lined up?"

"I'll be helping John Kingsley interview his two benefits fraudsters, and see if I can find out anything about the identity frauds but also the murder of Danuta Jankowski. I'll also be interviewing the dentist, Ben Alexander, but I'm not sure if I'll be involved in the interview with Jack Inglis."

Jack Inglis was now on police bail, and had been released from hospital but he was struggling to cope with the crutches, not that he didn't know how to use them, but the broken ribs were creating pain when he walked on the crutches. He was sitting on the settee at home watching television, thinking about what he should be saying to get any sentence reduced. He did not like the idea of naming Wendy Carson and Frank Sinclair, but he knew Frank was dead and he doubted if he would ever see Wendy again. Wendy had phoned him once and he hadn't reported that to the police and he was hoping that he wouldn't hear from her again. There was no point carrying on the identity fraud business.

It was then that his phone rang.

"Hello"

"Hello Jack, its Wendy."

For a moment Jack was speechless but then managed to say a few words.

"I'm surprised to hear from you Wendy. I saw the television programme last week and I've been reading about you in the papers."

"Don't believe in everything you see or hear, it's not all true."

"What do you mean?"

"Forget that for now. Are you still interested in giving me some work to do, I'm sure you still want to earn some extra money. I can be with you in a couple of hours?"

"Not anymore. I've been arrested for the identity fraud and I'm currently on bail. I also got beaten up for using the names of the twin boys who had died."

"I presume that you haven't mentioned my name to the police."

"No, of course not Wendy."

"If you have to give a name, tell them it was Frank."

"He's dead."

"I know that but I'm sure that you don't want to go the same way as him?"

"Are you threatening me Wendy?"

"No, I'm just telling you to be careful in what you say to the police."

The phone went dead and he tried dialling 1471, but the number had been withheld.

Michael Davis and Felicja Jankowski heard the bell go in the front door and Felicja went to see who was outside. The postman handed her two letters being sent Special Delivery and she signed the receipts. She walked back into the lounge and gave one to Michael and opened the one addressed to her. They were from the Benefits Agency Fraud Investigators and a man named John Kingsley had arranged for them to be interviewed, separately, three days later. It was also recommended that they bring a solicitor with them, when they were to be interviewed, formally, on a variety of benefit frauds. They were also being asked to phone John Kingsley within twenty four hours to confirm they would be attending, and the name of their solicitor. Further action would be taken if they failed to comply with the requirements specified in the letters.

Felicja turned to Michael saying.

"They must know all about us and that I'm claiming unemployment in Agnieszka's name using your other address. I told you that you couldn't go running when you were claiming invalidity benefits and I bet they know that you've been working for the builder. It's all your fault because you put me up to this and told me what to do."

"Don't go blaming me, you've been receiving the money and enjoyed spending it as well as sending money back home to Poland."

"I haven't been able to help poor Danuta. She was murdered by that Wendy Carson, but you told me I couldn't go to the police because they would find out about the frauds that we were committing. At least I'll be able to tell the police what I know about that woman and Danuta. Maybe I'll be able to live in peace once I've told them everything I know about Danuta and maybe they'll find Wendy Carson. I don't care what happens to me, I want revenge for Danuta. I'll admit everything when I speak to this John Kingsley."

"Let us have a think about what we're going to say, we'll have to try and make excuses or blame somebody else. Don't you go telling him that there's nothing wrong with me, I'll deal with him myself, but don't you start saying it was my fault. You knew everything that was happening and you can take care of yourself."

"It says that we have got to have a solicitor with us, do you know one?"

"Yes, I'll contact my solicitor. We are being interviewed separately and I'm not sure if he can act for both of us. If there's a problem, I'm sure one of his partners will represent you."

Ben Alexander had been living with his parents as a temporary measure. He was still working in his Dental Practice, but there was no sign of his girlfriend, Sue Patterson, returning to work nor did he expect her to return to work following the birth of Mandy, but that was now well over a year ago.

He had phoned Sue several times but she was adamant that their relationship was now over, and he decided to make a visit to the house that he had bought for Sue. He knocked on the door, rather than use the key and was surprised when the door was opened by a man.

"Hello, is Sue in?"

"Yes, who are you?"

"I'm Ben Alexander."

The man look startled for a few seconds, but then replied.

"I think you'd better come inside."

They walked into the lounge, where Sue was feeding Mandy. Ben then asked Sue.

"What's going on Sue, who is this man?"

Before Sue could speak, the man said.

"I'm Karl. I've been Sue's boyfriend for three years. I only heard about you a few months ago and before you ask, Mandy is our child, not yours. Once I found out that Sue had an affair with you, I had some checks done and Mandy is definitely my daughter. I've forgiven Sue and I know that she's been trying to break it off with you, but you keep pestering her. I suggest that you leave her alone and go back to your wife and children."

"What's he talking about Sue? That's a load of rubbish."

"It's not Ben and I've tried to let you down easily, but you've given me money and bought this house for me. I found it hard to stop taking the money, gifts and all the other things you kept buying me. I'm only human but I've been trying to tell you for a few months."

"You let me buy this house and you've always told me that Mandy was our daughter."

"I know, but now you know the truth. It's all over between us Ben. Let Karl, Mandy and me live our own lives. Do as Karl says, go back to your wife. You told her that Mandy was your daughter but now you know she isn't, it might help you get together again."

"I paid for this house and I want my money back."

"You bought it for me Ben. There were no conditions that I'd have to give it back if we split up."

"We'll see about that. I'll take legal advice. You haven't heard the last of this and if I go to prison, you'll be going with me."

Ben then stormed out of the house.

24

David drove the journey to Chester for the interviews with Felicja Jankowski and Michael Davis. He had allowed sufficient time to arrive just after 9 o'clock and it was only a short walk to the Audit Agency of the local hospital. He had arranged to meet John Kingsley at 9.30 a.m. and the interview with Felicja Jankowski was due for 10.30 a.m.

On entering the Administration Department of the local hospital, he made his way to the second floor and followed the signs for the Audit Agency and rang the buzzer to gain entry. He was well known to the Audit Agency staff having used their facilities to complete work and hold previous interviews. The door was opened by Kate.

"Good morning Kate."

"Morning David."

"We will be holding two interviews today and a colleague, John Kingsley, from the Benefits Agency will be arriving shortly."

"He's just arrived David and he's sitting in the end room on the right which you have been allocated for the day. John's having a coffee and I presume you'll be having the same?"

"Yes please Kate. I'll go down and meet John as we need to have a chat first. The first lady to be interviewed is Felicja Jankowski and she's due at half past ten. The second interview will be with a Michael Davis and that's arranged for one o'clock this afternoon."

"I suppose they'll both have solicitors with them as usual"

"Yes, I haven't got their names yet, but John will know and I'll give you the details."

"Thanks David. I'll get the coffee and bring it down."

David walked down the corridor and met up with John Kingsley who was just finishing setting up the tape machine for the two interviews.

"Hi David. Did you have a good journey?"

"Not bad except for a bit of a queue at the Runcorn Bridge."

"Who's representing Felicja and Michael? I'll tell Kate when she comes in with the drinks."

"Felicja Jankowski is being represented by Alan Parsons and Michael Davis's solicitor is Simon Devonish. They're both from the same practice."

"I've met Simon before, but I don't know Alan Parsons."

"Reverse. I know Alan Parsons but I've never met Simon Devonish. I did speak to him on the phone. Give me a couple of minutes and I'll update you on a few things and go through the paperwork, I presume you'll then want to discuss tactics?"

"Yes, hopefully it should be fairly straightforward, at least I hope so."

Kate arrived with the mug of coffee and David gave her a note with details of the people to be interviewed, their solicitors and the times of the interviews.

"Thanks Kate. When they arrive sit them on the two chairs in the corridor and let us know and we'll then go and collect them."

"Okay David."

John handed David a copy of the pack of disclosures that he would be giving Alan Parsons and they flicked through the pack. It was all clear and the interview relating to the benefits fraud was being led by John, with David operating the machine and joining in if necessary. John then advised David.

"The Benefit frauds have been going on for less than two years for Felicja and we know she's been using the name Agnieszka Kowalski for the frauds. We have totalled the Unemployment Benefits, Jobseekers Allowance, Council Tax Rebate and the Housing Benefits and by our reckoning, we are looking at twenty one thousand, four hundred pounds. When I spoke to her solicitor, he did not seem surprised and I have a feeling that she's already admitted it to him but we never know. I'll question her about the benefits fraud and then bring you in to find out how she obtained the documents relating to Agnieszka Kowalski. It'll do no harm saying that you are looking at the identity fraud element. I won't mention that you may also want to discuss the murder of her sister, Danuta."

"That's fine John. I think it's possible that's she's held back coming forward about her sister because she's been involved in false claims from the Benefits Agency. The phone call to Criminals Captured was anonymous but we think it was her who made the call. I'm hoping that if she admits to your frauds, she'll tell us everything she knows about the identity fraud, the murder of her sister and anything else she knows about Wendy Carson. Does Alan Parsons know that I'm assisting you today?"

"No I didn't tell him it would be you. I just told him there would be a colleague assisting me which he knows, is normal practice. It should be a nice surprise, seeing that you know him."

"Yes, but he's okay. If he asks about my presence, I'll just say that I'm interested in the identity fraud. If it gets to the stage when she mentions Wendy Carson, I might stop the tape for a minute and tell her that I'm going to discuss the murder of her sister on behalf of the Metropolitan Police. Kevin Donnelly knows all about the interview and is happy to leave it with me."

David and John then finished the necessary preparations, obtained a jug of water and some glasses, and were having a general chat when there was a knock on the door and Kate popped her head round.

"They are both in the corridor sitting down."

"Thanks, we'll bring them in shortly," said David.

John then turned to David.

"I'll bring in Alan Parsons first, give him some background information and present him with the pack of disclosures, he will then be able to go back to his client and discuss the documents that we've given him."

John went outside to where Alan and Felicja where sitting.

"Hello Felicja, I am John Kingsley and I presume you are Alan Parsons?"

"Yes, are you going to provide me with some disclosure documentation?"

"Yes, if you'd come with me, we are only next door; I'll go through the disclosure pack."

John and Alan left Felicja Jankowski alone in the corridor and walked to the next room to join David who knew Alan fairly well, having met him on several previous occasions.

"Good morning Alan."

"Hello David, what have we done to deserve the honour of Mr Fraud?"

"I'm assisting John with the Benefit Frauds but my main involvement will be with how Felicja obtained the fraudulent documents relating to Agnieszka Kowalski. I'm hoping that Felicja will help us with my enquiries into that. It might do her some good in the long run."

"You'll put a good word in with Judge, in due course?"

"That depends on how helpful Felicja is with my enquiries."

"I'll have a word with her and suggest that it might be to her benefit if she helps you."

John then started the proceedings

"A present for you Alan," and he then handed him the Disclosure Pack before both he and David opened their copies.

John then explained some of the contents to Alan.

"It's fairly straight forward Alan. We have listed all the claims made with respect to the four areas, initially Unemployment Benefits, Jobseekers Allowance, Council Tax Rebate and Housing Benefits. You will see that the claims relate to Agnieszka Kowalski and the address is Nine Hayes Avenue, Chester. We know that Felicja lives at Seventeen, Crossland Street, Chester with her partner Michael Davis. Crossland Street is rented but Michael Davis owns the property in Hayes Avenue and Felicja, or should we say Agnieszka, has been stating she is renting this from a private landlord, hence the claims for Council Tax rebate and Housing Benefits. You will also see that we're looking at a fraud in excess of twenty one hundred pounds and do feel that admissions of guilt will be better for your client, but you'll understand that."

"I'll show this information to my client and I'll mention what you've said. I'll also inform her that the famous Mr Fraud, David Parish, is in attendance."

"I'm honoured Alan."

Alan smiled as he left the room with the Disclosure Pack to join Felicja Jankowski and discuss the contents. John turned to David.

"Do you think that Felicja will own up to everything and mention Wendy Carson? She might have something to say about Michael Davis, but I doubt it. I think she'll try and act dumb when we mention Michael Davis but she'll have to admit something about him."

"I'm certain she will, but I'm hoping that she'll tell us all she knows about Wendy Carson. I'm hoping that she has a guilt complex about her sister and not coming forward when she was murdered. Let's see how it goes."

There was only a delay of about fifteen minutes before Alan Parsons returned to the room with Felicja Jankowski who looked quite pale and had obviously been crying and did look quite distressed. They all sat down and David turned to Felicja.

"Would you like a glass of water?"

"Yes please. I saw you on the television on the Criminals Captured programme. I want to tell you what I know about Wendy Carson. She killed my sister, Danuta."

"We have to leave that until later, Felicja. John wants to talk to you first about the claims that you have been making."

Felicja turned to Alan who said.

"That's correct Felicja. You'll be able to talk about that later."

John then spoke to Felicja.

"I just want to check that you understand what we are going to do. David will operate the tape machine and you will hear a loud noise before the start of the interview, this is normal. Has Alan explained what we are going to discuss and the procedures that will take place?"

"Yes, I understand, I'll tell you what I've been doing but you'll have to ask Michael about what he's done. That's nothing to do with me."

"Okay, David will you start the tape please?"

David started the tape and the noise appeared before John started the interview with the opening procedures.

"This Interview is being tape recorded, it is the twenty fifth of March, two thousand and eight and the time by my watch is ten fifty five a.m. I am John Kingsley a Fraud Investigator for the Benefits Agencies. The other officer present is."

"David Parish, a Fraud Consultant also representing the Benefits Agencies, the Health Authority and the Metropolitan Police."

"I am interviewing, please state your full name, address and date of birth."

"Felicja Jankowski, Seventeen Crossland Street, Chester. Date of birth, twenty eighth of April, nineteen seventy seven."

"Also present is."

"Alan Parsons, Pemberton and Willis, Solicitors, Chester."

"We are in the Audit Agency Department of the Hospital Authority, Chester. At the end of the interview, I will give you a notice explaining the procedures for the dealing with the tapes and how you can have access to them. Before the interview begins I must caution you."

"You do not have to say anything, but it may harm your defence if you do not mention when questioned something which you later rely on in court, anything you do say may be given in evidence. Do you understand the caution?"

Felicja looked a little bit startled but then replied.

"Yes."

"You are not under arrest and you are free to leave at any time. The reason for this interview is that we are investigating fraudulent benefit claims made by you, using the name of Agnieszka Kowalski. Do you understand the reason for this interview?"

"Yes."

"If at any time you wish to speak to your solicitor in private or if you wish me to stop the interview for any reason, then tell me and I will stop the interview."

At this stage, Felicja turned to Alan Parsons, who smiled and said.

"That's okay Felicja."

"I know that you're going to ask me about the claims that I've been making but I'll also talk to you about how I got the documents in the name of Agnieszka Kowalski and that woman Wendy Carson, who murdered my sister."

John then continued.

"Have you looked at the documents in the pack with your solicitor which relate to claims made for unemployment benefits, jobseekers allowance, council tax rebate and housing benefits?"

"Yes, he's showed me them."

"They are claims made in the name of Agnieszka Kowalski and total twenty one thousand, four hundred and twenty three pounds. You will have seen a photograph, in the pack, of you in the Benefits Agency office and the staff member confirms that the person in the photograph is known to the Agency as Agnieszka Kowalski, but that photograph is you, isn't it Felicja?"

"Yes that's me."

"Do you confirm that you have been making claims in the false name of Agnieszka Kowalski?"

"Yes."

"Do you admit to all the false claims, which are itemised in the pack and total twenty one thousand, four hundred and twenty three pounds?"

"I've no idea how much I've claimed but it did all start just under two years ago. The figures look right and I've spoken to my solicitor and I've decided to admit to all the charges. I want to get it over with and tell Mr Parish about my sister."

"I would like you to confirm that you have been working for the hospital as a Healthcare Assistant for the past two years under your real name of Felicja Jankowski?"

"Yes and I'm still working in the hospital and I've got the day off today."

"You have been making claims on Nine Hayes Avenue, Chester, but you live at Seventeen Crossland Street, Chester. Is that correct?"

"Who owns Nine Hayes Avenue?"

Felicja turned to Alan, and asked.

"Should I tell them?"

"If you know, then you should tell the truth."

"Michael owns Nine Hayes Avenue."

"Does Michael Hayes know all about your fraudulent claims made on the Benefits Agency?"

"I'm not sure what Michael knows, you'd better ask him yourself."

Alan Parsons then interrupted.

"I think you shouldn't ask my client about Michael Hayes. I know that you are interviewing him this afternoon and I've advised my client not to talk about him, but she's quite willing to talk about other matters. She will assist David with his enquiries and has admitted her part in claiming the various benefits under the name of Agnieszka Kowalski."

"Okay, we'll leave Michael Hayes out for the moment. Can you repay the money?"

"I don't have that amount of money, most of it has been spent."

"How much money would you be prepared to pay back?"

"I don't know."

"Have a think about what I've said and let your solicitor know"

John turned to David.

"Is there anything else that we need to mention as far as the Benefits Frauds are concerned David?"

"No, I think we have got enough for today. I think it's the right time to discuss the other matters relating to the identity documents of Agnieszka Kowalski."

David then directed a further question to Felicja.

"I'd like to ask you how you obtained the documents in the name of Agnieszka Kowalski."

"I was talking to some other Polish immigrants to this country and they mentioned that they knew how to obtain false documents and it was easy to claim extra money. They also knew how to get bank loans and credit cards in other names but I didn't do that. I went to London for a weekend trip with a few of them and they introduced me to Wendy Carson and her boyfriend, Frank Sinclair. She made it sound easy and I

needed some extra money. I borrowed a couple of thousand pounds and I got the documents in the name of Agnieszka Kowalski. Wendy Carson also told me how to make benefit claims and open bank accounts, get loans and credit cards. I only made the benefit claims. It seemed so easy and I told Danuta all about it. She wanted extra money for some studies and was unable to pay Wendy Carson but Wendy offered to give her some extra time to pay. I think she gave her a month but Danuta couldn't raise the money in time and went to explain this to Wendy Carson. I saw her go into Wendy's friend's house, I think his name was Denis and I went shopping and I never saw Danuta again until she was dead."
Do you wish to add anything further or clarify any point or anything you have told me?"
"No."
"Here is the notice which explains your entitlement to a copy of the tape used in this interview. This interview is concluded at eleven twenty five a.m. on the twenty fifth of March, two thousand and eight. Switch off the tape recorder."

David then spoke to Felicja again.
"I will talk to Kevin Donnelly from the Murder Squad about your sister. He might want to contact you himself, but there's nothing else you can remember, which might be important?"
"I don't think so. She was a nice lady when we first met and she was quite helpful. I recall telling her that I didn't like big cities like London and quite liked Chester. I told her that it was near Wales, and we often had a few trips to different parts of Wales. She told me that she used to go quite often to Anglesey, that's a small island, and you cross a bridge from the mainland. She said she'd love to go and live there and had been making some enquiries. Maybe she's gone to Anglesey."
"I'll get Kevin to make a few enquiries."
"Anything else?"
"No."

They left the room and David sat thinking about the phone call to Criminals Captured from a retired police officer, who was convinced he had seen Wendy Carson in Llangollen. Maybe she was headed for Anglesey.

The formal interview with Michael Davis was due to take place later that day, when he would be questioned by John and David. He was being represented by Simon Devonish, from the same partnership, Pemberton and Willis, which employed Alan Parsons.

It was just before one o'clock when Sue informed David and John that Michael Davis had arrived with his solicitor Simon Devonish. The preparations had been completed and both Michael and Simon would be aware of what Felicja had said. Neither David nor John had any concerns that they would have some background information, as the admissions by Felicja would prove useful in the taped interview.

John went outside to where Simon and Michael where sitting.

"Hello Michael, I am John Kingsley and I presume you are Simon Devonish?"

"Yes, I assume that you are going to provide me with a disclosure pack?"

"Yes, if you'd come with me, we are only next door; I'll go through the disclosure pack with you."

John and Simon left Michael Davis alone in the corridor, where he had decided to stand, and walked to the next room to join David who knew Simon, having met him on a couple of previous occasions.

"Good morning Simon."

"Hello David, I did hear on the grapevine that you were involved."

"Alan must have told you."

"That's right; we are both surprised to be dealing with the famous Mr Fraud?"

"I'm assisting John with the Benefit Frauds but my main involvement will be with the fraudulent documents relating to Agnieszka Kowalski. I'm hoping that Michael will help us with my enquiries into that. It might do him and her some good in the long run and you'll know that Felicja has given us some assistance."

"What type of assistance?"

"You know that I won't reply to that Simon."

"No harm in trying but I presume that you'll put a good word in with Judge, in due course, if my client is cooperative?"

"That depends on how helpful Michael is with my enquiries."

"I'll have a word with him and suggest that it might be to his benefit if he wishes to be helpful. I wouldn't guarantee that as he'll probably end up being sarcastic and unhelpful. That's normal for him."

John then started the proceedings

"A present for you Simon," and he then handed him the Disclosure Pack before both he and David opened their copies.

John then explained some of the contents to Simon.

"It's fairly straight forward Simon. We have listed all the claims made with respect to the four areas, initially Invalidity Benefits, Council Tax Rebate, Sole Occupancy and Housing Benefits. You will see that the claims relate to Michael Davis and the address is Seventeen Crossland Street, Chester. We know that Felicja lives at Seventeen,Crossland Street, Chester with Michael Davis. Crossland Street is rented but Michael Davis owns the property in Hayes Avenue and Felicja, or should we say Agnieszka, has been stating she is renting this from a private landlord, hence the claims for Council Tax rebate and Housing Benefits. There will probably be some conspiracy charges relating to Felicja and Nine Hayes Avenue Chester, but this is in the hands of the Legal Team. You will also see that we're looking at a fraud in excess of thirty three thousand five hundred pounds and do feel that admissions of guilt will be better for your client, but you'll understand that."

"I'll show this information to my client and I'll mention what you've said. I don't think he's that keen on the involvement of Mr Fraud, he saw you on television."

"I'm honoured Simon. I'm sure John and myself will take it easy with him."

Simon was laughing as he left the room with the Disclosure Pack to join Michael Davis in order to discuss the contents. David then spoke to John.

"I don't think he'll know any more about Wendy Carson than Felicja did, but you never know."

"I think he'll probably admit everything but will try and avoid the conspiracy charge which could end up more serious than the frauds he has committed."

"I'm certain he will. Simon will know the seriousness of a conspiracy charge and will tell him that he should let us know about Wendy Carson. They know that Felicja has admitted everything which involves Michael. Let's see what he has to say."

There was a delay of about twenty five minutes before Simon Devonish returned to the room with Michael Davis who looked quite annoyed and had obviously been having some words with Simon. John had offered them a private room rather than talk in the corridor and they had accepted the offer. They all sat down and David turned to Michael.

"Would you like a glass of water?"

"No thanks."

John then spoke to Michael.

"I just want to check that you understand what we are going to do. David will operate the tape machine and you will hear a loud noise before the start of the interview, this is normal. Has

Simon explained what we are going to discuss and the procedures that will take place?"

"Yes, I've seen it on television and I'll tell you what I know and no more."

"Okay, David will you start the tape please?"

David started the tape and the noise appeared before John started the interview with the opening procedures.

"This Interview is being tape recorded, it is the twenty fifth of March, two thousand and eight and the time by my watch is one forty five p.m. I am John Kingsley a Fraud Investigator for the Benefits Agencies. The other officer present is."

"David Parish, a Fraud Consultant also representing the Benefits Agencies, the Health Authority and the Metropolitan Police."

"I am interviewing, please state your full name, address and date of birth."

"Michael Davis, Seventeen Crossland Street, Chester. Date of birth, twenty sixth of April, nineteen seventy five."

"Also present is."

"Simon Devonish, Pemberton and Willis, Solicitors, Chester."

"We are in the Audit Agency Department of the Hospital Authority, Chester. At the end of the interview, I will give you a notice explaining the procedures for the dealing with the tapes and how you can have access to them. Before the interview begins I must caution you."

"You do not have to say anything, but it may harm your defence if you do not mention when questioned something which you later rely on in court, anything you do say may be given in evidence. Do you understand the caution?"

Michael looked a bit disinterested but then replied.

"Yeah."

"You are not under arrest and you are free to leave at any time. The reason for this interview is that we are investigating fraudulent benefit claims made by you. Do you understand the reason for this interview?"

"Yeah."

"If at any time you wish to speak to your solicitor in private or if you wish me to stop the interview for any reason, then tell me and I will stop the interview."

At this stage, Michael looked at Simon and said

"Get on with it."

"I know that you're going to ask me about the claims that I've been making but I didn't conspire with Felicja. We both did our own thing and I don't know what she's done but she must have told you. She's more interested in that woman Wendy Carson, who murdered her sister."

John then continued.

"Have you looked at the documents in the pack with your solicitor which relate to claims made for invalidity benefits, council tax rebate and housing benefits. You also said that you lived alone and claim as a single occupier?"

"Yes, my solicitor has showed me them."

"They are claims made in your name for a total thirty three thousand, five hundred and forty seven pounds. You will have seen a photograph, in the pack, of you running in the Marathon in Leeds. That's a distance of just over twenty six miles and you did it in three and a half hours. That's a good time and one of the organisers confirms that the person in the photograph is known to him as Michael Hayes, that is you, isn't it Michael?"

"Yes that's me."

"Do you admit to all the false claims, which are itemised in the pack and total thirty three thousand, five hundred and forty seven pounds?"

"How am I supposed to know how much I've claimed? If you say it's over thirty three thousand pounds you might be correct but I don't know. I've been advised to admit this by my solicitor and I will. Okay I admit it."

"Do you own Nine Hayes Avenue, Chester, but live at Seventeen Crossland Street, Chester?"

"Yeah."

"Who lives at Nine Hayes Avenue, Chester?"

"Nobody lives there at the moment. It's empty."

"Do you get rent from the property?"

"No. It's an investment but friends and relatives use it now and then and I don't charge rent."

"You have also been seen working for a builder, climbing a ladder and working on a roof. Is that correct?"

"I only worked one or two days, just to repay a bloke out who did some repair work on the house in Hayes Avenue. I didn't get any money for that."

"We'll be informing Inland Revenue about this and the Builder."

"That's got nothing to do with me."

"Can you repay the money that you've claimed over the past three years?"

"What money, do you mean the thirty three thousand? You must be joking. I haven't got that much money."

Simon then interrupted.

"I would like to have a quick word with my client please. Will you stop the tape?"

David stopped the tape saying.

"It is one fifty eight p.m. and the tape machine is being stopped at the request of Simon Devonish."

Simon and Michael left the room for a few minutes. When they returned David asked Simon.

"Is it okay if we restart the tape machine?"

Simon replied.

"Yes, but I would like Alan to ask Michael the question about repaying the money."

Davis switched on the tape machine saying.

"It is now two, seven p.m. and we are restarting the interview with Michael Davis. The people present are."

"David Parish."

"John Kingsley."

"Simon Devonish."

"Michael Davis."

John then spoke to Michael again.

"Can you repay the money that you've claimed over the past three years?"

"How much money are you talking about?"

"Thirty three thousand, five hundred and forty seven pounds"

"I don't know how much I can get together, but I'll discuss this with my solicitor and we'll let you know. I know that I've done wrong and I want to try and make amends."

John turned to David.

"Is there anything else that we need to mention as far as the Benefits Frauds are concerned David?"

"No, I think we have got enough for today. I think it's the right time to discuss the other matters relating to the identity documents of Agnieszka Kowalski."

David then directed a further question to Michael.

"I'd like to ask you what you know about the documents in the name of Agnieszka Kowalski."

"I know that Felicja had some documents and that she met a couple of people in London. They were Wendy Carson and Frank Sinclair, but you'll have to ask Felicja about those documents. It was nothing to do with me but I think she knew some other people from Poland, and her sister was also involved with Carson and Sinclair. Felicja did tell me that her sister wanted extra money to help with her studies and she tried to borrow it off Felicja but she didn't have it. She asked me but I wasn't going to lend money to someone I hardly knew. I know her sister asked Wendy Carson and I think she offered to give her time some extra time to pay. She gave her a few weeks to raise the cash but she had some problems and couldn't repay her. We saw her sister go into Wendy's house,

at least I think it was her house but Felicja never saw her sister again until she was dead."
Do you wish to add anything further or clarify any point or anything you have told me?"
"I've never conspired with anybody. I did my own thing and that's it."
"Here is the notice which explains your entitlement to a copy of the tape used in this interview. This interview is concluded at two seventeen p.m. on the twenty fifth of March, two thousand and eight. Switch off the tape recorder."

David then looked at Michael and said.
"I am going to report back to Kevin Donnelly from the Murder Squad about your Felicja's sister Danuta. He might want to contact you himself, but there's nothing else you know, which might be important?"
"Off the record. Felicja was worried about her sister and she persuaded me to ring Wendy Carson and ask her if she knew anything about the murder of her sister and who might have done it. I rang her the next day, when Felicja was not around. When I asked her, she told me to mind my own business, or I would go the same way as her sister. I decided enough was enough and I never contacted her again."
"Do you have anything else to tell us?"
"I don't think so. I know that you're trying to find her. Did Felicja mention that she Wendy Carson liked going to Anglesey in Wales?"
"Yes, she did."
"Just a thought."
"Anything else?"
"No."

They left the room and John and David reviewed the two interviews that had taken place during the day. John remarked.

"There will be no further investigations required until the capture of Wendy Carson, but this will be dealt with by Metropolitan Police because of the more serious nature of the crime that Kevin Donnelly is leading. I'll commence the legal proceedings but this should now be a formality with the admissions made by Felicja Jankowski and Michael Davis in their formal interviews."

"What do you think they'll get?"

"I would think that Michael will go to prison for a couple of years, but Felicja would probably only get a sentence of one year. It is up to the legal team to suggest she is returned to Poland after serving the prison sentence."

25

Ben Alexander was at home talking to his wife, Lynn.

"I've been a complete idiot, Lynn, I love you and the children and I don't know why I had the affair with Sue. I've been conned and she's got me involved in a fraud at the Dental Practice, which means that I'll be going to prison soon. She even conned me into believing that she had my child, but that's untrue. The father of her child is her boyfriend, Karl. They've just told me that and I bought her a house thinking that Mandy was my daughter."

"You told me that she had your daughter."

"I know, but I was trying to be honest with you. I'm in a state of confusion, but I do know that I want you to forgive me. I know I don't deserve it but I'm begging you."

"You've only decided to try and mend our marriage, now that you've found out about her daughter and she's finished with you. You had nowhere else to go and decided that you might as well try and come back here. The pair of you have been defrauding the Health Service and using the money to buy her a house, lovely furniture, a nice car and whatever she wanted. You can't even come back here because you'll be going to jail for a few years. You're just feeling sorry for yourself, Ben. Don't come sobbing to me because you don't know what to do, now that she's finished your relationship. It's all over, Ben, and your children and me have got to live with the shame that you're going to put us through. We might lose this house if we can't pay the mortgage or the Health Service might sue you for the money that you've stolen and they might force us to sell the house to get the money back. Dad was telling me that they can do that type of thing these days. Why don't you sell her house or tell your solicitor that it was bought with the money that you two have fiddled from the Health Service. They might shorten your prison sentence but that's got nothing to do with me."

"I hadn't thought about it and I will tell my solicitor about the house."

"You haven't thought about anybody apart from yourself. You've cheated on us and you wouldn't have come back if she hadn't kicked you out. It's no good coming back to me as your second choice. It's all over, Ben, and I'll be getting a divorce. Go back to your parent's house, you can get round them but you can't get round me. Get out of here, Ben."

"I'll go for now, Lynn, but I won't give up. I want you and the children back and I'll make sure that you keep the house."

"You mean by using the stolen money. I don't want to be part of your fraud, give the money back to the Health Service, that's if you've got any left and haven't spent it all on your girlfriend."

"She's not my girlfriend anymore."

Ben then got up and left the house and when she heard the door close, Lynn broke down in tears.

Mark Weston, Ben's solicitor, was checking his paperwork before meeting with Ben, who had phoned yesterday afternoon, asking for a meeting. The formal interview with David Parish would be taking place early next week. His phone rang and one of the secretaries informed Mark that Ben Alexander was waiting in reception.

He went outside to meet Ben.

"Good morning Ben, let's go through to my office."

They sat down before Mark started the meeting.

"When you phoned yesterday Ben, you said you'd had some thoughts and possible offers you were considering making, in the hope they may take it easy on you. Perhaps you should give me the full picture."

"I know I've been an idiot and made to look stupid. I had an affair with one of the receptionists in the Dental Practice and she became pregnant and had a baby girl. I was led to believe that this was my daughter but it turns out it wasn't and is the daughter of her long time boyfriend. I bought this girl a house, completed renovations, and fitted the house out with furniture and everything that she wanted to make the house look nice. I even bought her a car. This was all purchased with the money gained from the fraudulent claims. She has now broken off the relationship and my wife wants nothing to do with me and is going to seek a divorce. I can't say that I blame her, but my receptionist, Sue Patterson, has taken full advantage of my misdemeanours."

"Whose name is the house in?"

"Sue Patterson but I've heard that this could be repossessed by the courts. Is that correct?"

"The Proceeds of Crime Act, two thousand and two, has set up an Assets Recovery Agency who will look at this type of thing. It's more often used with the moneys raised from drug dealing, but it could also be appropriate in your case, if they can prove the fraudulent monies were used to buy the house."

"I will tell them that I used that money to pay for the house. The purchase was completed by one of your solicitors who are involved on the conveyance side. I think it was Sarah Duncan, is she still here?"

"Yes, Sarah still works for us. How did you send her the money?"

"I had accounts in a couple of Building Societies, and the money was transferred from them direct to your firm's bank account. It cost two hundred thousand pounds but needed a lot of renovation, which cost me another fifty thousand pounds, but it must now be worth three hundred thousand pounds. I want the courts to get this house and kick Sue Patterson out."

"There shouldn't be any trouble in proving that you paid for the property. Our records will show all the details, but is this just an act of vengeance because the pair of you have split up."

"It is vengeance but I want to do a deal to try and get any prison sentence reduced. When we met David Parish and Brian Lewis, they did not say the amount of the fraud, but I've been checking and I think it is nearly six hundred thousand pounds. You should also know that some of the claims were made when I was on holiday. Sue Patterson must have claimed them on her own, but the money did come to the Practice Bank accounts. She had made many of the other claims that I did know about. Anyhow, if I have benefited by six hundred thousand pounds, there is a chance that I could repay the money. There is the three hundred thousand pounds from the sale of that house, two hundred thousand pounds that I have got in various banks and building societies, which then totals five hundred thousand pounds. The family house is worth about four hundred and fifty thousand pounds, but has a mortgage of a hundred and ten thousand pounds, which gives a profit of three hundred and forty thousand pounds. If that was sold, we could use a hundred thousand which would repay the Dental Board and leave my wife the balance of two hundred and forty thousand pounds. She can have that as part of the divorce settlement. How does that sound?"

"You want to sell the family house as well?"

"Well yes. It is half mine, but I'm giving my wife and children more than half. It seems fair to me and I have tried to patch up the marriage but it was no good. Lynn isn't interested and she was a manager in Human Resources before we had the children and I'm sure she can get a good job again. She has also run an upmarket clothing shop for the past few years. It was a struggle at first but it's doing quite well at the moment. I will support them when I come out of prison."

"I'm not sure how you stand with getting your job back in the Health Service. You'll also end up being disciplined by your professional body."

"I know all about that but I've got some contacts and friends in the Dental world. I've spoken to an old friend who I studied with at University, and we've retained contact over the years. I told him what I'd done and obviously, he called me an idiot, but in the end, he will help later. He has a big Dental Practice, which is private, and does not complete National Health Service work. He knows that I am a good dentist and will employ me as a dentist, not a partner, providing it has all been cleared by our professional body, but he will stand by me, and we reckon they will give me clearance to practise there."

"You seem to have done your homework and quite a bit of research."

"I had no choice in the matter and I've got to think of myself first at this time, but my wife and children will be okay, and I couldn't care less about Sue Patterson."

"Okay Ben, I've listened to what you have said, and I'll make the notes and bring it up next week at our formal interview with David Parish. Does your wife know about your thoughts on selling the family house?"

"No, not yet, but I presume it will all be sorted out as part of the divorce settlement."

"That's right, but it might be worth giving her some advance warning."

"I suppose so. I'll let her know, it does seem reasonable Mark."

"The formal interview will be held in Southport and they will provide full details of the frauds that they've uncovered. They will write to your surgery giving the time and place of the interview but I will be speaking to David on the phone."

"There haven't been any frauds for over a year, since Sue went on maternity leave. I just wish I'd never got involved, but that's my own stupid fault. I want you to tell David Parish that

I did not do this on my own. I'm sure that he'll ask me at the interview, but I want him to know beforehand and it'll give him time to arrange to see Sue. Hopefully, by cooperating, it might help me when it gets to court."

Ben then handed a piece of paper to Mark.

"This is Sue's address and phone number. I've also listed her mother's address and phone number if he's having trouble making contact."

"If that's what you want, Ben, I'll let him know, but he has probably realized that somebody else may be involved, and I'm sure he'll have got word that you were having an affair with Sue Patterson. Are you still managing to work at your Practice, without any problems?"

"Yes. The staff know that I have been involved in some fraudulent activity but they've no idea how much. That'll come out soon I imagine, but the patients don't seem to know anything or care apart from their teeth."

Ben and Mark shook hands and Ben left the office.

Mark then rang David on his mobile but it was switched off. Rather than leave a message, he tried the home phone number and heard a female voice answer the phone.

"Hello"

"Oh hello, it's Mark Weston from AGK Solicitors. Is David there please?"

"No, this is Alisa, I would think that he'll be back in the next hour or two. Have you tried his mobile?"

"Yes Alisa, but it has been switched off."

"He must be driving then. Can I take a message?"

"Yes, if you would. David is interviewing Ben Alexander next week and I'm representing Ben. I have a message to give him from Ben. Will you tell him that Ben wants him to know that he was not acting alone and somebody else is involved. I've got the details of this second person and contact numbers. I've got David's email address and I'll send them through straight away. Will you tell him to check for messages when he gets home?"

"I will tell him. Thank you Mark."

26

David returned to his Liverpool home to find that Alisa had returned from London.

"Hello Alisa, I didn't expect you back today. This is a nice surprise or is there something that you've got to tell me?"

"Yes, but before I do, I've just taken a phone call from Mark Weston. You're interviewing Ben Alexander next week?"

"That's right."

"It seems that Ben wants you to know that he was not acting alone. He has given Mark the details and he has emailed you the information. You've got to check your messages."

"That'll be the name of somebody who worked at the practice. She was having an affair with Ben. I'll check it now."

David switched on the laptop and checked that the message had arrived. It was there and named Sue Patterson, as well as giving some contact details.

"Just as I thought, anyhow have you got something to tell me?"

"I suppose you could say that. I have now completely finished with my work in the United Kingdom. I've packed up all my belongings from the flat in London and they're all in the dining room."

"You seem quite happy about that."

"I think so but I've enjoyed the spell in this country but once I knew that it was ending, I felt that it was time to finish and I'm glad to be up here. I'll have to book a flight to Seville in about a week's time and arrange the move from Seville to Murcia. I did speak to an Estate Agent in Seville about selling my property and he said that it would sell very quickly, and he even has a waiting list of people who want to move into the area where I live."

"That's great news. I think that I should be able to come with you to Seville and help you move up to Murcia."

"Have you got time with the investigations that you are working on at the moment?"

"It's not too bad actually. John Kingsley has now taken over the benefit fraud and will link up with Kevin Donnelly, because of the connection to Wendy Carson. He'll keep me in touch but I shouldn't be needed now. The identity fraud involving Jack Inglis is being taken on by Anne Graham, and she also has to report to Kevin Donnelly because the murder investigations take priority. I will inform Sally O'Brien of the up to date situation because of the involvement of her twins, but she is pretty much up to date. I've got to give Kevin Donnelly a ring soon and update him with the benefit fraud and the links to Wendy Carson, but that only leaves our dentist, Ben Alexander, and the formal interview will take place early next week. I'll be completing that interview with Brian Lewis and he knows what's going on. I might try and contact this Sue Patterson to arrange an interview in the middle of next week, hopefully, Brian will be available. The documentation concerning the payroll fraud involving Wendy Carson is all up to date, but there's nothing I can do there, until she is finally arrested, but Kevin Donnelly will lead all investigations concerning her and he will only involve us at a later stage."

"Do you think they will find her?"

"I think they'll catch her in the end. I reckon she is still in this country or maybe somewhere in Wales. Her luck will run out eventually and hopefully, nobody else will be murdered in the meantime."

"She is some bad woman. I can't think of a case like this in Spain. A woman who gets annoyed when somebody upsets her, or betrays her, and then decides to kill them."

"The police in this country feel the same way. Kevin was saying he couldn't find a similar case and they do check all different types of murder to see if any patterns emerge. She's murdered three people that we know about, but for all we know, there may be more. She's committed the payroll fraud in the London hospital and she seems to be supplying this identity fraud service, where people pay her for the false documents and then go away and commit identity fraud. It's weird, and we have no idea how much money she's made from the identity fraud scam."

"I'm pleased that you can come with me to Seville. Once I've sold my property there, I'll buy somewhere in Murcia, but I have been provided with some temporary accommodation. It's not in a police station and you are allowed to stay."

"I should hope so. Don't book the flights for a couple of days until I've sorted everything out."

"That's okay. When I finished yesterday evening, I had a drink with a few colleagues. We were talking about the links between the U.K. and Spain but one of the other blokes works mainly with Interpol, and he was telling us about some of the enquiries they get from members of the public. He was saying that people are desperate for help at times, but have no one to turn to and they couldn't really help on many occasions. It got me thinking on what we could do if we retired early, or even if we both gave up our current jobs. I'll tell you about it when we have a drink and something to eat later."

"It sounds interesting Alisa. I'd better give Kevin Donnelly a ring to bring him up to date and find out if he knows anymore."

"Hello, Kevin Donnelly."
"Hi Kevin. It's David Parish."

"I was going to give you a ring later but you've saved me the job. How did you get on with Michael Davis and Felicja Jankowski?"

"I completed the formal interviews with John and the pair of them virtually admitted everything as far as the benefit frauds are concerned. I thought that Felicja was glad it was all over and to be honest, all she wants to do is sort out her sister, Danuta's murder. She did know her sister owed Wendy Carson some money and was going to see her. They saw her sister going in to see Wendy, but the next time she saw her sister, she was dead. As far as Felicja is concerned, it was Wendy Carson that murdered Danuta. Felicja also admits buying fraudulent identity documents off Wendy Carson and Frank Sinclair. She also mentioned during a friendly conversation, that she liked Chester and Wales. Wendy then told her that she liked Wales especially Anglesey where she'd been many times."

"I did contact the police in North Wales and they were circulating the information throughout North Wales including Anglesey. How about the interview with Michael Davis?"

"He admitted his part in the benefit frauds, but tried to deny any involvement in the frauds that Felicja had committed. He did know about the meeting between Danuta and Wendy Carson and was with Felicja, in London, at that time. He also saw Danuta going in to see Wendy and thought there were no problems. After the body was found, Felicja was distraught and kept asking him to contact Wendy, to see if she knew what had happened to Danuta. Interestingly, he did eventually ring Wendy and did speak to her. He asked Wendy if she knew what had happened to Danuta and he was told to keep out of it or he would go the same way as Danuta. He then decided to keep out of it all together and he believed that he could be in danger and he might have problems with their fraudulent claims on the Benefits Agency. I did say to both of them that you may want to speak to them about the murder of Danuta."

"Thanks David. Interestingly, Anne Graham spoke to Jack Inglis about the identity frauds, and he did name Wendy Carson and Frank Sinclair as the people who gave him the fraudulent documents to complete the identity frauds on the O'Brien twins. He did obtain the birth certificates himself, but they would have saved him the trouble at an extra cost. I had to go to Manchester yesterday about another case and thought that it might be useful if I had a word with Jack Inglis, while I was there. I cleared it with Anne and got an update, but when I went to see him, he tried to keep Wendy Carson out of it, and indicated that it was all down to Frank Sinclair. I could see he was holding something back and started to put pressure on him. In the end he admitted that he had received a phone call from Wendy a few days ago, asking him if he wanted to help with her side in the identity fraud. He declined saying that he had been caught by the police and had been beaten up by a couple of blokes on behalf of the twins' father. He said he didn't want anymore to do with it. She then told him not to mention her name as it wouldn't be in his best interests. He knew what that meant and that's why he was trying to avoid mentioning her. She also said that she was only a couple of hours away and he did check for the source of the phone call, and no information was available, but she was still in this country or Wales, I suppose."

"So, Michael Davis and Jack Inglis have been threatened on the phone and they are both, clearly, frightened. This Wendy Carson must have something about her which creates fear."

"It's the knowledge of the murders that she has committed. She doesn't know when to stop."

"I'll send you the copies of the interviews with Felicja Jankowski and Michael Davis, but it looks as though it's all in your hands for the time being. I've got a formal interview with a dentist next week, but I'll then be going over to Seville with Alisa and help her move to Murcia. You've got my mobile number if you need to contact me."

"Thanks David and I'm sure I'll be in touch sometime soon."

David then rang Sue Patterson and the phone was answered fairly quickly.

"Hello"

"Is that Sue?"

"Yes, who is that?"

"My name is David Parish. I am a Fraud Consultant with the National Health Service and I'm currently working with the Dental Board, looking at some of the claims made by the dentist, Mr Alexander, where you used to work. I have been given some information concerning the claims that have been made and I feel it advisable that we should have a formal interview next week. Would Wednesday suit you, say ten thirty in the morning."

"I don't know."

"I would advise you to be accompanied by a solicitor. Do you have a solicitor?"

"I can't remember his name. I need time to think."

"It would be in your best interests to attend this interview. I'll send you a letter confirming the time and place that the interview will take place. I'll also give you my contact details and you or your solicitor will be able to give me a ring to confirm that you and he will be attending."

"I need to speak to my solicitor."

"I look forward to seeing you next week. It is best if you attend and I look forward to hearing from you or your solicitor."

David and Alisa went for a leisurely walk for an hour through the local park before returning to the house. Alisa had already prepared the evening meal and when they returned, she placed the Spanish type Chicken Casserole in the oven for about half an hour. David did the honours and poured two large gin and tonics and they then sat at the table with a few nibbles, whilst the chicken was being cooked.

David then smiled as he spoke to Alisa.

"Go on, then tell me what the bloke from Interpol was talking about which has made you so intrigued."

"It was just interesting listening to what he had to say. He mentioned that Interpol, themselves, had received many phone calls asking for help. It was often a case of people missing and parents would ring up with distress stories. Their sons or daughters had fallen out with them and hadn't made contact but they knew they were somewhere in Europe, more often than not in Spain or England. Crimes had been committed in one country but the villains were known to be in another country. Fraudulent activities, which you'll know about, had been aimed at foreign people, often aimed at those who were trying to buy properties in different countries. The cases are endless, but in all cases they had tried to contact their local police but the lack of manpower, international difficulties and all sorts of problems, prevented them from getting the full help that they required. On many occasions, the people were willing to pay for help, but Interpol would not be able to recommend anybody."

"It must be sad for many people. I've heard of many cases help but they've had no one to turn to."

"Anyhow, he started joking about the two of us. He knew of my role with Interpol, Foreign Police forces and the ability to communicate in different languages. I do speak Spanish, English and a little Italian. Then we spoke about you and your fame throughout Europe where you are known as Senor Fraudo and Mr Fraud. You speak English, Spanish and a little French. He then suggested that we form an Agency and he and his colleagues would be quite happy to refer all the problem cases. He even said that we could become officially accredited to Interpol and many foreign police forces. We all had a good laugh about it but I got to thinking about it the next day. It is a thing that we could probably do, maybe not now but possibly in the future. We could have a base, together, somewhere, probably Spain or England. It was just a thought."

David smiled as Alisa was speaking and listening to what she had to say.

"It does sound quite intriguing. I know that we have agreed that we are going to keep travelling between Murcia and Liverpool and will be seeing each other for a few days each month plus holidays, but we will be apart. We both want to carry on working and we've assumed that is me carrying on as a Fraud Consultant, mainly in this country and you with the Spanish police in Murcia. I think we assumed we'd have to carry on our present jobs, but if it meant we'd be together, still working, and enjoying the work, it is worth thinking about. I'm not sure how it would work out with Interpol, but we'd need to have enough investigations to keep us going and we'd make sure we had enough time for each other. I think that type of thing may be a possibility. You probably know a bit more than me, but it does sound interesting."

"In that case, I'll make some more enquiries over the next couple of months with Interpol and in Spain."

"I've got plenty of contacts in this country. I'll see if such an idea was a possibility in their eyes."

"It would mean that I'd have to work with you David, all the time. How would you cope with a female boss?"

"I don't know what you're talking about. I'd have to be in charge."

"Okay. I'll let you think that you're the boss, but I'll end up having it my own way."

"I'm sure you will, Alisa Garcia."

They both finished their gin and tonics, and David opened a bottle of Rioja to go with the Spanish chicken casserole. They both then had an enjoyable evening, enjoying the meal and talking about the possibilities of being together, without the tedious journeys between the two countries.

The next morning David phoned Sally O'Brien with an update on the twins' identity fraud. He was unable to speak to Sally initially, but she rang him back later in the morning.

"Hello"

"Hello David, its Sally, I believe you've been trying to get hold of me?"

"Yes, it's just an update on the identity fraud. Anne Graham from Cheshire Police interviewed Jack Inglis about the fraud, and as you know he admitted it, but did say the fraudulent documents were obtained from Wendy Carson and Frank Sinclair. Kevin Donnelly was in Manchester on another matter and he also spoke to Jack Inglis. Apparently, Jack tried to push the blame on Frank Sinclair, but Kevin eventually found out that he had spoken to Wendy on the phone who had threatened him. My part of the investigation is now virtually over and Kevin will lead the ongoing investigation because of the murder situations. We know who did the identity fraud on the twins and who supplied the documents and the legal process will take its natural course. I suppose their might be a follow up on Criminals Captured if they haven't caught Wendy but that's it for now."

"That's fine with me David and I appreciate the help that you've given me. Send me your bill but keep in touch if you feel it necessary."

"I will do. Thanks a lot Sally and best of luck with the television programme."

27

It was a nice sunny day as Wendy Carson sat outside the cottage on the bench having a cup of coffee and a cake. She was watching the pheasant priming itself and strolling through the grass near the small bushes when a rabbit appeared and the pheasant flew gracefully through the sky to a place of safety.

Wendy was thinking about her future as she had done, on several occasions, since arriving at the cottage in Anglesey over a week ago. It was a lovely area and she was quite content to stay there at the moment, but she was wanted by the police and she had seen photographs on both the television and the newspapers. She had disguised her appearance, especially with the changes to the colour and style of her hair, but she recognised herself in the photographs and surely somebody would, if they were continually shown on the television and the papers. Maybe she would become unimportant, and not headline news in a few weeks and she would then be able to start leading a normal life.

The previous day, she had gone to the local market and as she was walking around, she noticed the occasional look from other people. Perhaps this was just the normal thing but she was becoming a little obsessed and at times feeling a little uncomfortable. She had made no more contact with her mother or daughter and she had ceased to look at being involved in the fraud business and especially the provision of the false identity fraud documents. This was, she thought, an area where the police might have contacts and lead to her capture. She did despise that David Parish who had arranged for national coverage on Criminals Captured, and gave full details of the type of things that she had undertaken in the fraud world. The policeman, Kevin Donnelly, also told the viewing public of the murders she was suspected of committing. They were both fairly accurate in what they had said, but it was David Parish that she thought had gained the public's interest and he would be at home enjoying himself with his Spanish girlfriend, while I'm hiding in Anglesey. She was even cautious when she went to the local shop, but would still have to go today and get some food and perhaps a couple of bottles of wine.

Wendy got up off the bench and went inside the cottage and locked all the doors before making the way to her blue, Fiat Punto car.

She drove out of the cottage, past the old church and cemetery and headed for the little village where the local shop was situated. It was only a ten minute drive and she was able to park in front of the shop. She went inside the shop and collected a basket from by the front door. It took about five minutes to complete the shopping, buying the food that she required and two bottles of Australian red wine. The same lady always seemed to be in the shop when Wendy was there, and she gave her a smile as Wendy went to the counter to pay, in cash, for her shopping.

"Hello, it's a lovely day today. Are you here on holiday?"

"I'll probably be here for a couple of weeks."

"Where are you staying?"

"Not far away."

Wendy handed over a twenty pound note, thinking to herself, why are you so nosy about what I'm doing and where I'm staying, but maybe she was getting a bit neurotic with herself. She collected her change but thought that she was getting a funny look from the shopkeeper.

"Thank you."

Wendy left the shop and put the shopping on the passenger seat of the car. She was about to drive away, when she remembered that she had forgotten to pick up a tub of margarine. She returned to the shop and picked up the margarine and went to pay the lady. As she got to the counter, she saw the lady was not there but she could hear her talking on the phone in the little office next to the counter. The door was open and the lady had her back to Wendy, but was talking in Welsh so Wendy couldn't understand what she was saying. She then heard the lady say four words, which Wendy understood quite clearly. The words were Wendy Carson, Criminals Captured.

She was startled for a second but knew, straight away, that she had been recognized and it was probably being reported to the police. The lady put the phone down and Wendy attacked her from behind, there were little groans, but it was too late. She was dead just like the other people who had crossed Wendy Carson.

Wendy moved quickly to leave the shop and get into her car for the drive back to the cottage. She was going to quickly pack all her belongings and leave the island of Anglesey. She had failed, however, to notice the inside security cameras which was still working, taking a film of all the activity which took place inside the shop. It did not cover the little office, but it would have shown Wendy entering the shop twice, and then leaving, the second time in rather a hurry.

Wendy spent less than half an hour packing her luggage, loading the car and locking the cottage. She did, surprisingly, put the keys back through the letterbox. As she joined the A5 and headed towards Bangor, she suddenly thought that she had to cross the Britannia Bridge. Surely the police would not be at the Bridge stopping traffic looking for her already. After fifteen minutes she reached the Britannia Bridge but there were no police and she was able to cross quite easily. She decided to leave Wales on a different route than when she arrived from London, and followed the coast road and the signs for Conwy. This road was the A55 and would pass Conwy and eventually make its way towards Chester. She made sure that she kept within the speed limits and avoided being photographed on any of the speed cameras.

A local policeman had reached the small shop in response to the telephone call and as he was about to enter an elderly lady came rushing to the door screaming.

"I think she's dead."

"Who?"

"The lady shopkeeper. She's on the floor in the office by the counter."

He made his way to the office and checked for a pulse, but he already knew that she was dead and immediately made contact with his office.

"It's David Williams. I've got a body at the shop. It's the lady shopkeeper who reported seeing Wendy Carson. I think she might have gone the same way as the others who fell foul of Wendy Carson. You'd better send some support and an ambulance. There is a security camera and it sounds as though it's still working. It might show us something. We don't know where Carson is staying, she might go into hiding or she might leave the island pretty quickly. If we get a photo from the camera we will probably need to make some local enquiries to see if anyone recognises her."

Within the hour, the police had removed tapes from the camera and had found Wendy Carson entering and leaving the shop on two occasions. They also got some photographs of her current appearance. Local enquiries were being made when Detective Inspector John Jones of the North Wales Police phoned Kevin Donnelly in London.

"Hello, Kevin Donnelly."

"Hello Kevin, its D.I. John Jones from North Wales Police. I think we have some news on your Wendy Carson, not good I'm afraid."

"Go on, tell me more."

"We had a phone call from a shopkeeper, Karen Jones, in Anglesey, saying she was convinced that she had just served Wendy Carson in her shop. A local policeman was sent around and probably arrived within fifteen to twenty minutes. When he arrived at the shop, he found her dead. The Scene of Crime is there now and the body has been taken away, but we think she's been murdered in the same way as the others. One good bit of news, there was a security camera in the shop and we've looked at the tape. There is film of a lady entering the shop on two occasions and the second was the same time as the phone call was being made, before she left in a hurry. It is an old camera still using video tapes but we've taken photographs of the lady. She does look different to the published photographs of Wendy Carson, but it's definitely her. We have given out copies of the photographs to local police and they are making enquiries within an area of about three miles. It's not that heavily populated in that area of Anglesey and if she lived more than three miles away she wouldn't have gone to that shop. We have stationed a couple of police cars near Menai Bridge and Brittania Bridge, but she would have had time to leave the island. When we were warned that there was a possibility she may have been on the island, we were told that she may have a blue Fiat Punto. We are looking for that but for all we know she might have got rid of it. Is there anything else that you have or we need to know?"

"To be honest John, you appear to have done everything that you can. Let us know what your local search turns up and the results of the post mortem but let me have copies of the photographs."

"I've got our specialists trying to improve the quality, but I'll get them to fax them to you or send you an email. We'll also take a copy of the tape and check some others. We'll send you anything that may help."

"Thanks John. I'll be in touch."

Later that evening David Williams was making enquiries into the whereabouts of Wendy Carson and he knocked on the door of a local plumber.

"Hello, we're trying to find where this woman is staying. Have you seen her around?"

He then showed the photograph.

"Oh yes, that's the lady who's been staying at Lloyd and Hilary's cottage. They let me know if somebody is staying there and I keep an eye on the place. I believe her name is Colette Brady. She isn't in though, I saw her driving away in her blue Punto a few hours ago and she hasn't come back."

"Which is the cottage?"

He pointed out the cottage to David.

"Did you ever speak to her?"

"No, she kept herself to herself, and never spoke a word to anybody. What has she done?"

"She's a suspect in a few murder enquiries."

"You don't mean Karen Jones, at the local shop today?"

"When did you hear about that?"

"It's all the local gossip and we've had a couple of phone calls."

"We will probably need to go into the cottage. Do you know who has any contact for the owners?"

"I have their home telephone number and their phone number in Spain. I've also got a set of spare keys."

It was not too long before forensics arrived at the cottage and did a thorough search. It had been left tidy with no physical evidence linking to Wendy Carson. The team did take swabs of evidence which might give a DNA profile as well as several sets of fingerprints. The police had spoken to the owners who were in Spain, but were returning the day after tomorrow, although they confirmed that they had never actually seen Wendy Carson. The booking had been completed through the internet and several phone calls but they had been paid for three months. Cash had been paid into their bank account. They also said that the local neighbour, the plumber, would always keep an eye on the cottage. He was a great help to them.

Kevin Donnelly had received enough information to request an update on the next days Criminals Captured programme, with a recent photograph of Wendy Carson and film from Anglesey, being shown to the television audience by Sally O'Brien.

28

David had a meeting with Brian Lewis before the formal interview with Ben Alexander. The meeting was being held in the Human Resources Department of the Health Authority office in Southport, and Ben was to be represented by Mark Weston.

They had both prepared for the meeting and only needed to set up the equipment and have a quick update on Ben Alexander, but David needed to update Brian on the phone call from Mark, and his dealings with Sue Patterson.

"First of all, do you have any questions on the interview with Mark? I presume that you've had chance to read the file notes and the disclosure packs?"

"Yes David. It all looks fairly straight forward and I don't think that he'll argue the case from what I've heard on the grapevine. Do you have any more information on Sue Patterson?"

"That's what I want to talk to you about now. I had a phone call from Mark updating me on a meeting he'd had with Ben. Ben had told Mark that his relationship was all over with Sue, and he told him that she was involved in the fraud from the beginning. He, himself, had never entered a claim for dental treatment. All the entries on the computer system had been input by Sue, but he accepted that the monies from the Dental Board had gone into his bank account. He even admitted that some of the entries had been made when he was not in the practice and was on holiday."

"That ties up with the research that we have done. I knew that he was not in the dental practice on several dates when claims were made. That's why I've highlighted them in the disclosure pack."

"He also provided some details on what had happened to the money he had received due to their fraudulent actions. It appears that he bought Sue her house for two hundred thousand pounds and then spent a further fifty thousand on renovation. He seems to think it is now worth three hundred thousand pounds. He wants to do some type of deal by repaying the six hundred thousand pounds and wants the courts to repossess the property under the Proceeds of Crime Act."

"That'll be down to the Assets Recovery Agency and I'm sure that they wouldn't have any great problems, providing it can be proved that he paid the money."

"I don't think that will be a problem. He can also provide a further two hundred thousand, which he has hidden in various bank accounts. The balance of one hundred thousand pounds would be made by getting a new mortgage on the family home."

"Is he back with his wife?"

"I don't think so."

"Will she go along with this new mortgage?"

"Ben must think it will all be part of a divorce settlement."

"How about Sue Patterson? Does she know all about this proposed offer?"

"I've no idea. I did phone her and told her that we wanted to interview her as part of this investigation."

"What did she say?"

"She was a bit shocked but wouldn't commit herself to an interview on the phone. She didn't give the name of any solicitor and I told her I'd contact her again within a day or two. I've tried ringing her with no response and I've even tried ringing her mother but she denies that's she's staying with her.

I wanted her to sign an acknowledgment of a letter which gave the details and time of the appointment but we've failed to make contact when I sent a delivery company with the letter. They tried half a dozen times including evening visits, but failed to get any response. They did post one letter through the letter box but I've no idea if she has seen that letter. That's why I asked you to duplicate the disclosure packs, just in case she turned up. I did suggest this afternoon, but I haven't heard anything, so I doubt if she'll turn up."

"Have you contacted the police yet?"

"No. I'll wait until this afternoon before I speak to Inspector Anne Graham. She'll contact the local police and they'll put out an arrest warrant and I'll ask them to circulate the airports and ferry ports in case she intends to do a runner, but I don't think she will. She has a daughter and a boyfriend and I think she'll be with him somewhere."

"I wonder if Ben Alexander or Mark has any more information."

"Good question. I don't know but we'll ask them."

David and Brian then finished, flicked through the packs and completed the necessary preparations, obtained some bottled water and some glasses, and were having a friendly discussion when there was a knock on the door and the receptionist came inside.

"The two gentlemen are both in the room next to the reception desk."

"Thanks, we'll collect them in a few minutes," said David.

David then spoke with Brian.

"I'll bring in Mark Weston initially, give him some detailed information and present him with the pack of disclosures, he will then be able to go back to Ben and discuss the documentation that we've given him."

David then went outside to reception and knocked on the door to the room where Mark and Ben where waiting.

"Hello Mark, Hello Ben."

"I assume that you're going to provide me with one of your disclosure packs?"

"Yes, if you'd come with me Mark, we're just down the corridor and I'll go through the disclosure pack."

David and Mark left the room and walked along the corridor and into the room to join Brian, who had met Mark in previous interviews involving David, as well as some of his own investigations.

"Good morning Mark."

"Hello Brian, we meet again. Mr Fraud and partner?"

David then updated Mark on the situation with Sue Patterson.

"Thanks for the information about Sue Patterson, but I haven't been able to get confirmation that she'll attend the formal interview. She is due to see us this afternoon but I doubt that she'll turn up. I did speak to her the once, but I've tried ringing her since, without success, and her mother doesn't seem to know where she is. We did drop a letter off at her house, and we've tried to get some type of proof of delivery without any luck. I'll see if she turns up, but if not, we'll arrange for the police to be involved."

"She did ring Ben and told him that you'd phoned her. She asked him what he'd told you and he told her to mind her own business, but he did say to her that she'll need a solicitor pretty quickly. I've not heard if she's coming to the interview later. Sometimes other people's solicitors do talk before the interview, but nobody has tried to contact me."

"Thanks Mark."

"What did you think about Ben's proposals to pay the money back?"

"I think that the Assets Recovery Agency should have success in getting the Sue Patterson's house sold if we can get the evidence that Ben provided the money."

"The house purchase was completed by our firm and we have evidence that the money came from accounts in the name of Ben. Apparently his wife will go along with the hundred thousand pounds from the matrimonial home. I don't know if she will get another mortgage or whether her parents will give her a hundred thousand pounds, but they are going to get divorced, and she wants to retain the family house."

"It should help him in court."

"You'll put a good word in with the Judge, in due course?"

"That depends on the assistance that Ben provides, but it's got to help his sentence by paying the money back, I don't know what will happen to his role in the Health Service, that's out of my hands."

"There's always private dentists, who don't do any National Health Dentistry work."

"Quite a lot these days."

Brian then started the proceedings.

"Here is a copy of the disclosure pack Mark."

He then handed him the Disclosure Pack before both he and David opened their own copies.

Brian then explained some of the contents of the pack to Mark.

"We've listed the fraudulent entries on a year by year basis and an annual list is in front of the entries. You will see in nineteen ninety-eight to nineteen ninety-nine there are two hundred and fifty claims totalling forty nine thousand and eight hundred pounds. They increase each year until the last year, which was two thousand and five to two thousand and six, when there were four hundred and eighty-six claims at a total cost of ninety seven thousand six hundred pounds. In total, there are two thousand, nine hundred and twenty six fraudulent claims at a total cost of five hundred and eighty-six thousand, seven hundred pounds."

David then joined in the conversation.

"The last claims were made in the year, 2006, which no doubt you'll be aware, is when Sue Patterson left to go on maternity leave. She has not returned to work and no claims have been made since that date. You'll also see that Brian has highlighted claims that were made when Ben was on holiday and not in the Dental Surgery."

Mark then commented.

"I think we all know that Ben has never made an entry on the computer system with respect to a claim. All that work was done by Sue Patterson."

David replied.

"The money all went into Ben's Practice Bank account though."

"I'm sure we'll be discussing that later at the formal interview."

"I'll go through this with Ben and I'll mention what you've said about Sue Patterson."

"Thanks Mark."

Mark then left the room with the Disclosure Pack to join Ben and discuss the contents.

Brian then remarked.

"Do you think that Ben knows the whereabouts of Sue?"

"To be honest, I don't think he does, but if he did, he might tell us."

There was a wait of twenty-five minutes before Mark Weston returned to the room with Ben Alexander. They all sat around the desk and Ben turned to David.

"I believe that Sue's gone missing?"

"Not for long. She might turn up later for all we know."

David then spoke to Ben.

"I just want to check that you understand what we are going to do. Brian will operate the tape machine and you will hear a loud noise before the start of the interview, this is normal. Has

Mark explained what we are going to discuss and the procedures that will take place?"

"Yes, I understand."

"Okay, Brian will you start the tape please?"

Brian started the tape and the noise appeared before David started the interview with the opening procedures.

"This Interview is being tape recorded, it is the thirty-first of March, two thousand and eight and the time by my watch is ten thirty five a.m. I am David Parish a Fraud Consultant with the National Health Service. The other officer present is."

"Brian Lewis, a Fraud Specialist also representing the Health Authority and the Dental Board."

"I am interviewing, please state your full name, address and date of birth."

"Benjamin John Alexander. I'm currently living at my parent's house, Thirty one Arundel Lane, Preston. Date of birth, twenty first of March, nineteen sixty nine."

"Also present is."

"Mark Weston AGK Solicitors, Manchester."

"We are in the Human Resources Department of the Health Authority, Southport. At the end of the interview, I will give you a notice explaining the procedures for the dealing with the tapes and how you can have access to them. Before the interview begins I must caution you."

"You do not have to say anything, but it may harm your defence if you do not mention when questioned something which you later rely on in court, anything you do say may be given in evidence. Do you understand the caution?"

Ben obviously knew this was coming and replied.

"Yes."

"You are not under arrest and you are free to leave at any time. The reason for this interview is that we are investigating fraudulent dental claims made by your Dental Practice. Do you understand the reason for this interview?"

"Yes."

"If at any time you wish to speak to your solicitor in private or if you wish me to stop the interview for any reason, then tell me and I will stop the interview."

"I understand."

"I know that you're going to ask me about the dental claims over an eight year period but I want to put it on record that I was not acting alone. I did not actually enter the fraudulent claims on the computer system at the Dental Board. That part was completed by Sue Patterson."

"I will be asking you about that during the interview, but your comments have been noted."

David then continued the interview.

"Have you looked at the documents in the pack with your solicitor which relate to claims made for various types of dental treatment?"

"Yes, he has showed them to me."

"They are claims made in your name relating to dental treatment at your Dental Practice. A full list of all the treatments are provided in the pack, but they cover an eight year period from nineteen ninety-eight to the year two thousand and six. There are a total of two thousand nine hundred and twenty-six claims totalling five hundred and eighty six thousand, seven hundred pounds."

"Yes."

"Do you admit to all the false claims, which are itemised in the pack and total five hundred and eighty six thousand, seven hundred pounds?"

"I don't have an exact figure for the claims, but I think Sue Patterson may have the information, but I do accept your findings. I recognized many names on the lists that I know are no longer my patients."

"What was the role of Sue Patterson?"

"Sue worked at the practice and was responsible for the day to day running. She would complete most of the records of the patient's treatment, and make all the appropriate claims from the Dental Board. I started having an affair with Sue in nineteen, ninety eight. It was only a fling to begin with and we got talking about how easy it would be to claim for patients who had died, or who had left the practice. Sue tried it a few times before I found out and I, stupidly, did not stop her doing it. She then started making many claims and it all seemed to get out of hand. She eventually persuaded me to buy her a house and all the extras that went with it. I needed the extra money to keep Sue happy and keep the family home going. We did have money problems for several years and my wife lost money in some ventures to begin with. They seem to have improved now and no claims have been made since Sue left the practice to go on maternity leave. I thought it was my child, but it turns out she had a boyfriend at the same time and the child is his. I've got no excuses but you have been informed that I want to repay all the money."

"Okay, let's not discuss Sue Paterson for the moment. I have been informed of your intention to repay the fraudulent claims. For the record, on tape, how do you intend to repay the money?"

"I will repay two hundred thousand pounds from existing bank accounts. The house that I purchased for Sue Patterson is now worth around three hundred thousand pounds. My solicitor can prove that it was money from my bank accounts that purchased the property and I understand that you can make this happen. Is that right?"

"Yes. There is a Proceeds of Crime Act, which introduced the Assets Recoveries Agency. They will repossess the property and then sell it, with the proceeds being returned to the Health Authority. I'm not sure how much Sue Patterson knows about this but it will be explained in due course. That totals around five hundred thousand pounds and how is the rest to be repaid?"

"I am getting divorced and part of the settlement will allow me to receive a hundred thousand pounds, with my wife having full ownership of the matrimonial home. I thought she might get a mortgage, but her parents are fairly well off and they may just hand over the hundred thousand pounds. I am just hoping that by arranging repayment in full, I may receive a more lenient sentence. Is that correct?"

"It is all down to the judge, but he will have been informed of the repayment has been made or the current situation with the Assets Recoveries Agency."

"Is there anything else that we need to mention as far as the Frauds are concerned Brian?"

"No, I think we have all the information that we require. I think you wanted to discuss the whereabouts of Sue Patterson."

David then asked a further question to Ben.

"Are you aware that we are having some difficulty contacting Sue Patterson?"

"Yes. Mark informed me before the interview."

"Do you know where she is?"

"No. If I knew I'd let you know immediately. If she's not at home, I thought she might have been with her mother. I gave you the details, but if she isn't there she will probably be somewhere with the boyfriend. Her mother will know where she is. She and Sue are close and always talking on the phone. I'm sure if the police go round to her mother's house, you will be able to find out where she is."

"If you are in contact, will you let your solicitor know, and he will contact us."

"Yes, that's no problem. I want you to find her."

"We will and you never know, she might turn up this afternoon."

They all smiled as David made that comment.

"Do you wish to add anything further or clarify any point or anything you have told me?"

"No."

"Here is the notice which explains your entitlement to a copy of the tape used in this interview. This interview is concluded at eleven fourteen a.m. on the thirty-first of March, two thousand and eight. Switch off the tape recorder."

David and Brian collected some sandwiches and a coffee from the staff canteen and sat down passing time, before they had to return to the interview room prior to the possible one o'clock interview with Sue Patterson. They returned at a quarter to one, but decided, after a half an hour, that there was no longer a requirement to stay, not having received any contact from Sue or her representative.

Before leaving David phoned Anne Graham at Cheshire Police.

"Hello, Anne Graham."

"Hi Anne, its David Parish."

"Hello David. What can I do for you?"

"A favour please."

"Go on, tell me all about it."

"We've been investigating a fraud by a dentist. It has been going on for several years and we are looking at nearly six hundred thousand pounds. We've interviewed him and he has admitted his part but he had an accomplice at the dental practice, a woman he was having an affair with who entered all the claims and they seem to have shared the gains. I did telephone her asking for an interview but she's done a disappearing act. She's not at home and her mother denies knowing her whereabouts. The dentist has said her mother will definitely know where she is but we need the police to find her, which will mean you will be required to be involved in the investigation."

"Where does the mother live?"

"It's in Cheshire. I'll email you all the information that you require and, hopefully, find where she has gone. She has a young daughter and a boyfriend and we don't think that she's left the country, but I don't know."

"Send me the details David and I'll let you know once we've got some more information."

"Thanks Anne, I'll be in touch."

"Bye David."

David turned to Brian.

"I'll email Anne with all our information and she'll find Sue Patterson. I'll let her have one of the disclosure packs, but they'll probably lock her up and interview her once they get hold of her. I'll update you once I hear from Anne."

David quickly sent the information to Anne, and they then both left the Health Authority Building.

29

Wendy Carson drove along the A55 in North Wales until she saw the signs for St Asaph, when she then left the main road and made her way to St Asaph and parked her car in a secluded spot. She went to the boot of her car and found the small carrier bag that she wanted before getting back into the car. The wig that she was looking for was grey in colour and she flattened her hair before putting the wig on to make sure it fitted correctly. She then took out the make up and using the skills she had developed over the years, carefully used the different types of make up to make herself look older with her facial appearance now suiting the grey haired wig. This was one of the three wigs that Wendy had kept in the bag, always knowing that she may have to change appearance in order to avoid capture, either by the police or to avoid members of the public recognising her from photographs in the newspapers or what was being shown on television.

It would not be long before the police knew her hair had changed from the natural blond to the dark colour that she had previously used to dye her hair. She looked at herself in the make up mirrors and the car mirror and was quite satisfied that her appearance was sufficiently different to that shown to the public.

She then left the car, putting the carrier bag back in the boot, and walked along the row of shops until she found a small café and purchased a chicken wrap and a cup of coffee as well as a salad dish that she would eat later in the evening. A newspaper was on the table and she flicked through finding nothing of interest. News of the murder in Anglesey was not yet in the papers.

Wendy then walked back to her car and drove away, returning to the A55 and heading for Chester. It was only about a half hour later when she found a hotel for travellers on the outskirts of Chester. She was now Amanda Jeffers and had the appropriate documentation under that name. Colette Brady would now be headline news as well as Wendy Carson.

The room was booked for two nights under the name of Amanda Jeffers. She took the essential luggage to the room again parking her car in the far side of the car park. She was concerned that details of her car may be provided to the media and felt it may be necessary to get rid of the car and find some other transport.

Later that evening, Wendy was sitting in her room, enjoying a glass of red Shiraz wine, watching television. She was waiting to watch Criminals Captured and then the news to see if there were any updates on Wendy Carson or Colette Brady.

Criminals Captured started and Sally O'Brien and her co-presenter mentioned some of the cases that they were going to discuss. She then said she would start with an update on the search for Wendy Carson, which had been discussed on an earlier programme.

Kevin Donnelly then appeared and he told the viewers that another murder had occurred in Anglesey, which they believed was the work of Wendy Carson, who was using the name of Colette Brady. Although she had changed her appearance, the shopkeeper in Anglesey thought she had come into the shop a couple of times. When she entered the shop a third time, she was convinced it was Wendy Carson and rang the police. They arrived twenty minutes later and found the dead body of the shopkeeper, Karen Jones, who had been killed in the same manner as Frank Sinclair, Denis King and Danuta Jankowski. The police did a local search and found out that Wendy Carson had been renting a cottage under the name of Colette Brady, but had left the cottage within fifteen minutes of the murder of Karen Jones. A bigger search had been made on the island with no trace of Wendy Carson. It was believed she had now left the island driving a Blue Fiat Punto. Photographs of Wendy with long blonde hair and short dark hair were then shown and the public were told not to approach her because of the dangers that would create.

Wendy felt that her new appearance was good but felt she would have to move the Fiat Punto. It was now dark and she decided to leave the hotel and drive to Chester. She had made up her mind to drive the car to a large multi storey car park and leave the car there. In the morning she would obtain a hire car in the name of Amanda Jeffers. She returned about an hour later, having got rid of the Punto and got a taxi for the short journey back to the hotel.

After spending a couple of days in Chester and twice walked around the Chester City Walls, which is a two mile walk around the city centre and allows the walker to see many of the city's key heritage sites, she was able to browse through many of the city's shops, bought a street map of Liverpool and arranged for the hire of a car, this time a red Ford Ka. Wendy was also able to supplement her holding of cash using cash cards for the several bank accounts she held in various names.

It was during these walks that Wendy decided what would be the next course of action that she would undertake. David Parish, Kevin Donnelly and Sally O'Brien had brought her name and appearance to the whole country using the television programme, Criminals Captured. It was time to seek revenge and a visit to Liverpool was now her next step, she knew the address of David Parish.

Anne Graham had sent two police colleagues to Sue Patterson's mothers address and when she answered the door, they saw a child's push chair in the hall of the house. Although she had initially denied any knowledge of her daughter's whereabouts, they soon gained access to the property and found Sue Patterson with her daughter, Mandy.

Sue was arrested and taken to the police station to be interviewed by Anne Graham. Once under interrogation by Anne, Sue soon admitted that she had been involved in the fraud with Ben Alexander, the dentist. She had been flattered at first, and had a longstanding affair, although still in a relationship with her boyfriend Karl, the father of Mandy. Ben had been infatuated with Sue, and soon supplied her with money and other luxuries, which continued and ended with him buying her a house and having it renovated. She knew, from the threats that Ben had made, that the police would know that the house had been purchased with the monies gained from the fraudulent claims. It was only a matter of time before she would lose the house and end up going on trial with Ben Alexander for fraud.

She also knew that Karl would not support Sue, once she was in prison and without the financial benefits supplied by Ben Alexander. Her mother would have to take care of Mandy.

Once she had heard that Ben was planning to repay all the money taken in the fraudulent claims, which included the sale of her house, she hoped that she might be able to avoid a prison sentence, and helped the police in every way possible. This was wishful thinking according to her solicitor, who thought she may have played a strong part in the fraud by making all the claims on the computer system, some of which were completed when Ben Alexander was not even present in the Dental Practice. She had been bailed by the Magistrates Court and it was now a question of waiting for the Crown Court appearance with Ben.

30

Wendy Carson booked out of the hotel the following morning and got into the hire car for the journey to Liverpool, which she estimated would take about three quarters of an hour. She had checked the map and took the A41 through Wirral towards the Mersey Tunnel, paid the toll fee and then she took the inside lane into the tunnel. There was an exit to the left just before the main exit, which Wendy took and emerged by the Pier Head, where she looked at the Liver Building with the famous Liver Birds on the roof of the building.

She followed the road, past the Albert Dock and continued on this road which ran parallel with the River Mersey, before veering left towards one of the main roads into Liverpool. She turned away from the directions of the Town Centre and looked for Liverpool Cricket Club and when this came into sight, she turned towards the area where David Parish lived. Within five minutes, she turned into the road and looked for his house and slowed down slightly as she passed the house.

The driveway had been extended and there was a Black Ford Fiesta parked in front of the house, but no car parked in the driveway. It was only a two door car and Wendy thought that this would not belong to David Parish but would belong to his Spanish girlfriend, who she had seen with David a year ago, when he was working on the travel fraud case in the hospital where Wendy worked.

She continued driving to the top of the road, which led to a large Park. Wendy parked the car and decided to take a walk around the park, while she considered her next course of action. She passed a café and thought that she would call back there for a cup of tea, before she returned to the car. It was a pleasant circular walk around the park, part of which was in the open with plants on one side and grassland on the other, with a children's play area. The path then curved through an area where it was darker with trees growing on either side and she had to smile when she saw a young boy hiding behind a tree, with his mother and father, pretending not to know where he was, shouting for him. He then jumped out and they both pretended they were frightened, which made him laugh.

Wendy continued the walk and eventually returned to the café where she enjoyed a cup of tea and a scone, before returning to her car. She looked at the street map and then turned down a couple of the side roads, before again locating the beginning of the road where David Parish lived. The idea was to see if he had returned in the hour that she had been on the walk and had a drink in the café.

As she neared the house, she suddenly saw a lady walk out of the driveway and walk down the road in the direction of the park. Wendy recognised her as David's girlfriend and noticed that she started to walk briskly wearing a pair of walking shoes. She suddenly thought that she may be going into the park for a walk and drove quickly past and parked the car near the entrance to the park.

She then went into the park and took the same pathway, but stopped about a hundred yards ahead to see if his girlfriend entered the park. It was only a matter of two minutes before Alisa came into the park and headed towards Wendy, who then started walking again, briskly, past the café and towards the area where the trees darkened the path and where she saw the young boy hiding earlier. She glanced back as she turned towards the trees and smiled as she saw who was following her. It might not be David Parish, but this was perhaps a better target. Once she walked into the tree covered area, she left the path and hid behind a tree.

Alisa was now in sight and she started walking past the trees and as she passed the tree where Wendy was hiding, she had no idea what was to happen shortly. Wendy moved from behind the tree to just behind Alisa. Her martial arts involvement had taught her how to move quietly and quickly. She soon reached and grabbed her from behind before Alisa had time to turn and look who was behind her.

It was the surprise element which had allowed Wendy to overcome and murder Danuta Jankowski, Frank Sinclair, Denis King and the lady in the shop in Anglesey. She had forgotten her name although she had heard it on television. Wendy was now confident that she would be able to murder whoever she wanted in the same way as the others.

Alisa grimaced as she was grabbed around the neck from behind, but there was no surprise element. Her training and skills in self-defence had taught her to react immediately depending on where the attack came from. As the hold became tighter, Alisa lifted her right leg, turned slightly and brought her foot down, heavily, into the foot of Wendy. The sound of breaking bones in the instep and the metatarsals in Wendy's right foot was followed by a scream and the grip around Alisa's foot loosened. Alisa raised her right elbow to head height and turned sharply as Wendy's grip loosened. The elbow smashed into the right side of Wendy's face and the familiar sound of bone crushing occurred again as her nose was broken, the cheek bone splintered and pushed up into the eye socket.

Wendy was now screaming and fell to the floor. It was then that Alisa turned to see who her attacker was, and immediately recognised her as Wendy Carson. She pulled off the wig to make sure, but this was definitely the blood splattered face of Wendy Carson.

Alisa took out her mobile phone while Wendy was lying on the path of the park. Before she could make a call, a man and woman rushed across to see what had happened. The lady asked.

"What have you done to her?"

"She has just tried to kill me and I acted in self-defence. I am a police officer and I'm just going to ring for the police and ambulance. Will you wait here please?"

Alisa dialled 999 and when the call was answered she replied.

"Police please."

The call was directed to the police.

"My name is Alisa Garcia. I am a Spanish Police official, currently seconded to the Home Office and Metropolitan Police in London. A lady has just tried to kill me, but didn't realize that I am trained in self-defence. I managed to stop her attack but she is currently lying on the floor with broken bones in her foot and her face. She will need an ambulance but the police should be here before the ambulance. You may know the lady, she is being sought by the police for a series of murders. Her name is Wendy Carson."

"How do you know that it's Wendy Carson?"

"My boyfriend is David Parish, and he has been working with police investigating some frauds that this lady has also undertaken."

"So you're the girlfriend of the famous Mr Fraud?"

"I'm afraid so."

"Right Alisa, where are you?"

"To be honest I'm not sure. I'm in a park but don't know the name. There is a lady and gentleman here. I will put the gentleman on the phone and he'll explain where we are."

Alisa handed the phone to the man and asked him to give the police directions. She heard the man give directions while she spoke with the lady.

"I heard you say Wendy Carson. Is this the lady who has been committing the murders and has been shown on Criminals Captured."

"Yes. I don't know why she picked on me, presumably because David's my boyfriend, but I don't know how she managed to track me down."

The man finished with the phone and handed it back to Alisa.

"The police are on the way and the ambulance will follow. They should be here in five minutes. They asked who was screaming in the background and I told them it was Wendy Carson. She just laughed."

"I'd better ring David and let him know what's happened."

She dialled the number on the mobile.

"Hello Alisa."

"Hi David, where are you?"

"I've just come in, where are you?"

"I'm in the park at the top of the road, waiting for the police and an ambulance."

"Why?"

"Wendy Carson has just tried to kill me but she obviously didn't know about my skills in self-defence. She's lying on the floor with a broken foot and broken nose and cheekbone. Her eye doesn't look too good either. The police and ambulance will be here in five minutes."

"Whereabouts are you in the park?"

"I was walking round and I went past the café and then continued to where the trees are on both sides of the path. That's where we are now."

"I know where you mean, I'll be there in ten minutes. Wait for me."

"Okay David. I'll see you in ten minutes."

When David arrived at the scene in the park, the police were out in force and there was an ambulance, with the paramedics attending to Wendy Carson. The man and woman who had come across the incident were obviously enjoying the activity, especially now the famous Mr Fraud had arrived on the scene. Wendy Carson was then placed in the ambulance accompanied by two police officers. The look on her battered face and eye was clearly a look of hatred as she stared at Alisa and David.

A police sergeant had now appeared on the scene and approached David and Alisa.
"It's Alisa Garcia and David Parish, isn't it?"
David replied.
"Yes. I think we have a lot to thank this lady for don't we? Anybody who thinks they can attack Alisa Garcia and come out unharmed must be a bit crazy, but then she must be mustn't she?"
"I can see the result. Are you okay?"
"Yes, I'm fine."
"You should go to the hospital for a check up. It might be worth it just in case our friend tries to change the story. You should also tell them how she sustained her injuries. I know its self-defence but you should make sure they do all the checks on her, so they coincide with your statement."
"That's probably a good idea. Is there anybody special to ask for?"
"Yes. Go to the General Hospital, and make your way to Trauma and Orthopaedics. When you get there, ask for the Consultant Mark Davidson. He does work for the police and I'll let him know that you are coming in."
"I'll go down later today."
"We will need to take a statement off you sometime Alisa. It's just a formality."

Alisa replied.

"Yes, I understand that. Do you want me to write it out and hand it to the local police station?"

"That's okay. It saves me doing it"

"I'll do it when I'm waiting at the hospital and hand it in later this afternoon. Is that okay?"

"Yes. Give them your contact details in case we need to contact you. I will inform the appropriate people that we have Wendy Carson in custody. She has hired a car we've just taken the keys off her. We don't know where it is, a red Ford Ka."

David then remarked.

"I saw a Red Ka when I entered the park. It's by the side entrance."

"Thanks we'll go and check it now."

"I'll give Kevin Donnelly from the Metropolitan Police a ring, and give him the full story. He'll probably enjoy it."

David and Alisa then made their way out of the park, hand in hand. As they left the park, the Sergeant and another police officer had just opened the Ford Ka. The Sergeant had opened a suitcase and showed the contents to David and Alisa. It was full of twenty pound notes."

Later that afternoon when David and Alisa had returned from the hospital and dropped off the statement, they were having a coffee, when the phone rang which was answered by David.

"Hello."

"Hi David, its Kevin Donnelly."

"I was just about to ring you Kevin."

"I've just been told that Wendy Carson is in custody. She tried to kill Alisa but ended up in hospital herself. It's such a shame isn't it?"

David could hear Kevin laughing on the other end of the phone.

"She's in hospital with a police guard but she'll be moved here tomorrow or the day after. Did you know that they found just under a hundred thousand pounds in the back of the car?"

"I knew they'd found money, but I didn't know how much. It makes you wonder how much money she's got hidden away."

"We'll try to find it, but it will probably be difficult. More important, how's Alisa?"

"She's fine and she's just completed the police statement."

"Give her my thanks."

"I will. Bye for now Kevin."

31

David had travelled to Seville with Alisa, and helped her in the move to Murcia. Initially, Alisa lived in temporary accommodation provided by Guardia Civil, but within a matter of weeks had found suitable accommodation only a half hour drive from Murcia Airport, which provided direct flights to Liverpool.

He had been updated on the fraud cases that he had investigated and both he and Alisa had been informed that they must return to London for the forthcoming trial against Wendy Carson. That was to commence in two days' time and David and Alisa had arranged their flights back to Liverpool and would travel to London for the court case.

The minor accomplices in the payroll fraud had already appeared before the courts and Chris Sugden, Jim Barrowcliffe and Tom Crouch had all received sentences of twelve months. The Judge accepted that they were working for Wendy Carson but had opened fraudulent bank accounts and received fraudulent salaries into the bank accounts, which had been arranged by Wendy Carson. They had taken a large share of the proceeds and had given Wendy a large portion of the money they had obtained. Wendy Carson had not appeared at this trial as the murder trials were of a higher priority. She would be charged with fraud as well as the three murders of Danuta Jankowski, Denis King and Karen Jones. She was also charged with the attempted murder of Alisa Garcia.

Her solicitor had initially reported that Wendy was going to plead guilty to the fraud and the three murders but not guilty to attempted murder of Alisa. The case that the police had now obtained was now overwhelming, with DNA evidence from Wendy Carson being found on all three bodies, as well as sightings of her entering the premises where the murder of Karen Jones took place and video evidence providing stronger proof. It was unclear why she would be pleading not guilty to the lesser charge of attempted murder but David had his thoughts. He thought that Wendy Carson did not want to be having shown to be a failure in attempting to murder a lady or she wanted to try and blame Alisa for the attack.

The New York Police Department had issued the extradition documentation to the Metropolitan Police for Wendy in respect of the murder of Frank Sinclair. They were aware that it would be many years before they would be able to have her sent back to the United States, but insisted that this must take place.

Ben Alexander and Sue Patterson had given guilty pleas which avoided the necessity of David having to appear in court. Ben had returned over six hundred thousand pounds to the courts, which was the result of the sale of Sue's house, the money he had hidden in several bank accounts, and a remortgage of the family home which was part of the divorce agreement with his wife, Lynn. Sue's relationship with Karl, the father of her daughter Mandy had also broken up, but there was no reconciliation between Ben and Sue.

Ben was sent to prison for three years, with the judge indicating that it would have been four years, if he had not returned the monies gained from the proceeds of the fraudulent activities. Sue was sent to prison for eighteen months and her daughter was left in the care of her mother.

Manchester prison was now the home of Jack Inglis for the next fifteen months. The case had made bigger headlines, because of the involvement of Sally O'Brien. The use of the deceased twins' names in the fraud had disgusted the public, especially the regular viewers of Criminals Captured. Sally had received massive support and had used this case to warn the public of identity fraud and precautions they should take. There had been a big public response and names of many fraudsters had been provided to the police.

32

David and Alisa went into London Crown Court, where they then met Kevin Donnelly and Brian McAndrew, the barrister acting for the prosecution. It was Brian who then updated Kevin, David and Alisa.

"I've just had a chat with Peter Morton, Wendy Carson's barrister. He read the report from Mark Davidson, the Hospital Consultant and then spoke to Wendy and has persuaded her to change her plea on the attempted murder charge from not guilty to guilty. The report was quite thorough and mentioned the bruising and marks that he had seen on your neck and back. He also stated that the broken bones in the foot were caused by the stamping from the back of a heel from a person immediately in front. The broken cheekbone could only have been caused by the elbow of a person having her back to Wendy, with the arm being raised in an upwards direction. He then confirmed that the marks on your neck were firm to begin with but then minor scrapes when the grip was released. Mr Davidson also states that it was remarkable that you weren't murdered and only a person with a high level of self-defence skills could have prevented the murder. If you hadn't acted within five seconds you would be dead."

They all then made their way into the court to listen to Wendy Carson make her pleas to the charges that were being brought against her. David and Alisa sat whilst they heard all the charges being made against Wendy Carson. A guilty plea was given to the murders of Danuta Jankowski, Denis King and Karen Jones. She pleaded guilty to the attempted murder of Alisa Garcia, but glared at Alisa after she had made the plea. A further guilty plea was provided for the fraud on the payroll at the hospital and guilty pleas to a sample of charges relating to the provision of forged documents which assisted in several cases of identity fraud. Two of the identity fraud cases related to the twin boys of Sally O'Brien, Paul and John O'Brien, who had died in a road accident twenty years ago.

Judge William Lawson, who was presiding in the Crown Court listened intently and then looked at the Prosecution Barrister, Brian McAndrew.

"Mr McAndrew."

"Thank you your honour. I have very little to say but the murder of three people, which might have been four, but for the self-defence skills of a Spanish Police official, Alisa Garcia. There is fraudulent activity on a large scale that has been brought to our attention, but identity fraud is becoming much more active with the involvement of people like Wendy Carson. This case has become high profile with the showing on national television and requests of help from the public. I am sure the sentence will show the severity of these crimes, but we have also been served with an extradition warrant by the New York Police Department in respect to the murder of Frank Sinclair in New York. It is their wish that Wendy Carson be sent to New York, if she is ever released, to be charged with the murder of Frank Sinclair."

Judge William Lawson then turned to the Defence Counsel, Peter Morton.

"Mr Morton."

"Thank you your honour. My client has helped the courts by admitting her guilt to all the charges that have been put before her. Mrs Carson has had no previous record until she met her ex boyfriend Frank Sinclair, who introduced her to fraudulent activity, having served a sentence for fraud in New York. She was besotted with him and she has now committed the most serious criminal activities for which she is full of remorse. The fraud on Euston General Hospital was for six hundred thousand pounds, but I understand that they will now have received back four hundred thousand pounds."

Judge Lawson interrupted Mr Morton.

"Mr Morton. I should point out that this money was not returned by your client. It was only the quick work of David Parish and the Bank Investigators that allowed the freezing of bank accounts, which blocked three hundred thousand pounds being claimed by Mrs Carson. The further one hundred thousand pounds was found in the back of her car when she was arrested."

"Yes, I understand that your honour. My client will be receiving a long prison sentence and will be an elderly lady when she is released from prison. I feel that sentence will reflect all her guilt, but any extradition to New York, at this stage of her life will be unfair. I am asking this court to refuse the extradition in view of the time she will have served for her crimes in this country. My client, Wendy Carson is now at the mercy of this court."

"Mr Morton. The two countries have a reciprocal arrangement as far as the extradition of criminals is concerned. I accept that your client has not been found guilty of any murder in the United States, but they have issued extradition proceedings in the correct manner and we feel there is a case to be answered in New York. This will be held on file until a sentence has been served in this country, when she will be extradited unless the authorities in New York agree to waive any charges, which is probably unlikely."

The Judge then addressed Wendy Carson.

"This is, without doubt, one of the most horrendous cases heard by the courts in this country. The murder of a young lady, Danuta Jankowski from Poland, who came to this country to work and better her education, but was murdered because she was short of the money to pay you for fraudulent documents. Then there is the murder of one of your accomplices, Denis King, because he provided the police with some information. Finally, a shopkeeper, Karen Jones, in Anglesey was murdered because she rang the police to help. You then made the mistake of trying to kill Alisa Garcia, but you were unaware that she was a self-defence expert. This lady stopped all your criminal activities which would, no doubt, have continued. A fraud in one of our hospitals was undertaken for sheer greed. You were in a position of trust, but succeeded in obtaining six hundred thousand pounds by setting up an organised crime, with accomplices working to your instructions. Your next area of crime was identity fraud, where you provided the documents to complete the frauds, and allowed the use of children who had died, tragically, many years before. I accept that another criminal, now in prison, serving a sentence for his part in that fraud, provided you with the information, but you supplied the documents which allowed the fraud to be successful. The sentences for the murders of Danuta Jankowski, Denis King and Karen Jones are life imprisonment, and taking into account the admission of the attempted murder of Alisa Garcia, I will recommend that you serve a minimum of twenty one years. The sentence for the fraud committed at the hospital and the provision of identity fraud documents is four years and that will be served consecutively with the sentences for murders. The extradition warrant relating to the murder in New York will remain active and they will be contacted prior to any release from a prison in this country."

It was three years since Wendy Carson had been sent to jail and her daughter, Pauline, had never visited her mother nor had she ever made contact. It was a situation that would never change as Pauline could not forgive a person whom had committed such evil acts. She had difficulty in holding any relationships as the daughter of a multi-murderer and a fraudster. Employment was virtually impossible and she was living on the basic benefits that the State provides.

Wendy Carson's mother, Mary Longridge, was in constant contact with Wendy, and enjoyed the benefits. She had been going on two luxury cruises each year and spent other holidays staying at luxury hotels in various part of the world. Her new wealth was evident in her house, and there was still no shortage of the money being made available to support this lifestyle. The police were aware of the luxury living of Mary Longridge, which had to be from hidden funds of Wendy Carson, but they had little success in pursuing this matter. Mary had offered money to her granddaughter, Pauline, but this was refused. Pauline was aware of the source and her relationship with her grandmother was also non-existent.

Ben Alexander had been released from prison, but found it impossible to obtain employment as a dentist. He had been hoping to obtain a post in the private sector but had failed. He also tried unsuccessfully in the National Health Service but knew he would not get employment in the public sector. At the present time, he is working as a taxi driver.